Bamidele Isaac Akinlabi is a Nigerian author and storyteller known for weaving rich narratives that explore the complexities of the epic fantasy genre. Born and raised in Nigeria, his writing is infused with the vibrant culture and traditions of his homeland, blending them seamlessly with imaginative worlds and intricate plots. Bamidele's work delves deep into the realms of fantasy, offering readers a captivating journey through tales of heroism, magic, and moral dilemmas. With a passion for storytelling, he continues to craft stories that inspire, challenge, and transport readers to new and extraordinary worlds.

I dedicate this book to God, my family and friends, whose love and support have been the bedrock of my journey.

Bamidele Isaac Akinlabi

THE MYSTERY TREE HOUSE

GENESIS

AUSTIN MACAULEY PUBLISHERS
LONDON * CAMBRIDGE * NEW YORK * SHARJAH

Copyright © Bamidele Isaac Akinlabi 2024

The right of Bamidele Isaac Akinlabi to be identified as author of this work has been asserted by the author in accordance with sections 77 and 78 of the Copyright, Designs and Patents Act 1988.

All rights reserved. No part of this publication may be reproduced, stored in a retrieval system, or transmitted in any form or by any means, electronic, mechanical, photocopying, recording, or otherwise, without the prior permission of the publishers.

Any person who commits any unauthorised act in relation to this publication may be liable to criminal prosecution and civil claims for damages.

This is a work of fiction. Names, characters, businesses, places, events, locales, and incidents are either the products of the author's imagination or used in a fictitious manner. Any resemblance to actual persons, living or dead, or actual events is purely coincidental.

A CIP catalogue record for this title is available from the British Library.

ISBN 9781035885787 (Paperback)
ISBN 9781035885800 (ePub e-book)
ISBN 9781035885794 (Audiobook)

www.austinmacauley.com

First Published 2024
Austin Macauley Publishers Ltd®
1 Canada Square
Canary Wharf
London
E14 5AA

Thank you for always believing in me and pushing me towards my dreams. And to all those who dare to dream big and create: May your imaginations continue to inspire and shape the world.

Table of Contents

Preface 11

Prologue 12

Chapter One: The Birth of a Legend 15

Chapter Two: The Tree of Resilience and Unity 23

Chapter Three: The Horror Race 28

Chapter Four: The Landers 32

Chapter Five: The Mountain 38

Chapter Six: The Plan 46

Chapter Seven: The Arrival 55

Chapter Eight: Angel of Death Scare 60

Chapter Nine: The Hundredth Step of Horror Race 64

Chapter Ten: The Awakening of Demetrious 70

Chapter Eleven: Secrets, Betrayal and Shifting Alliances 80

Chapter Twelve: Web of Ambition 89

Chapter Thirteen: Miracle the Wizard 97

Chapter Fourteen: Revelations and Burdens 103

Chapter Fifteen: Secrets, Power and Destiny	108
Chapter Sixteen: Shadows of Destiny	114
Chapter Seventeen: The Moon Cave	125
Chapter Eighteen: The Ravens	131
Chapter Nineteen: Crown	136
Chapter Twenty: The Ambush	142
Chapter Twenty-One: More Conspirations	147
Chapter Twenty-Two: Gandoki's Mission (1)	151
Chapter Twenty-Three: Gandoki's Mission (2)	156
Chapter Twenty-Four: The Werewolf	162
Chapter Twenty-Five: Akika's Agreement	168
Chapter Twenty-Six: The Right-Hand Man	174
Chapter Twenty-Seven: Negotiations	180
Chapter Twenty-Eight: Voyage to Sanctuary	188
Chapter Twenty-Nine: The Great Ganjak	194
Chapter Thirty: Requin	201
Chapter Thirty-One: Asylum	206
Chapter Thirty-Two: Hillside	210
Chapter Thirty-Three: The Slavers' Bay	215

Preface

Amidst the vast ocean, a colossal tree stands; its roots shrouded in mystery. It sits in the middle of the ocean, about fifteen thousand feet tall, and it occupies four thousand, three hundred and fifty acres of what appears to be an island; its roots spread across the landmark. The Mystery Tree House, it both shelters and curses those marooned upon its massive roots. A diverse group of shipwreck survivors, including West African sailor Warriorisborn, discovered the life-sustaining properties of the tree's water, sparking the foundation of a new community.

As years pass, secrets and betrayal take root within the tree house, threatening their paradise. Warriorisborn faces not only internal challenges but also mysterious forces that govern the tree's existence. *The Mystery Tree House* weaves themes of leadership, sacrifice and destiny against a backdrop of ancient magic and enduring hope…

Prologue

The tempest raged with a fury unimaginable to those who had not witnessed its wrath. The sky above was a churning mass of ominous grey clouds, sporadically illuminated by violent streaks of lightning that seemed to split the very fabric of the heavens. The wind, like an unleashed banshee, screamed through the air, driving the sea into a wild frenzy. Towering waves crashed against one another, their white, frothy crests reaching for the sky before collapsing back into the tumultuous ocean with deafening roars.

Amidst the chaos, a solitary sailor from the western coast of Africa struggled to maintain control of the beleaguered ship. Years of battling the sea had left his hands rough and calloused, his eyes sharp with determination. His vessel, a fragile speck amid the storm's fury, was at the mercy of each monstrous wave threatening to engulf it. The sailor's hands, rough and calloused from years of battling the sea, clung to the wheel with all his might. Rain lashed his weathered face, and the sting of saltwater burned his eyes, yet he pressed on, fuelled by an unbreakable will to survive.

The ship was a clipper, renowned for its speed and elegance. Its long, narrow hull was painted a deep black, designed to cut through the waves with minimal resistance. Tall, sturdy masts supported an expansive array of sails, now billowing wildly in the tempest. Despite its current plight, the clipper had an air of resilience, its sleek lines and robust structure hinting at countless voyages across treacherous seas. The deck, though slick with rain and seawater, was meticulously maintained, a testament to the crew's pride and the ship's storied past.

Hours passed like a never-ending nightmare. Each moment was filled with relentless peril. The ship groaned and creaked under the strain. Its wooden hull strained against the ocean's unyielding assault. Just when the storm seemed to offer no respite, a new danger loomed. With a sickening crunch, the vessel struck a hidden obstacle, sending the sailor and his crew sprawling across the deck. The air filled with the sound of splintering wood, a grim testament to the collision's force.

"Hold fast!" the captain roared, his voice barely audible over the howling wind. "We've hit something!"

Scrambling to their feet, the crew discovered the source of their calamity: a massive, rough-surfaced object jutting from the depths. Initially baffled, they struggled to comprehend what had ensnared their vessel. Closer inspection revealed the truth—a colossal tree root, its gnarled and twisted form improbably rising from the ocean floor.

"What in Neptune's name is that?" a sailor gasped, eyes wide with disbelief.

"It's a root!" shouted another, his voice tinged with awe and fear. "A tree root in the middle of the ocean!"

The survivors of the crash were a diverse and motley group, hailing from various corners of the globe. Most were Africans, but among them were also Europeans, Arabs and Americans. Their reasons for being at sea were as varied as their backgrounds. Some were traders seeking fortune in distant lands, other explorers driven by an insatiable thirst for discovery. A few harboured darker intentions, aiming to exploit the riches of new territories.

In the face of the storm's fury, their differences became inconsequential. The relentless tempest had bound them together in a shared struggle for survival, weaving a tapestry of camaraderie from the threads of their disparate lives. As they stood on the deck of their shattered ship, gazing at the colossal tree root that had become their unexpected refuge, they understood that their journey had taken an unforeseeable turn. The storm had not only altered their course but had also forged a bond among them, born from adversity and the indomitable spirit of those who dared to challenge the seas.

"Captain, what do we do now?" a young sailor asked, his voice trembling with both fear and hope.

"We survive," the captain replied, his gaze steely and resolute. "We salvage what we can and make the best of our situation. Together."

The storm's roar faded into the distance, leaving behind an eerie silence punctuated only by the gentle lapping of waves against the hull. The survivors, exhausted and battered, looked around at their fellow companions with newfound respect and unity. Their shared ordeal had stripped away the veneer of differences, revealing the core of human resilience and solidarity.

As dawn broke, casting a golden hue over the turbulent waters, the crew set to work assessing their situation. Despite the damage, their spirits were unbroken. They salvaged what they could from the wreckage, pooling their resources and skills to ensure their survival. In the face of overwhelming odds, they had found strength in each other, a testament to the unyielding human spirit.

The storm had tested them beyond measure, but it had also given them a gift—a profound sense of kinship and an unshakeable determination to persevere. As they navigated the uncertain waters ahead, the memory of the tempest remained a constant reminder of their resilience, and the bonds forged in the heart of the storm.

"Together, we can overcome anything," the captain declared, his voice filled with conviction. "This storm may have broken our ship, but it has forged an unbreakable crew."

With renewed resolve, the survivors faced the horizon, ready to embrace whatever challenges lay ahead. Their journey had only just begun.

As the sun climbed higher, casting long shadows across the debris-strewn deck, the crew gathered to assess their supplies. Waterlogged barrels of provisions were dragged from the hold, and a makeshift inventory was taken. Despite their ordeal, a sense of purpose permeated the air.

"We need to ration our food and water," said a seasoned sailor, his voice steady despite the exhaustion etched into his features. "There's no telling how long we'll be out here."

"Aye," agreed another, "but we've got a strong crew and plenty of skills among us. We'll make it."

It must be established, however, that no matter the motivational speaking that the captain would do, there was great hunger and shortage of stock. And, as shown throughout history, hunger begets selfish and wicked men; for one is born with the instinctive need to look out for one's self.

Chapter One
The Birth of a Legend

Warriorisborn grew up in the vibrant and bustling regions of western Africa, where the sun blazed golden and the air was filled with the scents of rich, red earth and blooming flora. From a young age, he was immersed in the rhythm of the marketplace, where traders from distant lands converged, bringing with them exotic goods and tales of faraway places.

With a keen mind and an insatiable drive for wealth and power, Warriorisborn carved a niche for himself in this thriving hub. He transported foreign passengers across treacherous waters in exchange for valuables, forging connections and amassing treasures along the way. His most prized commodity, however, was iron glass—a rare and mysterious material in high demand for its unique properties.

The iron glass Warriorisborn traded was unlike anything else. Legend had it that these gleaming shards were remnants of an ancient weapon, buried deep within the African landscape by ancestors long gone. The iron glass was long, strong and sharp, with a quality so burnished that it shimmered like the finest mirror, reflecting the world in its smooth surface. Its origins were shrouded in mystery, and its value was immense.

Intelligent and charismatic, Warriorisborn knew how to wield his charm to his advantage. His striking appearance and flamboyant style made him a magnetic presence, drawing women and business partners alike into his orbit. He had an aura of confidence and power, his every movement a testament to his self-assured nature. Whether negotiating a trade or sharing a laugh over a drink, he was always the centre of attention, his words weaving a spell over those around him.

In his homeland, spirits were highly coveted, and Warriorisborn capitalised on this demand by trading large quantities of iron glass for the finest liquors.

These spirits were more than just a beverage; they were a symbol of status and luxury, a key to unlocking the admiration and respect of his peers. With every successful trade, Warriorisborn's influence grew, his name becoming synonymous with wealth and sophistication.

As he navigated the complexities of commerce and human nature, Warriorisborn remained ever-focused on his ultimate goal: to rise to the pinnacle of power and prestige. He understood the world around him and played it to his advantage, a master of his destiny. In the gleam of the iron glass, he would often look at his reflection—smirking at his ambition and the promise of a future forged by his own hand.

However, after the impact, many passengers and crew members were severely injured, and many died instantly. The survivors arose from the ship, their bodies aching and minds clouded with confusion and devastation. Despite this great loss, the ship's population was still extremely high, dropping from thousand to about seven hundred men, women and children aboard.

The once bustling and hopeful vessel was now a shattered wreck, its remnants strewn across the churning waves and wedged against the massive tree root that had brought about their downfall.

Blood mingled with seawater as the survivors clung to the splintered remains, their breaths ragged and their eyes wide with shock. Cries of pain and grief echoed through the air, a haunting symphony of the shipwreck's aftermath. Amidst the chaos, those who had the strength helped the more severely wounded, their hands shaking but their resolve firm.

After many unrested hours, the group, weary and disoriented, managed to pull themselves onto the gnarled tree roots. The roots, vast and ancient, provided a precarious refuge from the merciless sea. They sat there, a disparate band of individuals from different corners of the world, united by their shared calamity. To say that they were crestfallen was an understatement.

The air was heavy with the scent of salt and blood, and the roar of the ocean was a constant reminder of their ordeal. They sat in silence, their minds racing to make sense of their new reality. Faces that had once been strangers now reflected the same haunted expression, their shared survival knitting them together in a fragile bond.

They were like a generation of the walking dead.

Slowly, the initial shock began to ebb, replaced by a grim determination to survive. They took stock of their injuries, their losses and their meagre resources.

Resting on the rough, resilient roots of the tree, they found a momentary sanctuary to gather their thoughts and plan their next steps.

Though their journey had been violently interrupted, the survivors knew that they had to move forward. The tree roots, once a symbol of their disaster, now served as a foundation for their recovery. In the stillness of that moment, amidst the lingering storm and the wreckage of their ship, they began to forge a path towards hope and resilience.

Warriorisborn was angry and frustrated about the situation, feeling guilty that he had led them into a calamity. After a full day of salvaging any and everything they can for food (that was not already lost to the sea), hunger broke in again, afresh, and they became very thirsty.

Warriorisborn was desperate to get the survivors out of their predicament. He went to the deck of the ship, pondering his next move. Lying on the floor were thousands of iron glass shards, a few metres away from where he stood.

These might have been priceless, out there, he reasoned, but over here, it was as valueless as the gold and silver now lying across the remains of the ship.

Suddenly, a woman's sharp gasp and piercing groan caught his attention from a distance. He traced the voice and found a woman well into her fifties crawling on the floor, seeming to be in a desperate need for help.

She looked weak and feeble but had a very hard-to-not-notice aura that made Warriorisborn wonder how he had not earlier noticed her.

He carried the frail woman out of the wreckage, her weight barely a burden despite his own exhaustion. She clung to him, her eyes wide with a mixture of relief and fear, yet confidence.

"You are the chosen one," she murmured, her voice barely above a whisper.

Warriorisborn looked at her, puzzled. "What do you mean?"

The woman took a deep breath, gathering her strength. "My name is Aza. I am what some call a blossom whisperer, a keeper of ancient secrets and powers. You saved me, and now, I will help you save us all."

He frowned, sceptical but intrigued. "How can you help? We are stranded, and our supplies are dwindling. Many are injured and weak."

"There is always a light at the end of the tunnel," Aza said, her voice gaining strength. "You must trust me. The iron glass on your ship—its power is beyond what you know. It can cut through the toughest of materials, including the tree root that holds us here."

Warriorisborn hesitated. "Iron glass? We use it for trade, but how can it help us now?"

Aza fixed him with a steady gaze. "The tree root we are trapped against holds the secret to our survival. Cut through it, and you will find a source of life, a way to sustain and heal us. You must act quickly before it's too late."

Desperation gnawed at him, and he felt the weight of these people's lives on his shoulders. He nodded. "I will do it. But if this fails, we may not have another chance."

"It will not fail," Aza said firmly. "Trust in the power of the iron glass and in yourself. You are destined for greatness."

Without another word, Warriorisborn raced back to the deck of the ship. His heart pounded as he spotted the iron glass shards glinting in the sunlight. He grabbed one, its cool, smooth surface reflecting his determined face.

He hurried to the base of the massive tree root and, with a swift motion, slashed at it with the iron glass. To his astonishment, the shard cut through the tough root with ease. A stream of clear, fresh water burst forth, splashing his hands and face.

"The water is fresh and full of life," he exclaimed, his voice trembling with awe.

The other survivors, hearing his shout, rushed to the scene. They stared in amazement as Warriorisborn filled his cupped hands with the water and drank deeply. He felt a surge of energy and vitality course through him.

"This is it!" he shouted. "We are saved!"

People began to drink the water, their eyes lighting up with hope and relief. The injured were brought forward, and as they drank, their wounds began to heal miraculously. The air buzzed with excitement and disbelief.

Warriorisborn turned to Aza, who had followed him and now stood at the edge of the group, a faint smile on her lips.

"You were right," he said, his voice filled with gratitude. "Thank you, Aza. You have given us hope."

Aza nodded, her eyes shining. "The iron glass has many secrets, as does this tree. But remember, Warriorisborn, this is just the beginning. There will be more challenges ahead. But together, you can overcome them."

With newfound strength and resolve, Warriorisborn addressed the survivors. "This is the promised land," he declared. "We will build a new life here, stronger and united. Together, we can overcome anything."

Cheers erupted from the crowd, their spirits lifted by the miraculous turn of events. As they began to organise and plan for the future, Warriorisborn knew that with the help of Aza and the iron glass, they had the power to face whatever lay ahead.

Remaining were about three hundred and fifty strong men, one hundred and fifty-five women, forty-four children, including one old blind man and six old women who were dwindling. He called all of them together and promised them hope.

Five men from different backgrounds who understood his language stood against him. Their names were Alexandre, Charles, Muhammad, Cyril and Lambert. They all disagreed about his leadership after he had led them into calamity. They asked Warriorisborn about his plan. He told them about his vision to build a homelike environment and live there forever with the aid of the root water since they all believed the tree roots had healing powers. After a few private discussions, they decided to join Warriorisborn and assist him in convincing the rest of the survivors to follow his vision.

Cyril was not happy with the decision. He suggested they should build a ship and sail to their intended destination, but since he could not achieve this by himself, he decided to join the others.

With the help of the iron glass, the strong survivors started carving into the tree to build a shelter. As they drank the root water, they realised the more they carved, the stronger they became. They did this day and night for a long time without food but still felt fulfilled.

One day, the old blind man shouted, "Stop carving the tree! We are all going to die! I see redness of blood; I see despair." People ignored his words, believing he was hallucinating because of his age and disability. Unbeknownst to them, he sensed an unseen scar of war and strife.

The old blind man was a seer. He had been abandoned by his parents at a young age when they discovered he could not see, thinking he was evil. He was placed beside a river, but fortunately, he was found by an old woman who took care of him and helped him nurture his abilities. The old woman died when he was seven years old. Since then, he had survived using his instincts wherever destiny took him despite his blindness. People called him the 'soothsayer'.

The mystery tree craft was completed after five years and a few months of hard work. It felt like an afterlife, a feeling of hope. Everyone was happy. Most believed destiny had led them to the tree. It was a big relief for the travellers.

Even though they could have built a ship and headed back to land, they were astonished by how the injured victims had risen after ingesting the root water. Many children were born during that period, and the population of the inhabitants multiplied. However, a month after the completion, something unforeseen happened.

One morning, as the sun rose and cast a golden hue over their new home, a strange sound echoed through the tree craft. It was a deep, resonant hum, vibrating through the very roots of the ancient tree. The inhabitants gathered, curiosity and fear mingling in their expressions.

Warriorisborn stepped forward, his eyes narrowing as he tried to pinpoint the source of the sound. "Stay back," he commanded, his voice calm but authoritative. He approached the centre of the tree craft, where the hum seemed strongest.

Suddenly, a section of the tree root began to crack and shift, revealing a hidden chamber beneath. The survivors gasped, stepping back in awe and trepidation. From the chamber emerged a blinding light, illuminating the entire area. Warriorisborn shielded his eyes, peering into the brightness.

From within the light, a figure slowly materialised. It was Aza, the blossom whisperer, looking more ethereal and powerful than ever. Her presence was both comforting and unsettling.

"Do not be afraid," Aza spoke, her voice echoing as if coming from all directions. "I have come to guide you. The tree has chosen you as its protectors, but with this honour comes great responsibility."

The survivors exchanged glances, their initial relief giving way to a new sense of purpose and duty.

Aza continued, "This tree, the source of the iron glass and the healing water, holds immense power. It is a beacon of life and strength, but it must be protected from those who would seek to exploit it. You have been brought here to safeguard its secrets."

Warriorisborn stepped forward, his expression resolute. "We will protect it. We have already seen the wonders it can do. We owe it our lives."

Aza smiled, a hint of sadness in her eyes. "Be vigilant, for there are forces in this world that would stop at nothing to harness the power of this tree. You must be prepared to defend it, and yourselves."

With those words, Aza began to fade back into the light, her form dissipating like mist in the morning sun. The chamber slowly closed, the hum receding until all was silent once more.

The survivors stood in stunned silence, absorbing the gravity of their new mission. Warriorisborn turned to his people, his eyes reflecting the determination and strength that had always defined him.

"We have been given a great task," he said, his voice carrying the weight of their collective resolve. "This tree has given us life and hope. We must honour that gift by protecting it. Together, we are strong."

The survivors nodded, their spirits buoyed by Warriorisborn's words. They set to work fortifying their home, creating defences and strategies to ensure the safety of their newfound sanctuary. The tree, once a symbol of their disaster, had become a beacon of hope and unity.

Days turned into weeks, and weeks into months. The survivors thrived, their bond growing stronger with each passing day. They built homes within the tree, using the iron glass to craft tools and weapons. The tree's healing water continued to sustain them, and its roots provided a constant source of strength.

Warriorisborn emerged as a true leader, guiding his people with wisdom and courage. He often sought the counsel of the old blind seer, whose visions provided invaluable insights into the challenges they faced. The seer, once thought to be a harbinger of doom, had become a trusted advisor and a symbol of resilience.

One evening, as the sun set over the horizon, casting a warm glow over the tree craft, Warriorisborn gathered his people for a meeting. They sat in a circle, the firelight flickering on their faces.

"We have done well," he began, his voice filled with pride. "But we must remain vigilant. Aza warned us of dangers, and we must be ready to face them. Our strength lies in our unity and our resolve."

Alexandre, one of the men who had initially opposed Warriorisborn's leadership, stood up. "We have come a long way," he said, his tone respectful. "We have built a home and a community. But we must also remember that we are not alone in this world. We must be prepared for what lies beyond our sanctuary."

Charles, Muhammad, Cyril and Lambert nodded in agreement. They had seen the strength and wisdom in Warriorisborn's leadership and had come to respect and trust him.

Cyril, still harbouring a desire to explore the world beyond, spoke up. "We should send out scouts," he suggested. "To learn more about our surroundings and any potential threats. Knowledge is power, and we must be informed."

Warriorisborn nodded thoughtfully. "You are right, Cyril. We need to understand the world around us. We will organise scouting parties to gather information and ensure our safety."

With that, the meeting concluded. The survivors returned to their tasks, their resolve stronger than ever. They were not just surviving; they were thriving, building a future from the ruins of their past.

Months turned into years, and the tree craft became a thriving community. The iron glass was used to create intricate artworks and practical tools, the healing water ensured their health and vitality, and the tree itself provided shelter and sustenance. The population grew, and new generations were born into the safety and prosperity of their unique home.

One day, as Warriorisborn stood at the edge of the tree craft, gazing out at the horizon, he felt a sense of peace. They had faced incredible challenges and had emerged stronger. The tree, with its secrets and powers, had become a symbol of their resilience and unity.

Yet he knew their journey was far from over. The world beyond their sanctuary was vast and unpredictable, and they would need to remain vigilant and prepared for whatever lay ahead. But for now, they had built a haven of hope and strength, a testament to the power of unity and determination.

Warriorisborn turned back to his people, his heart swelling with pride and gratitude. Together, they had created something extraordinary, something that would endure. And as long as they stood together, they could face any challenge that came their way.

The tree craft, with its ancient roots and shimmering iron glass, stood as a beacon of hope and a reminder of the indomitable spirit of those who dared to dream and build a future from the ashes of disaster.

Chapter Two
The Tree of Resilience and Unity

Warriorisborn's vision after the crash was to create a homelike atmosphere in the tree. He pictured a structure that could house thousands of people, knowing it might be their home for a long time. Houses about twenty feet wide and fifteen feet tall were built around the tree, ascending to the top. Steps were constructed to each level of the houses throughout the entire tree, and a wide-open passage in the middle led to a large round platform, about three acres wide at the treetop, where they decided to store the iron glasses recovered from the ship's deck. This platform, situated at the upper part of the tree, opened to daylight, allowing the sun to shine through by day, while thousands of wooden torches illuminated the tree house by night.

There were thousands of steps linked together, leading to the top of the tree, with a wide central staircase that ascended to the large round platform. The steps could accommodate fifty people standing side by side, creating a grand and practical passage. However, this very staircase collapsed precisely at midnight one fateful morning.

The crumbling of the central staircase killed one quarter of the inhabitants, a great shock to the tree house residents. This catastrophe raised urgent questions; why had this happened? After days of study, they discovered some shortcomings of the tree house. They knew nothing could penetrate the mysterious tree except the iron glass, and while death was uncertain—evident by the still-living elderly—the collapse of the staircase was a bombshell. Despite this, not all secrets were uncovered, and as years passed, more mysteries were unveiled.

However, after the collapse of the central staircase, the platform where the iron glasses were kept remained intact, supported by the carved beams that extended into the tree's core. The members of the tree house were terrified, anxiously awaiting what might come next. Warriorisborn remembered the old blind man who had predicted this mysterious occurrence and decided to visit him.

The blind seer spoke to him, "This is just the beginning. More dangers lie ahead. Let us not create a world of power and greed. We should find a land, or else the tree shall destroy us all. We are not invincible, nor is the tree. There are four ways to die."

Warriorisborn, unwilling to listen further, stood up and left without the blind man's knowledge, dismissing him as delusional. At 12:00 noon, the following day, exactly twelve hours after the collapse, the tree reconstructed the central staircase in an astonishing display. The new step grew rapidly, so fast that the acceleration gave it a horrible, bumpy look. It appeared dangerous to climb, and panic spread among the occupants. After seven days of tension, the staircase suddenly shook violently, as if about to collapse again. Everyone was devastated, but after a few moments, it stopped, and the base of the step weakened. This became an annual occurrence, and over time, the inhabitants became accustomed to it, dubbing it the 'Step of Horror'.

Over the years, they noticed the base of the step became flimsy, but it always merged firmly every seven days before the collapse, regrowing twelve hours later, followed by a violent shake on the seventh day. This tremor would cause anyone on the step at that time to fall and die, and the step would be flooded with water for the rest of the year.

This dangerous cycle was ignored for many years. By about twenty-six years after arrival, the tree house population had increased, becoming congested and overpopulated. Warriorisborn realised more construction was needed. The challenge was retrieving the iron glass from the platform, which required climbing the Step of Horror within the narrow time frame before the next shake. Initially, it had taken seven days to climb the first, intact staircase; now, it would require more time to navigate the uneven and dangerous Step of Horror. The task had to be completed within seven days, before the big shake, to regulate the tree house population and establish more space.

Warriorisborn called his chiefs and asked if anyone had a solution. They devised a strategy, setting the inhabitants on a perilous course into the unknown.

In the dimly lit chamber of Aza the blossom whisperer, the air was heavy with the scent of flowers and herbs. Warriorisborn stood before her; his brow furrowed with concern as he sought her counsel on a pressing matter.

"Aza," he began, his voice betraying a hint of uncertainty, "we face a dilemma. Our tree house is overcrowded, and resources are dwindling. I fear we may not survive much longer if we do not take action."

Aza, her eyes clouded with foresight, listened intently, her fingers tracing patterns in the petals of a delicate blossom. She knew the path ahead was fraught with danger, but she also understood the necessity of Warriorisborn's plan.

"This is a dangerous path you tread, Warriorisborn," she cautioned, her voice barely above a whisper. "But sometimes, the greatest risks yield the greatest rewards. If you are to lead your people through this trial, you must do so with conviction and authority."

Warriorisborn nodded solemnly, the weight of Aza's words settling upon him like a heavy cloak. He knew that to enact change, he would need to assert his authority as leader of the tree house.

"And what of the population reduction?" he asked, his voice tinged with uncertainty.

Aza's gaze met his, steady and unwavering. "Sometimes, sacrifices must be made for the greater good," she replied cryptically. "You must do what is necessary to ensure the survival of our people, even if it means making difficult decisions."

With Aza's blessing ringing in his ears, Warriorisborn knew what he must do. He would crown himself as king of the tree house and rule with strength and determination, guiding his people through the challenges that lay ahead.

Understanding her meaning, Warriorisborn realised that to rule effectively and make extreme decisions, he needed to instil fear among his people. He devised a strategy that would lead the inhabitants into the unknown.

"We must climb the Step of Horror and retrieve the iron glass," Warriorisborn declared to his chiefs. "This is our only way to expand and survive. We will form teams, each with a specific task and time frame. We must be swift and careful."

Alexandre, one of the chiefs, voiced his concern. "But the risk is too great. Many will perish if we fail."

Warriorisborn nodded solemnly. "I know the dangers, but we have no choice. The tree house is overcrowded. If we do nothing, we will perish anyway. This is our chance to secure our future."

Cyril, another chief, who had previously disagreed with Warriorisborn's leadership, spoke up. "What if we build a ship and leave this place? Seek new lands as the seer suggested?"

Warriorisborn shook his head. "The tree has provided for us in ways no land ever could. The healing water, the iron glass…we cannot abandon it. We must make this work."

With the strategy in place, Warriorisborn rallied the inhabitants. "We will climb the Step of Horror and retrieve the iron glass. It will be dangerous, but together, we can succeed. We must expand our home and ensure our survival."

The inhabitants, driven by necessity and fear, agreed to the plan. They organised into teams, each assigned a specific task—some to climb, some to support from below and others to guard the base of the tree.

Warriorisborn and a group of the strongest and most skilled climbers began their ascent. The Step of Horror was treacherous, its surface uneven and jagged. Each step was taken with utmost caution, the iron glass glinting ominously in the sunlight.

The journey was arduous. Hours turned into days as they slowly made their way up the perilous staircase. The inhabitants below watched anxiously; their hopes pinned on the success of the climbers. On the seventh day, just before the tremor was expected, Warriorisborn and his team reached the platform.

With great care, they retrieved the iron glass and began their descent. The timing was crucial; they had to reach the base before the step's violent shake. As they climbed down, the tree began to tremble. The inhabitants held their breath, praying for their safe return.

Warriorisborn led his team with precision, his determination unwavering. They reached the base just as the step shook violently, sending shockwaves through the tree. But they were safe, the iron glass secured.

The success of the mission brought a brief respite. With the retrieved iron glass, they began expanding the tree house, creating more space to accommodate the population density.

However, the annual cycle of the Step of Horror continued to loom over them, a constant reminder of their precarious existence.

Years passed, and the inhabitants adapted to their unique way of life. The Step of Horror remained a symbol of both danger and salvation. Each year, they faced its tremors, knowing that their survival depended on their unity and courage.

Despite the ongoing challenges, Warriorisborn's vision had been realised. The tree house had become a thriving community, a home forged from adversity. The iron glass, the healing water and the tree itself were their lifelines, and they had learnt to protect and cherish them.

In the heart of the tree, Warriorisborn often reflected on their journey. The old blind seer's warnings, Aza's guidance and the courage of his people had shaped their destiny. They had created a sanctuary in the most unlikely of places, proving that with determination and unity, they could overcome any obstacle.

The tree house stood tall, a beacon of hope and resilience. Warriorisborn knew their journey was far from over, but he was confident that together, they could face whatever the future held. Their story was one of survival, courage and the unbreakable spirit of a people who had turned disaster into opportunity.

Chapter Three
The Horror Race

That, too, was not enough, for the population did continue to rise alongside the danger.

Warriorisborn and his chiefs devised a cunning plan to solve two pressing issues with one brutal solution. They invented an annual race, set in the tree house, to take place seven days before the crumbling of the big step. The dual motives of this race were to retrieve the iron glass from the platform and to reduce the population of inhabitants. This race was exclusively for sixteen-year-old male occupants of the tree house. Each participant had to prove their worthiness by racing up the Step of Horror within seven days before the big shake. They had to retrieve an iron glass and descend seven days after the big shake, or else they would fall and die.

The challenge of climbing the Step of Horror in seven days was daunting due to its perilous shape and the fact that the base of the step only merged firmly seven days before the race. The path was treacherous, full of sharp turns and sudden drops that would test even the most agile climber. The steps were uneven and slippery, covered in moss and the remnants of previous races. This left the participants with only one option; to race up the step seven days before the big shake and descend seven days after. The base would be flooded, and they would have to swim out holding their iron glass as a victory token.

Despite knowing the plan was a death sentence, Warriorisborn and his chiefs were indifferent. Their main goal was to keep the tree house sustainable. They did not expect everyone to survive the race, but they were willing to pick the strongest among the people and make them soldiers. After devising this malevolent plot, they needed someone to take responsibility for the inevitable bloodshed. Anticipating potential future revenge from the people, they decided to crown Warriorisborn as the tree house king to maintain their innocence.

Warriorisborn stood before the assembly of tree house inhabitants, his expression stern and unyielding. "We need to ensure the survival and strength of our community," he announced. "Therefore, we shall hold an annual race to determine the worthy. Only those who can retrieve the iron glass and survive the Step of Horror will dine with the king at the treetop."

He paused, letting his words sink in. The crowd murmured uneasily. Parents exchanged worried glances, and young boys shifted nervously.

"As your king," Warriorisborn continued, "I promise rewards for those who succeed. Each participant will keep the iron glass they retrieve, helping to create more rooms in our tree house. Those who pass the test will be ordained as soldiers. Remember, fatigue makes cowards of men."

Despite the king's attempt at motivation, many saw the race as a suicide mission. Some parents decided to hide their sons who fell within the age category, unaware of the severe consequences.

The tension in the tree house was palpable. The first race took place under a heavy atmosphere. A few boys managed to reach the top, grasping their iron glass with trembling hands. Many more fell from the step and died instantly, their bodies crumpling on the hard ground below. The plan worked as expected, leading to significant controversy and hatred against Warriorisborn. The people were both sad and angry, but they did not realise that Warriorisborn was not the sole person to blame.

Six qualified candidates were caught hiding during the race. They were arrested and imprisoned, awaiting Warriorisborn's judgement. He convened with his chiefs to decide their punishment. Despite their past barbaric decisions and sentences, including drowning, women and children were not excluded from these punishments. At this point, none of his chiefs were willing to make joint decisions, fearing retaliation from the people. They were content with their luxury lifestyles in the treetop chambers, leaving Warriorisborn to make most decisions. They hailed him as the king of the tree house.

A few days later, Warriorisborn decided on the punishment. He called for the prisoners and sentenced them to death by drowning. This decision shocked many people, who cried for the innocent boys. But no one had the courage to challenge his authority. Suddenly, a woman ran up to him from the crowd, crying loudly. She knelt before him and pleaded for her son's life, revealing that he was the king's son. Her son, Followmehome, had been caught and imprisoned with the others. Kala, his mother, revealed his identity to the entire tree house occupants, hoping the king would show mercy.

"Please, Warriorisborn," she begged, tears streaming down her face. "Spare my son. He is your blood."

Warriorisborn's face hardened. He had ignored Kala due to his numerous affairs with other women in the tree house. Many of these women gave birth without his knowledge. Kala moved to the lower section of the tree, fearing for her son's safety. Even though Followmehome was willing to participate in the race, Kala stopped him out of fear. She feared for her son's life, knowing the treacherous journey that awaited him. He was caught and imprisoned, and no one knew his identity until Kala revealed it.

Despite Kala's plea, Warriorisborn stood by his rules. He felt bitter but tried not to show weakness. Followmehome and the other five boys—Ravana, Samael, Satan, Seth and Chernobog—were thrown into the ocean. All but Followmehome drowned. He survived the ocean waves and made it to land. This punishment continued for many years. Some victims made it to shore and discovered a land hundreds of miles away from the tree house, with Followmehome being the first man.

On this new land, Followmehome constructed tents covered with leaves. The land was lush and fertile, with a variety of plants and fruits that provided ample sustenance. After a few months, he met a lady named Crown, who had been banished from the tree house for prostitution. Crown had lived a hard life, surviving on her own in the wild. They fell in love and had six children, the first of whom was a daughter named Wealth of God. Wealth of God was strong, beautiful and energetic, growing up toned and fit like the boys on the land. She became competitive and less emotional due to her close relationship with her father.

As the years went by, more survivors were rescued from the ocean by Followmehome and his crew. They took the survivors under their wing and reassured them. The land was abundant with natural plants and fruits. An astonishing discovery was made; every child born on the land stopped ageing once they turned sixteen. These children were of mixed race like those in the tree house but were more toned and fit due to their swimming training by Followmehome. Their survival instincts were sharp, and they were adept at navigating the treacherous waters that surrounded their new home.

Followmehome spent years building ships and constructing large castles to house people. He became the leader of the Landers and trained many in swimming and sailing. He saved numerous victims from drowning in the ocean, with the support of his daughter and crew members. However, despite their efforts, more bodies surfaced under the ocean after every race. Followmehome felt it was time to end the barbaric laws of the tree house, but he did not know how to achieve this yet.

Chapter Four
The Landers

Over the years, the tree house had built a formidable army from worthy candidates who survived the Step of Horror and earned themselves an iron glass. These soldiers had grown enormously in number and strength, and they were now respected and regarded as the warriors of the tree house. For many years, rumours had been spread by the tree house scouts. One rumour was about a man spotted rescuing people from the deep ocean; he was said to have a large ship and crew members and was seen a few miles away.

Warriorisborn and his chiefs heard the rumour and could hardly believe it. Warriorisborn decided to visit Aza the blossom whisperer to learn if the people he had sentenced to drowning were still alive. He was astonished by Aza's confession. She told him the victims of the ocean were the Angels of Death, and each would rise after living in the sea for one hundred years. Immediately, the king perceived unforeseen danger from Aza's revelation.

One day, as the sun dipped low on the horizon, casting a warm glow over the tree house, a guard hurried towards the king, his footsteps echoing through the grand halls. His face was etched with urgency, his eyes wide with excitement as he approached the throne room.

"The scouts, Your Majesty," he began, breathless from his haste, "they've returned with news. They've seen him again."

The king's brow furrowed in surprise; his interest immediately piqued. Beside him, his chiefs exchanged quick glances, their expressions mirroring his astonishment. The mystery man, elusive and enigmatic, had once again crossed paths with their realm.

"How is this possible?" the king pondered aloud, his voice laced with a mixture of disbelief and intrigue. "How does he venture into the depths of the ocean without running out of breath?"

The question hung in the air, unanswered yet laden with curiosity. It was not only the king's desire to uncover the truth behind this mysterious figure but also to validate the unsettling revelations shared by Aza, whose words had ignited a spark of unease within the hearts of the tree house inhabitants.

As the sun began its descent, casting long shadows across the tree house, the king convened with his chiefs in the war room. They gathered around a rough-hewn table; maps spread out before them, the flickering candlelight casting an eerie glow.

"We must find this mystery man," declared the king, his voice low and determined. "To unlock the puzzle of our myths."

"Aye, Your Majesty," nodded one of the chiefs, his brow furrowed in concentration. "But how shall we proceed?"

The king leaned forward; his gaze fixed on the map. "We'll need a boat," he said, his tone decisive. "A sturdy vessel to carry us across the ocean."

The following day, the king's orders rang out through the tree house, setting the servants into motion. They toiled tirelessly, hammering and sawing, until finally, a boat stood ready at the water's edge.

As the sun rose on the horizon, painting the sky in hues of pink and gold, the king, his chiefs, Gandoki and four trusted servants embarked on their journey. The boat creaked and groaned as it sliced through the water, the rhythmic sound of oars dipping and pulling filling the air.

At first, the journey seemed promising, the wind at their backs and the sun on their faces. But as they ventured deeper into the ocean, the mood aboard the boat grew sombre. The vast expanse of water stretched out endlessly before them, a daunting reminder of the challenges that lay ahead.

Days turned into weeks, and still, there was no sign of the mystery man. Hunger gnawed at their stomachs, the meagre rations dwindling with each passing day. Finally, the king called his chiefs aside, his voice low and urgent.

"We cannot continue like this," he said, his eyes dark with resolve. "We must make a sacrifice."

Gandoki, weakened by hunger and exhaustion, lay curled up in fitful sleep, unaware of the conversation taking place around him. With heavy hearts, the king and his chiefs made their decision, their words spoken in hushed tones, their faces etched with guilt.

And so, under the cover of night, the deed was done. Gandoki, still lost in slumber, was cast overboard; his fate sealed by the hands of his own kin. And as the waves swallowed him whole, the king and his chiefs turned to the four servants, their eyes gleaming with hunger and desperation.

It was a secret pact, forged in the darkness of the night, a grim reminder of the lengths to which they would go to achieve their goals. And as the boat sailed on, the echoes of their actions lingered in the air, a shadow that would haunt them forevermore.

It took months to reach the shore. The king was furious that he had to sacrifice his son for his selfish act, yet he was determined to do whatever it took to get him back. He felt disappointed but focused on the mission ahead. After a few days of trekking along the shore searching for the mystery man, they saw what looked like a big town from afar with many inhabitants. They were approached and guided to the head of the Landers, Followmehome.

As a respected man and king of the tree house, Followmehome welcomed him warmly and asked why he had come all this way. The king asked if he was the mystery man who rescued people from the deep ocean. Followmehome denied this but still wanted to know the purpose of the visit. Due to a lack of trust, he refused to admit he was the mystery man.

The king proceeded to make him an offer, asking if he could provide the name of the mystery man who rescued people from the deep ocean. He explained that Gandoki, his last son, fell overboard during a storm and was lost to the sea, and he needed him to be rescued. He never mentioned those who were slaughtered and promised to reward him with whatever he desired. Followmehome had waited for this moment, determined to end the barbaric acts of the tree house.

He felt this was his opportunity to gain access which would enable him to carry out his mission in the future. He requested from the king that Landers be allowed to participate in the tree house race if Gandoki was found. Warriorisborn agreed without hesitation, as he would do anything to recover his son. He could not forget how he had banished his first son, a heavy burden on his heart, and was ready to pay any price to bring back Gandoki.

None of his chiefs questioned his decision; they had lost concentration, believed they had sinned and were covered in guilt and fear. Followmehome promised to give him feedback by morning. A feast was thrown for the king, and people ate and danced around a bonfire all night, entertaining the tree house king.

Followmehome gathered his family and close advisors and revealed the conversation he had with the tree house king and his chiefs. He told them what he demanded and his intentions. He explained that if he was able to rescue Gandoki from the ocean, this would give the Landers access to the tree house race, reminding them of how much they needed iron glasses to protect themselves from unforeseen attacks. His plan was to negotiate with the tree house king to allow Landers to keep any iron glass retrieved from the race as a trophy. He promised not to reveal their source of strength, a fruit that grew on their land. Everyone agreed.

Meanwhile, the king stayed awake all night discovering the Landers' way of life, while his chiefs were in a brothel, intoxicated and bed, except Cyril, who sat with him all night to learn more about the Landers. They noticed one fruit the Landers were particularly interested in, and the king was curious if this might be what made them appear fit and strong. He told Cyril to pluck some on their way back. He also wondered why there were so many teenagers compared to adults, a puzzle he needed to solve.

Thereafter, Followmehome met with the tree house king and admitted he was the man they intended to meet. He agreed to look for Gandoki and appealed to the king, asking if the Landers could hold onto the iron glass retrieved from the race and take it back to the land. The king accepted and granted his request but asked for something in return; he wanted to know Followmehome's source of power.

Warriorisborn's intention was to empower himself only; he had no intention of sharing the source of power with the chiefs or any of the tree occupants. He wanted to be one step ahead of everyone else, to be able to swim across the ocean without drowning. He despised the fact that another ruler had access to a mortal secret, so he decided to establish a harmonious relationship with the Landers.

Followmehome, knowing how wise the king was, wanted to gather as much iron glass as possible in case of unforeseen situations in the future. His mother once told him, "The only way to destroy the tree house is to cut off all its roots with the iron glass." She claimed to have obtained this information from his father years ago during an affair, but no one knew how true the tale was.

Followmehome had a second meeting with his sons and advisors. They all wanted to prove to the tree house occupants that there was a better place to live than the tree. They all agreed and signed the deed.

The next day, Followmehome and the king boarded a ship, accompanied by Wealth of God and his crew members. They sailed towards where Gandoki was last seen. After several weeks on the ocean, Followmehome almost gave up, overwhelmed by seeing so many faces drowning in the ocean. But this time, he was on a mission to save one. It was tough on him, as he had been diving for weeks and unable to save any of the victims struggling beneath the ocean due to his objective. After several attempts, he spotted a boy who matched the description he was given, the last son of Warriorisborn, his stepbrother, Gandoki.

Gandoki admired his father and hoped one day to rule the tree house. He always wanted to prove his worth but had failed many attempts, making him dedicated to the service of the tree house, hoping for a chance to rule as king someday.

Gandoki returned to his father. In return, the king agreed to Followmehome's demands and gave the Landers access to compete in the Step of Horror race. However, there was a lack of trust between both parties. Followmehome decided to give the king an incorrect recipe of power (bitter leaf) instead of the fruit.

On the other hand, the king told his chiefs to pluck some fruits on their way back home. These fruits were covered in a hard shell and could be preserved for a long time. They set off to leave.

Followmehome, in a gesture of kindness, offered to assist the tree house king on his journey, guiding them across the deep ocean. With a sturdy ship and skilled crew, Followmehome ensured the king's safety amidst the unpredictable waves.

Grateful for this unexpected kindness, the tree house king found solace in Followmehome's hospitality. Relieved of the burdens of navigation and maritime challenges, he could finally relax, allowing a sense of tranquillity wash over him. As the days turned into weeks and the ship cut through the ocean's endless expanse, the king marvelled at the camaraderie and warmth displayed by the Landers.

Amidst the rhythmic lull of the waves, a bond of mutual respect and admiration blossomed between the two leaders. Conversations flowed freely as they shared stories of their respective lands and cultures, bridging the divide that once stood between them. Through laughter and shared experiences, they forged a connection that transcended their differences, fostering a newfound sense of unity and understanding.

After weeks of sailing, the king and his chiefs departed, extending their gratitude towards each other, and Followmehome headed back to land.

Warriorisborn and his chiefs decided to visit the Landers without any guards to gain their trust. They believed a man who saved people from the ocean would not hold them captive. They risked everything to seek power, but in the end, the men they fed on added to their guilt.

Chapter Five
The Mountain

The Landers were gearing up for the impending race. Followmehome gathered all sixteen-year-old male Landers and his six sons to prepare them for the task ahead despite only one of his sons being sixteen. He, along with his advisors, assembled the boys, both young and old, understanding the grave consequences if the king discovered they had stopped ageing. They resolved to keep this secret at all costs.

Years ago, Followmehome had discovered a colossal mountain named Ganjak, approximately four hundred and twenty-five miles from where the Landers had settled. Ganjak stood at an imposing height of nineteen thousand three hundred and forty-one feet above the land. It was a massive peak that would take days to climb. Followmehome intended for the qualified Landers to race to the top, giving them a foretaste of the challenges that lay ahead.

He led them on a long journey through the forest, taking several months. Eventually, they spotted what appeared to be a high wall in the distance. As they drew nearer, the wall grew larger, and some among them were astonished, while others felt fear. Upon reaching the base of Mount Ganjak, they realised the true enormity of the mountain. None had ever seen ground rise to such heights before. Followmehome instructed them to camp at the mountain's base for the night, in preparation for the next day's task.

Years prior, Followmehome had embarked on an adventure where he first encountered Mount Ganjak. This discovery piqued his curiosity, compelling him to explore what lay at the summit. His upbringing in the tree house had instilled in him the belief that treasures were always hidden at the top. Denied the opportunity to race on the horror step in his youth, he was eager to satisfy his curiosity and ambition. Despite the arduous journey, it took him six days to reach the peak of Ganjak. Along the way, he made many astonishing discoveries on land beside Mount Ganjak though he kept these findings to himself.

Now, standing at the base of the mountain once more, Followmehome reflected on his past adventure. He knew that the race up Mount Ganjak would be a formidable test for the young Landers. They would need to summon all their strength, courage and determination to reach the top. The race was not just about the climb but about preparing them for the unknown challenges of their future.

As the sun set behind the towering mountain, casting long shadows over the camp, Followmehome addressed the boys. He spoke of the importance of perseverance and the rewards of courage. He reminded them that this race was not just a test of physical endurance but a journey of self-discovery and growth. They would face their fears, push their limits and emerge stronger for it.

The boys listened intently, their eyes wide with anticipation and resolve. They understood the significance of the task before them. As they settled into their tents for the night, their thoughts were filled with the challenges that awaited them on the morrow. The climb would be difficult, but they were determined to prove themselves worthy of the task.

With the first light of dawn, the Landers would begin their ascent, embarking on a journey that would shape their destinies. The race up Mount Ganjak was more than a physical challenge; it was a rite of passage, a test of their very essence. And with Followmehome's guidance, they were ready to face whatever lay ahead.

At dawn, the air was crisp as Followmehome gathered the boys, their breaths visible in the morning chill. "Prepare yourselves," he commanded, his voice steady.

He made sure to reveal nothing of the mountain's height. He set the challenge: reach the top of Ganjak within four days or be eliminated from the tree house race.

The boys exchanged uneasy glances, staring up at the mountain that pierced the sky, its peak lost in the clouds. They couldn't fathom its height, but there was no turning back. This was a test they had to pass, and they steeled themselves for the climb.

The weight of the task settled over them as Followmehome explained the stakes. Only those who reached the top in time would earn the right to face the Step of Horror. With determination etched on their faces, they pledged to prove their worth.

Meanwhile, Warriorisborn, back in the tree house, gathered the members to announce the inclusion of the Landers in the upcoming race. His announcement sparked a mix of excitement and concern. Whispers spread, questioning why the Landers, previously banished, were now being welcomed back. Only Warriorisborn's closest advisors knew of the secret bargain with Followmehome.

In a secluded corner of the tree house, Lambert and Alexandre met in secret. Their love was a dangerous secret, punishable by death, as they had tragically witnessed with a fellow teenager. Driven by fear and the need for change, they plotted to dethrone the king. They believed their plan was foolproof and undetectable.

Tensions simmered within the tree house community. The decision to include the Landers was met with grumbling, yet no one dared to question Warriorisborn, except for his most trusted warrior, Godhascome. Known for his intelligence and bravery, Godhascome had conquered the Step of Horror in a record-breaking five days. This feat had earned him the king's trust and respect. In the private chambers, Godhascome approached Warriorisborn, his steps weighted with determination. "My lord," he began, his voice steady yet tinged with uncertainty, "may I inquire about the inclusion of the Landers in the upcoming race?"

Warriorisborn gestured for Godhascome to take a seat, his own posture exuding authority as he poured a drink. "It's a matter of strategy," the king replied, his tone measured. "The Landers, though banished, possess unique skills and strengths. Their participation will add an element of unpredictability to the race, keeping our contenders on their toes."

Godhascome furrowed his brow, unconvinced. "But my lord, are we not risking further unrest by allowing them to compete?"

Warriorisborn's expression softened slightly, betraying a hint of weariness. "Trust me, Godhascome," he said, meeting the warrior's gaze. "I have weighed the risks carefully. This decision is not made lightly, but I believe it is necessary for the future of the tree house."

Godhascome nodded though his doubts lingered. With a respectful bow, he took his leave, the conversation weighing heavily on his mind. Though he longed for further clarification, he knew better than to press the matter any further.

Followmehome and the boys began their ascent of Ganjak. The climb was gruelling, and the mountain's unyielding slopes claimed their energy. One of

Followmehome's sons lagged behind, unable to match the pace. On the fourth day, the summit was within reach. Followmehome, five of his sons and thirty-three boys stood at the peak, elation coursing through their veins. The view was breathtaking, and the achievement filled them with pride and hope for the tree house race.

They waited for the remaining boys, who eventually joined them without injury. After a night of rest at the summit, they began their descent, the journey taking several days. As they trekked back home, Followmehome spoke of the Step of Horror, omitting its unpredictable nature that shifted shape each year. The challenge was only months away, and tensions back at the tree house continued to rise.

Rumours of rebellion brewed, an alliance forming to oppose Warriorisborn's decision. Anger and bitterness festered among the people, their frustration growing as the race approached. Lambert and Alexandre, hidden masterminds of the dissent, aimed to end the king's regime and establish new, more lenient rules. They joined forces with Seditious, a shadowy figure, to lead the rebellion. The tree house community, unaware of the true instigators, teetered on the brink of upheaval, driven by a desperate desire for change and vengeance.

Four members of the alliance crafted a clandestine plan, vowing never to reveal it, even upon death. This secret transformed the tree house into a place of dread.

While Lambert and Alexandre were trying to form an alliance, they didn't reach out to Seditious alone; they contacted also a man known as the Anonymous. Anonymous derived his name from his nature, as no one knew his real name. He chose to live in the shadows on the downside of the tree house and stay away from the spotlight. However, he only interacts with a few, and these few regarded him as a powerful man due to his high intellect and wisdom. Besides, none of these few could truly describe him since one could only meet him in dark and hidden places.

Anonymous was fully aware of every plan and happening at the top. He gets firsthand information as he has ears in every nook and cranny of the tree house that reports to him, with Malachi being one of his favourite informants. Malachi brought the most critical news in detail.

Anonymous was well aware of Warriorisborn's tyranny. Although he wished he could fight the king, he knew he could not defeat Warriorisborn in direct confrontation. He declined to be part of Lambert and Alexandre's alliance, believing their plan would likely fail. He knew Warriorisborn was cunning and sensed their plan was doomed from the start.

Gandoki, the last son of Warriorisborn who induced the agreement made by both parties, had gone missing. He had not been seen for days and had not resumed his duty, as a result. Godhascome asked one of the guards to pay him a visit and find out why he had been absent from his post, but when the guard arrived at Gandoki's room, the door was ajar, but the room was empty.

Around three in the morning, a guard recalled seeing someone in the passage near Gandoki's chamber. The man's attire marked him as an outsider, unlike the king, his family, chiefs and soldiers, who lived at the tree's top and wore distinct garments.

In the heart of the tree house, skilled hands wove wonders from wool harvested from the trees. Creative women, their fingers nimble with talent, transformed nature's bounty into exquisite textiles. Yet, despite their artistry, their creations bore the mark of a divided society.

This discrepancy in dress mirrored the authoritarian rule that cast its shadow over the tree house. The unequal distribution of garments served as a visual reminder of the power dynamics at play, reinforcing the divisions within the community.

Garments of various styles and qualities were available, and each tier of society was distinguished by its own unique design. The king and his family were adorned in the highest quality; their attire bespoke of their elevated status. Chiefs followed, wearing garments of slightly lesser quality but still distinct in their design. Soldiers, at the lowest rung of the hierarchy, wore simpler attire, reflective of their position.

This stratification in clothing created an atmosphere of inequality, a constant reminder to the inhabitants of their place within the rigid social structure. The disparity in dress served as a stark visual cue of the authoritarian rule under which they lived.

On the night of Gandoki's disappearance, a man from the lower levels of the tree house was sighted near his chamber by a guard named Servant of Allah.

Servant of Allah's origins were shrouded in mystery and tragedy. Born during the great storm that caused their current residency in the tree house, his parents perished in the tempestuous waves, leaving him orphaned at the tender age of one. Miraculously, he emerged unscathed from the wreckage, discovered nestled in a cloth and sheltered within a wooden box. Beneath this makeshift cradle lay a hidden compartment containing enigmatic items—a metal cup, a bottle of poison and peculiar voodoo artefacts. These relics hinted at a past steeped in secrecy and mystique, casting a shadow of intrigue over Servant of Allah's upbringing.

Warriorisborn, moved by compassion and curiosity, took Servant of Allah under his wing. The enigmatic artefacts discovered with the orphaned child only deepened the mystery surrounding his origins. Despite their unknown significance, Warriorisborn kept them in his possession, convinced of their protective power. He raised Servant of Allah as his own, imparting knowledge and skills as a father would to his son.

As Servant of Allah matured, his calm demeanour and striking Arabian features belied a fierce determination. He proved his mettle at sixteen, fearlessly undertaking the daunting Step of Horror race. His performance was nothing short of exceptional, earning him admiration and respect. Notably, an ancient tattoo adorned his neck, a symbol of his formidable spirit and untamed nature. Warriorisborn watched with pride as Servant of Allah emerged victorious, a testament to his strength and resilience.

The figure spotted by the guard was none other than Dino, a member of the Alliance and the nephew of Seditious. Known for his rebellious nature and penchant for violence, Dino and his cohort orchestrated Gandoki's kidnapping as a ploy to sow chaos and distrust among Warriorisborn's ranks. Their plan aimed to inflict pain and confusion, disrupting the king's plans and instilling fear within his soldiers.

Dino and his comrades, identifiable by subtle symbols woven into their clothing—a clandestine emblem, perhaps, or a discreet mark—seized Gandoki and spirited him away to the middle of the ocean, where they callously cast him into the depths for a second time. Warriorisborn, consumed by anger and frustration, ordered a frantic search for Gandoki, but the young man remained elusive.

Captured and confined to a cell, Dino faced interrogation by the leader of the soldiers, Godhascome. Despite relentless questioning and torture, Godhascome remained unconvinced of Dino's innocence. However, Warriorisborn, trusting in Servant of Allah's judgement, dispensed swift and severe justice. Without due process, he raised his iron glass and condemned Dino to death—a decision that sent shockwaves through the Alliance, igniting further animosity towards the king.

As tensions simmered, the Landers prepared for the upcoming Step of Horror race, while Wealth of God harboured resentment at the gender-based discrimination, fuelling her determination to compete.

In the aftermath of Dino's demise, Warriorisborn's fury intensified. Unaware of Seditious's involvement, he ordered the arrest of Dino's parents, who confessed to knowing some Alliance members but remained ignorant of Seditious's leadership. Panic gripped the tree house as arrests ensued, and the Alliance braced for the king's wrath.

Anticipating Warriorisborn's retaliatory measures, the rebels plotted their own counterattack. Disguised amongst the populace, Seditious and his agents lurked in the shadows, their ranks swelling with discontented souls eager to challenge the king's authority. As Servant of Allah and his men ventured into the lower levels of the tree house, they were ambushed by the rebels, catching the soldiers off guard. In the ensuing chaos, many soldiers were overpowered, and the true extent of the rebellion's reach became chillingly clear.

A few soldiers of the tree house were arrested and beheaded under the supervision of Seditious.

Dino's family had a reputation for stirring up trouble. While they often fought for what they believed was right, their methods sometimes veered into the realm of rogue behaviour. Their relentless pursuit of justice, while commendable in intention, often led them down questionable paths, earning them notoriety for their unconventional and sometimes disruptive actions. Despite their noble motivations, their tendency to resort to extreme measures occasionally cast them as outlaws in the eyes of others.

Before Dino's beheading, anger simmered in the hearts of the Alliance. They sought a fearless leader to guide them through the unforeseen challenges that lay ahead, placing their trust in Seditious to lead them into the impending battle.

At this juncture, the Alliance had swelled to thousands in population, with numerous individuals rallying against the ruler of the tree house and uniting with the intention to dismantle the regime. Seditious served as the decoy, shielding the true masterminds of the Alliance, akin to the deceptive nature suggested by his name.

As Servant of Allah and a handful of soldiers staggered back to the king's side, their clothes torn and faces grim with the aftermath of the battle, they recounted the harrowing ambush. Warriorisborn's brow furrowed in disbelief as he absorbed the tale, his usual aura of authority momentarily shaken by the unexpected assault.

Sensing the gravity of the situation, Warriorisborn dismissed his council of chiefs, his gaze shifting to the intricately carved patterns adorning the walls of his chamber, symbols of his reign now cast in shadow by the threat from within.

Alone in his sanctum, Warriorisborn summoned his trusted right-hand man, the flickering torchlight casting dancing shadows across their faces. With a terse nod, he instructed his confidant to craft a strategy, a web of intrigue and deception designed to ensnare the elusive leader of the Alliance and bend the remaining rebels to his will.

Chapter Six
The Plan

The king, Warriorisborn, stood on the balcony of his grand tree house palace, gazing over the vast forest kingdom. He knew that a direct confrontation with the Alliance would result in a horrific bloodbath, with innocent lives lost in the chaos. His heart heavy, he decided to request an interpersonal meeting with the leader of the Alliance, Seditious. The aim was clear: to resolve their disputes peacefully and lay past grievances to rest.

Summoning his most trusted advisors, Warriorisborn announced his plan. The room fell silent, the gravity of his words sinking in. He then stepped onto the balcony, addressing the gathered crowd below. His voice, steady and reassuring, carried through the air, promising his people that there would be no bloodshed. He gave them his word that the purpose of the meeting was to seek an agreement with the Alliance, a chance for peace.

Seditious, always suspicious, was intrigued by this sudden offer of compromise. He sent two of his rebels, stealthy and cunning, to visit the king. Their mission was to request that the meeting be held publicly, where both leaders would meet openly before the eyes of the crowd. When they arrived at the palace, Warriorisborn received them with unexpected kindness. Without hesitation, he agreed to the public meeting, his eyes revealing nothing of the calculations behind his decision.

A few hours after the agreement, Warriorisborn made a public announcement. He informed the people about the upcoming discussion with Seditious, assuring them once more that no harm would come to anyone. The announcement sparked a mixture of hope and apprehension among the people, who longed for peace but feared betrayal.

In the depths of his study, Warriorisborn examined the metal cup he had been studying for years. From the outside, it looked like any other cup, but its inner workings were a marvel. Two concealed layers allowed the lower part to fill with liquid first, sealing off before the upper part filled, creating an illusion of normalcy. This cup would play a crucial role in his plan.

Seditious got the feedback from the king, a date was set the Alliance were confident they got him to come to an agreement.

News of the meeting spread quickly, and the Alliance felt confident they had cornered the king into negotiating. But Warriorisborn had learnt something troubling about Seditious: he had a habit of making his men taste his food and drink before he did. This knowledge complicated the king's plan to poison him. Yet Warriorisborn was determined. He decided that the best way to defeat Seditious was through cunning rather than brute force.

On the day of the event, both parties arrived with their men, the atmosphere thick with anticipation. The meeting began, dragging on for hours. Tensions ebbed and flowed as the two leaders, Warriorisborn and Seditious, discussed their differences. As time passed, Seditious started to relax, a smug smile playing on his lips. He felt he had achieved the impossible—negotiating with the king. To him, this was the pinnacle of his accomplishments. Occasionally, he laughed, a sound that grated on Warriorisborn, who maintained a calm exterior while rage simmered beneath the surface.

Warriorisborn, ever patient, waited for the perfect moment. The hours of discussion seemed endless, but finally, an agreement was reached. The crowd erupted in cheers, believing they had witnessed the end of a long-standing conflict. Warriorisborn rose, his movements measured and deliberate, and clicked his fingers. A smile played on his lips as the metal cup was brought to the table.

He was poured a cup of spirit and, for the first time, stood up. The crowd fell silent, astonished. He drank from the cup, each swallow a display of his unwavering resolve. As he sat down, applause and cheers filled the air. The cup was then refilled for Seditious from a jar that contained a drop of poison. Warriorisborn had pondered whether the metal cup would conceal the poison, but ultimately, he decided to poison the entire jar to ensure the plan's success.

Seditious, basking in his perceived triumph, eagerly accepted the cup. Joy and arrogance were etched on his face as he lifted it high, acknowledging the crowd's applause. He drank deeply, emptying the cup without hesitation. For a moment, nothing happened, and a triumphant grin spread across his face. But then, his expression twisted in pain. His head suddenly ignited, flames engulfing him in an instant. He burned from head to toe, collapsing like a charred matchstick.

The silence that followed was heavy with disbelief and fear. No one could comprehend how the king had managed to kill Seditious without breaking his promise. Warriorisborn, having anticipated the possibility of Seditious's caution, had outwitted him with the poisoned jar. As the last embers of Seditious's body smouldered, Warriorisborn declared, "To kill a snake, strike at its head," his laughter filling the air as the Alliance bowed in submission.

Warriorisborn decided to take his shot, he perceived Seditious might have one of his rebel's drinks before him, and if the poison took effect, the Alliance would be aware of his intentions, and there would be bloodshed, he decided to put a drop of the poison in the jar of spirit, Seditious was indulged with the atmosphere, he felt comfortable and end up roasted.

In the aftermath, Warriorisborn addressed his soldiers, demanding the truth about Gandoki's kidnapping. Promising clemency to anyone who knew his whereabouts, he watched as Judas, trembling with fear, stepped forward. Admitting his role in the crime for which Dino had been beheaded, Judas confessed that Gandoki had been dropped into the ocean. The king's fury was palpable as he demanded the names of the other culprits. Judas, hoping for mercy, revealed Zacus and Fili, unaware that forgiveness was foreign to the king.

Zacus and Fili, pale and shaking, begged for their lives before the king. They were terrified of what would happen next, the tension growing within their hearts as they quivered before the lion-like eyes of Warriorisborn staring into their eyes.

Warriorisborn, his voice resonating with authority, demanded if anyone knew the exact spot where Gandoki had been dropped. Zacus, trembling but resolute, stepped forward, promising to help locate it. Without hesitation, the king drew his iron glass blade and swiftly executed Judas and Fili. The crowd gasped, their screams piercing the air. "No bargains in my tree house," the king declared coldly, "Anyone who wants to leave can swim to the land."

Meanwhile, Followmehome and his boys were fully prepared for the upcoming Step of Horror race, now just a few months away. One sunny afternoon, a royal messenger arrived by boat, bearing an urgent request for Followmehome's presence at the tree house. He gathered his family and advisors, sharing the message and their collective concerns. They all agreed that he should go and attend to the king.

Curious about the king's urgent summons, Followmehome decided to bring his daughter along for the visit despite his first son, Mighty, hoping to be chosen. Warriorisborn, desperate and guilt-ridden over the loss of his beloved son Gandoki, felt an insistent need for Followmehome's assistance. The pain of losing Gandoki gnawed at his conscience, and he was overwhelmed with the need to rescue his son once again, even if it came at a significant cost.

Calling his right-hand man, Godhascome, Warriorisborn and he brainstormed an offer that would entice Followmehome. Suddenly, Servant of Allah entered, bowing deeply before the king. "Apologies for the interruption, my lord," he said, his voice filled with conviction. "But I have a suggestion. Offer Followmehome the poison bottle. If he could save the people from the ocean, he doesn't have the intention to kill or destroy."

Warriorisborn turned to Servant of Allah, considering his words. "Your reason?" he asked, curious about the unexpected advice.

Servant of Allah straightened, meeting the king's gaze. "If Followmehome accepts the poison without hesitation, it will show his commitment to peace. It will prove his intentions are not to harm, but to protect and preserve."

The room fell silent as Warriorisborn contemplated the suggestion. Finally, he nodded slowly. "Very well. We shall test his intentions in this manner. Prepare the bottle and send word to Followmehome."

Godhascome, still uncertain but respecting the wisdom in Servant of Allah's proposal, bowed and left the room. The king's decision would soon reveal the true nature of Followmehome's intentions, a test of trust in these tumultuous times.

Followmehome, with his daughter and crew, sailed to the tree roots' edge. They dove into the ocean, swimming towards the tree house amidst the loud cheers and admiration from the onlookers. Guarded by soldiers, they walked into the tree house where the king greeted them warmly, declaring a grand feast. The night was filled with merriment, the air alive with celebration.

In the absence of any prying eyes, Followmehome visited his mother, Kala, in the lower section of the tree house, with his daughter.

Time had caught up with Kala, but her spirit was unbroken. She was excited to see him though her face held a mix of joy and regret. She was angry at herself for having done nothing when he was cast into the ocean years ago. How joyful she was to meet one of her grandchildren, for the first time!

Kala held Wealth of God so close to herself, as if to absorb her presence while she could.

Followmehome spoke gently, repeating all that had passed between him and the king. She listened quite attentively until he was done.

Kala's expression had turned serious. She then asked, "Does he know you're his son?"

Followmehome shook his head. "I'm not sure."

Kala continued, "Do not reveal your identity yet. You must stop him, and find a way to dry up the tree."

"Dry up the tree? How do I do that?" Followmehome asked, puzzled.

"The poison," she replied, and then, leaning heavily on her stick, she slowly got up and led them to the door. "It is currently your father's most treasured possession. This old woman has to get her sleep now. Goodnight, my lovely ones."

Followmehome had the door shut in his face before he could truly process the words of his mother. While all of these didn't sit well with Wealth of God due to her long-time admiration for the tree house and the tree house king, she remained composed and sincerely hoped her father would not get possession of the poison.

Our solution is poison?

The next morning, the king called a public meeting, ensuring that Followmehome and his daughter were present. The gathering was large, the crowd eager to hear what their king had to say. Warriorisborn began with praises, extolling Followmehome's bravery and humility, painting a picture of a loyal and valiant ally. However, he omitted one crucial detail—the story of how Followmehome had previously rescued Gandoki from the depths of the ocean. This secret was known only to Warriorisborn and his closest chiefs. The king feared that revealing this information might weaken his own image as a strong and capable ruler.

Standing tall before the assembly, Warriorisborn turned to Followmehome, his voice carrying a blend of authority and desperation. "Followmehome," he announced, "once more, I seek your unmatched courage. My son, Gandoki, is in grave peril, and I ask you to rescue him for the second time."

A murmur ran through the crowd, but the king continued, "In gratitude, I offer you something of great value—this poison bottle." He held up a bottle with a red skull imprinted on it. "Its contents are powerful, a symbol of control and ultimate power. Use it wisely or dispose of it as you see fit."

Followmehome's eyes gleamed with interest. He held his breath for a moment. Was this coincidence or fate? He was just thinking of how he would sneak into the king's chamber and steal it, yet here it was being presented to him on a golden platter. The poison bottle was not just a weapon; it was a tool of power and influence, something he could use to protect his people or solidify his position. He nodded solemnly, understanding the gravity of the task and the reward. The poison bottle represented a double-edged sword—an opportunity and a challenge.

With a deep breath, Followmehome agreed to the king's request. "I will find Gandoki and bring him back," he vowed, the weight of the mission heavy on his shoulders. His daughter stood by his side, her presence a reminder of what he was fighting for.

Warriorisborn felt a surge of relief. The guilt that had plagued him, the nights spent in restless torment over Gandoki's fate, now had a glimmer of hope. Followmehome's acceptance was a lifeline, a chance to make amends for the pain he had caused.

Immediately after, as the sun cast its golden rays upon the gathered crowd, Wealth of God seized her moment. She had been waiting patiently, biding her time to present her own demands. Stepping forward with a confident grace, she addressed the king directly.

"Your Majesty, if I may," she began, her voice clear and unwavering. "I have a proposal to put forth. For too long, women have been excluded from participating in the Step of Horror race. I ask for permission for women to join the upcoming race, and I personally request to be allowed to compete."

A murmur of surprise rippled through the assembly. Wealth of God stood tall, meeting the king's gaze with determination. "I promise to be the first to make it to the platform," she declared, her words carrying a weight of conviction.

Warriorisborn regarded her thoughtfully, the crowd's whispers growing louder. The idea was unconventional, yet the king saw in Wealth of God a strength and resolve that mirrored his own. He nodded slowly—screwing his eyes—acknowledging her courage and the merit of her request.

A wave of surprise swept through the crowd.

The king, taken aback by Wealth of God's boldness, turned to Followmehome. "What do you think of your daughter's opinion?" he asked, genuinely curious.

Followmehome, though initially displeased that Wealth of God had spoken to the king without his consent, figured that his mother's words had reached his daughter. Realising the significance of the moment and the potential for change, he decided to support her. He nodded, standing by his daughter. "I trust her judgement, Your Majesty. She has the heart and the strength to succeed."

She breathed out in relief.

Encouraged by her father's support, Wealth of God made another proposal. "Your Majesty, should I surpass all the male participants in the Step of Horror race, what would my reward be?"

Warriorisborn, intrigued by her confidence, smiled and asked, "What do you desire as your reward?"

Without hesitation, Wealth of God replied, "I wish to keep my iron glass blade, the poison bottle, and the metal cup."

Followmehome nodded, seeing his conjecture was right.

The crowd fell silent, astonished by her audacious request. The king, however, could not help but admire her spirit and determination. "Very well," he declared. "If you win, you shall have all that you ask for."

A cheer erupted from the crowd, the atmosphere electric with excitement. Both parties celebrated, the people of the tree house recognising the significance of this moment. Wealth of God's challenge symbolised more than just a race; it was a step towards greater equality and the breaking of old traditions.

The next day, Followmehome, accompanied by the king's guards and Zacus, sailed to the spot where Gandoki had been dropped. After several days of tireless searching, they found Gandoki and managed to revive him. The return journey to the tree house was filled with anticipation, and as they arrived, the people hailed Followmehome, the mystery man who had once again performed a miracle.

Upon meeting the king, Warriorisborn wasted no time. He drew out his iron glass blade and, with a swift motion, beheaded Zacus. "No sinner must go unpunished!" he declared, his voice resonating with a chilling finality. Followmehome stood there, dumbfounded. He could not believe what he had just witnessed. Thoughts raced through his mind—had Warriorisborn turned into a monster? He forced himself to remain calm and composed though anger churned within him.

Warriorisborn's brutal display of power was a clear message to his people: he ruled with an iron fist, making judgments based on his will alone. His absolute commands and authority were starkly opposed to Followmehome's beliefs in democracy and collective decision-making.

Later, in the privacy of the king's chambers, they poured themselves cups of spirit. Followmehome, still troubled, asked, "Why did you decide to behead Zacus?"

Warriorisborn's gaze was steady. "This is not land; this is the tree house. Here, there will always be a hierarchy. On land, all things can be levelled, but on a tree, sacrifices must be made for it to thrive, or else we become too much for it to carry."

Followmehome responded thoughtfully, "Maybe people are not meant to live on a tree in the first place."

Warriorisborn laughed, a sound filled with the weight of years of rulership. "What do you know? Maybe one day you will understand. Destiny chose us; we didn't choose destiny. Your bravery made you a leader of the Landers, just as my rules shape the tree house."

Followmehome said nothing more and retreated to his room.

The next morning, Followmehome called his daughter and set off for land. On arriving, he instructed her to prepare for a journey to Ganjak. On the way to the mountain, he revealed his plan with his daughter, Wealth of God as he felt it called for urgency. "You will win the race," he told her. "We need the poison and the cup. It's the puzzle piece that might end the rule of the tree house."

"Why?" she asked, slightly annoyed, though she suspected the answer.

"It could be the key to bringing balance," Followmehome replied, looking at her as if it was supposed to be obvious enough. "We must dry up the tree."

Wealth of God was conflicted. While she understood her father's intentions, she also had her own ambitions. She was power-greedy and wanted to carve her name in history, not just as a participant but as a champion. Despite her father's plan, she harboured her own secret hopes and dreams, ones she kept secret even from her father. They reached the mountain base, and she was in awe of its towering presence.

Her father laid out the challenge. "If you want to win the Step of Horror race and achieve your desires, you must reach the top in four days and descend immediately. I will wait here for your return, but you must come back in eight days. If not, I will leave and return home. Your time starts now."

Shocked and angered by the sudden demand, Wealth of God bit back her questions. She remembered how her father had accompanied the boys during their tasks and felt a pang of unfairness. Still, with a few fruits in her bag, she set off alone, determined to prove herself.

Followmehome, despite his intentions for her to receive the best training, was also irate. Her demands in the tree house without his approval had made him reluctant to accompany her. As he watched her leave, he hoped she would succeed, not just for the mission's sake, but to realise her own strength and potential.

Chapter Seven
The Arrival

The Step of Horror race was only a few months away, and anticipation buzzed through the tree house. Warriorisborn, standing before the assembly, addressed the eager crowd. His voice carried a promise of unprecedented excitement. "This year's race will be the greatest event in our history," he declared. "For the first time, the Landers will join us, and most importantly, Wealth of God, the first female participant, will compete."

The crowd erupted in murmurs. Parents exchanged worried glances while many females cheered enthusiastically. Warriorisborn continued, his tone firm yet encouraging, "This will give our women a chance to participate in future races, should she emerge victorious. However, I must stress that participation is not mandatory. Only those who are willing to join me at the treetop should take part."

His words ignited a mix of reactions. While some parents grumbled in concern, fearing the dangers their daughters might face, the younger females were invigorated by the opportunity. For them, it was a chance to break boundaries and prove their strength.

In the days that followed, the tree house was abuzz with preparations and training. The Landers also trained rigorously, their determination unyielding.

The tree house community was alive with energy, and Warriorisborn continued to rally his people, emphasising the historical significance of the event. He spoke of unity and strength, of the importance of courage and determination.

"We stand on the brink of a new era," he proclaimed. "Let this race be a testament to our spirit and resilience. May it bring honour to those who dare to compete and glory to our tree house."

The atmosphere was charged with a sense of impending change. The Step of Horror race promised to be more than just a competition; it was a symbol of potential transformation and the breaking of old traditions.

On the eighth day, Wealth of God descended from Mount Ganjak, her body aching from the arduous journey. Her father, Followmehome, welcomed her with pride and relief. "Rest for the evening," he told her. They set up camp around a fire, enjoying a hearty meal before settling down for the night.

As they sat by the flickering flames, Wealth of God broke the silence. "Was that training or punishment?" she asked, her voice tinged with exhaustion.

Followmehome, contemplating her question, remained silent for a moment. He understood the importance of the poison after his last visit to his mother. Although he wasn't entirely pleased with the demands Wealth of God had made to the king without his acknowledgement, he believed it was their opportunity to obtain the substance that could potentially end the tree house's barbaric laws. Torn between honesty and encouragement, he finally spoke, "It was both, my daughter. To strengthen you for what lies ahead and to prepare you for the challenges you'll face. I am proud of your bravery."

The Step of Horror race was fast approaching, and the Landers were busy preparing their ships for the journey. Excitement and anticipation filled the air. Followmehome and Wealth of God had just returned from their journey, and the news spread quickly. Followmehome gathered the Landers to announce the outcome of their visit to the tree house, carefully choosing his words.

"The females who might be interested in joining the Step of Horror race in the future may now have a chance," he said, "thanks to the demands my daughter made to the tree house king."

Someone in the crowd called out, "What were the demands?"

Followmehome replied, "Wealth of God will be joining the race as the only woman this time. She asked the king to allow women the privilege to participate if she completes the race. The king agreed, but he made it clear that it's not mandatory."

The crowd erupted in cheers, proud of their leaders and the strides being made for equality. Followmehome announced, "We leave in a fortnight." The joy and pride among the Landers were palpable.

Meanwhile, in the tree house, Warriorisborn was meticulously preparing for the race. He spoke with his right-hand man, Godhascome, expressing his desire for the event to be epic. "Many are called, but few are chosen," he said, his eyes gleaming with anticipation.

Godhascome took the king's instructions seriously, ensuring that all sectors of the tree house understood the high expectations. He warned them of the consequences of failing to meet these expectations, instilling a sense of urgency and discipline among the participants.

As the race day drew nearer, both the tree house and the Landers were abuzz with preparation and excitement. The stage was set for an event that promised to be historic, not just for the competition itself, but for the potential shift in traditions and the hope of a more inclusive future.

Wealth of God, though still recovering from her gruelling training, felt a sense of purpose and determination. She knew that her performance in the race could open doors for future generations of women. As she looked around at the bustling preparations, she felt the weight of her responsibility but also the thrill of making history.

A few days later, Aza the blossom whisperer visited the king in his private chambers. Her presence was always a mix of serenity and wisdom, and this visit was no different. "Warriorisborn," she began, her voice calm yet firm, "you must not give away the poison and metal cup. You know how powerful they are."

Warriorisborn sighed, acknowledging her concern. "I know their power, Aza. But I have already made a deal. Besides, I am confident that no female can win the Step of Horror race."

Aza's eyes flashed with intensity. "She is not just any female, she is the powerful one. You must understand that she stands a real chance of winning. Make her an offer she cannot refuse to keep her by your side."

The king digested her advice, realising the gravity of the situation. He nodded slowly. "Thank you, Aza, for your counsel. I will consider it."

Exactly a fortnight later, Followmehome, his children—Wealth of God, Monkey, Magnus, Moses, Mighty, and Miracle—the contestants, and a few advisors set off on their journey to the tree house. This time, experience had taught them well, and they found a faster route, significantly shortening their travel time.

As they approached the tree house, the anticipation grew. The contestants were eager, their spirits high, while Followmehome remained focused on the dual goals of the race and the larger mission at hand. Wealth of God, in particular, felt a mix of nerves and determination. She knew this was her moment to prove herself and secure a future for other women in her community, and largely to achieve her selfish dream.

After a few months had passed, the day finally arrived for the Landers to journey to the tree house territory. As their ships anchored near the tree house, the Landers, led by Followmehome, prepared to make their dramatic entrance. With a sense of purpose and anticipation, they dove into the ocean and swam towards the tree house.

The tree house occupants watched in awe and delight. The Landers moved with remarkable skill and grace through the water, their determination evident in every stroke. Among them, Wealth of God swam with a fierce resolve, her eyes fixed on the towering tree house that loomed ahead.

As they reached the shore and emerged from the water, the Landers were greeted with a mixture of admiration and curiosity. The tree house people had heard tales of the Landers' bravery and skill, but witnessing it firsthand was a different experience altogether.

Warriorisborn stood at the edge of the gathering, his expression unreadable. He watched as Followmehome and his children approached, their presence commanding respect. Beside him, Godhascome and other advisors murmured amongst themselves, impressed by the Landers' display.

The guards greeted them as usual and escorted them into the tree house. It was a glorious day, indeed. The Step of Horror race was just a few days away, and the Landers were prepared. They were about to witness the collapse of the horror step as the floor was said to be merging up firmly, according to the stories they had heard. They had six days and a few hours to go.

They were offered spirit to ease the cold. Followmehome, though not entirely agreeable to consuming spirits, could not deny the culture. Respecting the tradition, they all drank as they walked towards the entrance. The warmth of the spirit spread through them, contrasting with the cool air around them.

As they entered the tree house, the Landers were met with an astonishing sight. The grandeur of the tree house, with its sprawling network of wooden pathways and platforms intertwined with the massive tree trunks, left them in awe. Their eyes widened, mouths agape at the intricate beauty of it all. Everyone was stunned, except for Wealth of God.

Her composure did not surprise the others, as they knew this was not her first visit to the tree house. Wealth of God moved through the space with familiarity and confidence, unfazed by the wonder that captivated her companions. Her experience here had already steeled her against the initial shock.

Wealth of God was trained by her father to be resilient and composed, a training that made her less emotional. She neither laughed aloud nor cried in agony. The first time she laid eyes on the Step of Horror, she remained unfazed by its enormity. Without hesitation, she demanded to the king that she be allowed to race on the Step of Horror.

As the male Landers approached the daunting structure, their hearts sank. The sight was intimidating, and doubts began to creep in. Wealth of God's brothers suddenly thought she might be overambitious to believe she could win this race.

Seeing their apprehension, Followmehome decided to share a crucial rule to assist the Landers. "Never look down while climbing," he advised them. They nodded, absorbing his wisdom as they followed the guards to their place of rest to prepare for the race.

The tree house had evolved significantly, but disparities in the distribution of amenities were still evident. They had constructed manual wooden elevators that travelled swiftly to the upper parts of the tree, but these were accessible only to the king and his associates.

Before the race, Followmehome gathered the Landers. "Do not wait for one another during the race," he instructed. "This is a test of individual endurance and strength."

Chapter Eight
Angel of Death Scare

Followmehome entered the king's chamber, greeted by Warriorisborn with open arms. They sat down, and servants poured them cups of spirit. The open windows were draped with heavy red curtains, dimming the sunlight that filtered through. The room was filled with naked women, ready to indulge the king's desires at his command.

The king leaned back, a sly smile playing on his lips. "Tell me, Followmehome, what do you predict will be the outcome of this race? Remember, the agony of seeing loved ones fall from the Step of Horror is no small thing. As entertaining as it is, it's a game of death."

Followmehome took a sip of his drink, his eyes steady. "The Landers are superhumans," he replied confidently. "I promise you, they will all be victorious."

Warriorisborn raised his cup, his smile widening. "I admire your confidence. To victory, then!"

They clinked their cups together, the sound of their cheer mingling with the subdued murmur of the room. Despite the king's dark reminders, Followmehome maintained his composure, steadfast in his belief in his people's strength and resilience.

As the celebrations continued, Aza the blossom whisperer entered the chamber, leaning on her walking stick and shrouded in a black garment. The room fell silent, her presence commanding respect. Warriorisborn stood up, a frown creasing his brow.

"Aza, what brings you here?" he questioned, his voice edged with curiosity and caution.

Aza nodded and gestured for the king to follow her into his private chamber. Once inside, away from prying eyes and ears, Warriorisborn motioned for her to speak.

"Land is the future," she began, her voice carrying the weight of prophecy. "You must chase the future to avoid defeat."

Warriorisborn listened intently, understanding the gravity of her words but unsure of the path to take. "What should be done to achieve this purpose?" he asked, seeking her guidance.

Aza's eyes gleamed with a knowing light. "You must ensure that Wealth of God is within your reach. She is the key. Keep her close, and I will reveal the next steps when the time is right."

Warriorisborn nodded, absorbing her advice. The importance of Wealth of God in his plans became clearer. Aza, having delivered her message, turned and left the chamber, her black garment flowing behind her like a shadow.

As she exited, Warriorisborn sat back, contemplating his next move. He knew he needed to act swiftly and decisively to secure his future and the future of his kingdom.

Followmehome couldn't shake the sense of mystery surrounding Aza. Her presence had clearly unsettled the king, which indicated her immense power. Sensing that Warriorisborn might need some time alone after his sudden change in mood, Followmehome left the king's chamber and made his way to the down section of the tree, where his mother, Kala, resided. He was determined to find answers to the questions swirling in his mind, especially about Aza.

Entering his mother's chamber, Followmehome greeted her and immediately demanded some answers. He was not astounded by her reply.

"Aza the blossom whisperer," Kala began, "is the great witch of the tree house. Her family has been creating the deadliest poisons ever known. Their mastery over such dark arts is what makes the Blossom Whisperers so powerful."

Followmehome's eyes widened slightly, pieces of the puzzle falling into place. "Is this the same poison you spoke of when we last met?" he asked.

Kala nodded solemnly. "Yes, it is. Aza's family crafted that poison. Its potency is unparalleled."

This revelation clarified his doubts, reinforcing the importance of obtaining the poison. He believed that possessing it would give him the means to end the bloodshed and tyranny that plagued the tree house.

Determined, Followmehome felt a renewed sense of purpose. He returned to his quarters, contemplating his next steps. He knew he needed to tread carefully, balancing the need to protect his people while navigating the treacherous politics of the tree house.

Warriorisborn sat in his chamber, pondering the words of the blossom whisperer. As he poured himself a cup of spirit, lost in thought, Aza materialised before him once more, her presence unnoticed until she stood directly in front of him.

"Aza!" Warriorisborn exclaimed, startled. "I did not hear you enter."

Ignoring his surprise, Aza delivered her urgent message to the king. "Demetrious has risen," she announced, her voice grave with concern.

Warriorisborn was shocked by her statement. Standing up, he demanded, "What do you mean by this?"

Calmly, Aza explained, "The first victim who was sentenced by drowning would be unleashed in eight days' time, this would mark exactly one hundred years that Demetrious had been sentenced and, dear king, he shall rise again on that day. And he shall rise, not in human form, but as an angel; the Angel of Death."

Demetrious was a young boy who was seven years old, at that time, when the crash occurred. Unlike him, however, his parents hadn't been that fortunate. They had died instantly, losing their lives to the storm and ensuing crash.

The boy, Demetrious, had had a very feminine disposition over time and had even been caught getting laid with the tree house males, a few times. That information had gotten to the ears of the king and his chiefs and, after mutual agreement between Warriorisborn and his chiefs, a unanimous decision was made to have Demetrious sentenced to death.

He was banished and cast into the unforgiving embrace of the ocean for his transgressions, feared to corrupt others with his influence. While his accomplice was spared, Demetrious faced his punishment just two days after the harrowing commencement of his terrifying ordeal.

Demetrious and Crown became the inaugural individuals banished from the tree house for engaging in unauthorised sexual activities. Crown faced charges of prostitution, while Demetrious was condemned for his homosexuality. It was disheartening to note that the very crimes for which they were sentenced persisted among the lawmakers, who clandestinely engaged in similar acts.

Crown became the first woman to set foot on land after the banishment. Subsequently, Followmehome and five other boys—Ravana, Samel, Satan, Seth, and Chernborg—faced prosecution for avoiding participation in the step of the horror race.

Followmehome was the only survivor; the rest, who had drowned, were destined to transform into Angels of Death after enduring a hundred years of agony in the ocean's depths. In a matter of time, they too would be unleashed, seeking to devour humans to alleviate their torment.

Chapter Nine
The Hundredth Step of Horror Race

The event was a grand spectacle, filled with merriment. Everyone was drinking and revelling in the festivities. The contestants were ready, and the Landers were eager to witness the dramatic collapse of the Step.

Exactly at midnight, on the one hundred and seventh year after their ship had crashed into the tree house, the Step collapsed as usual. To the Landers, it felt like magic. They were amazed by the sight of the massive Step falling while the platform remained intact at the treetop, creating a magnificent spectacle. Although prepared, they feared the race would not be as easy as they had thought. Yet they were ready to proceed, even if it might spell the end of their existence. They awaited the start bell with trepidation.

Meanwhile, Wealth of God remained in her chamber, relaxing her muscles with her eyes closed. She meditated, envisioning the glory of emerging victorious in the Step of Horror race. The inspiration she felt boosted her courage, and she was determined to fulfil the vow she had made.

At twelve noon, the Step regrew as usual, but this time it had a horrible, bumpy appearance unlike anything they had anticipated. The Landers were shocked; they had not been informed of this aspect of its features. They had expected the Step to return to its previous shape, not to transform into an entirely new and unrecognised form. Even Followmehome was astounded, caught off guard by this unforeseen change.

Followmehome was as shocked as the rest of the Landers at the Step's new shape. He was amazed that none of the previous survivors had mentioned this aspect of its features; it seemed most had forgotten. The tree house contestants proceeded first, with the Landers following immediately. Wealth of God was the only female among them.

They all began their ascent on the Step of Horror, immediately realising the challenge that lay ahead. The surface was rough and treacherous, each step more precarious than the last. Determination turned to grim understanding; this was merely the beginning of their ordeal. As they climbed higher, the difficulty intensified.

Some tree house contestants lost their footing after just a few hours, plummeting to their deaths even from low altitudes. The onlookers from the tree house remained unfazed, cheering as the race continued. The king and his chiefs, alongside Followmehome, watched with bated breath, their anticipation palpable. Wealth of God, the lone female contestant, pressed on, her resolve unwavering amidst the peril.

However, the parents whose children were racing on the Step of Horror remained in their chambers, hearts heavy with hope that they would see their sons again in a few days. None could bear to witness the potential falls of their beloved children. Meanwhile, others gathered outside, cheering the contestants on. Spirits were served, and the revelry continued without pause, sleep eluding everyone as the event carried on for days.

By the third day, Wealth of God had ascended to the top of the leaderboard, her triumph evident to all spectators gathered to witness the race. Behind her, her brothers trailed closely, their progress observed with bated breath by the onlookers. However, her youngest brother, Miracle, struggled far behind, still at the bottom of the rankings.

Miracle, Followmehome's last son, possessed a different strength, one not measured by physical prowess alone. Though he may not have matched the physical might of his siblings, his indomitable will and unwavering enthusiasm shone brightly. Trained alongside his brothers in the ways of the male Landers, Miracle's determination to persevere amidst adversity was undeniable.

As the first light of dawn painted the sky with hues of gold and pink, Wealth of God ascended to the apex of the platform, her face illuminated by a mix of determination and exhilaration. With each step closer to victory, her expression shifted from focused intensity to radiant joy, mirroring the tumultuous journey she had endured.

Below, murmurs rippled through the crowd, a chorus of awe and disbelief mingling with whispers of admiration. The spectators, both Landers and tree house occupants alike, craned their necks to catch a glimpse of the historic moment unfolding before them. Amidst the murmurs, there were exclamations of astonishment and cheers of triumph, reverberating through the air and adding to the electric atmosphere of the occasion.

As Wealth of God reached the summit, a hush fell over the crowd, broken only by the pounding of her heart and the rhythmic beat of distant drums. The king, his eyes wide with astonishment, watched in shock as she stood victorious, a testament to the strength and resilience of the human spirit. Never before had he witnessed such bravery and determination in a woman, and he felt seriously disturbed at the sight of her triumph.

In that fleeting moment, as the morning sun cast its warm glow upon the scene, Wealth of God became more than just a victor; she became a symbol of hope and inspiration for generations to come. Her ascent to the top of the platform was not just a triumph of physical strength, but a testament to the power of courage, perseverance, and the unyielding spirit of humanity.

The king rose from his seat with a heavy heart, his mind swirling with the implications of Wealth of God's victory. With measured steps, he made his way to his chamber, the weight of responsibility pressing down upon him. He knew that much was at stake now that she had emerged as the winner of the race.

Once inside his chamber, the king wasted no time in summoning Godhascome. As he entered his summon, he noticed that the king's expression was grave, his thoughts consumed by the urgent matter at hand. With a sense of urgency, he laid bare his concerns, seeking guidance on how to ensure that Wealth of God remained within his grasp.

The king rose swiftly and strode into his chamber, a tumult of thoughts swirling in his mind. He called for Godhascome immediately upon entering, his tone urgent as he spoke.

"Godhascome, I need your advice," the king began, his voice tinged with concern. "Wealth of God has emerged as the winner, and I fear what that may mean for us. I promised her the poison and the cup if she won, but now I realise their importance. I must keep them within my possession. How can I ensure she remains within our reach?"

Godhascome, after a moment of contemplation, offered his counsel to the king. "Name her as your successor," he suggested. "Appoint her to take over the tree house laws when you are gone. This is an offer she will not reject, given her attitude towards power and fame."

The king pondered this advice, weighing the implications carefully. It was a strategic move, one that could potentially keep Wealth of God within his influence while securing the vital items he sought to retain. With a nod of understanding, he acknowledged the wisdom in Godhascome's words and resolved to act upon them.

The king, his decision made, issued a command to the guard. "Bring forth my metal cup and the poison," he instructed firmly.

As the guard hastened to obey, the king settled back onto his throne, his gaze fixed on the unfolding events before him. The race continued, but his mind was elsewhere, focused on the next steps he must take to secure his hold on power and ensure the loyalty of Wealth of God.

On the seventh day, all the Landers, alongside a handful of tree house males, had ascended to the top of the platform. The gruelling race had taken its toll, with many participants falling along the way. However, Miracle remained determined, pushing himself to the limit as he continued his arduous climb. Despite the odds stacked against him, he persisted, refusing to succumb to death's grasp.

As the tension reached its peak, Miracle's breath came in ragged gasps. With each step, his muscles screamed in protest, but he pushed forward, driven by an unyielding determination. The platform loomed tantalisingly close, a beacon of hope amidst the chaos of the race.

Suddenly, the ground began to tremble beneath his feet. Panic surged through Miracle as he struggled to maintain his balance. In a heart-stopping moment, he felt himself teetering on the edge of the precipice. Then, with a deafening roar, the ground gave way beneath him.

A collective gasp rippled through the crowd as they witnessed Miracle's harrowing fall. Spectators held their breath, their eyes wide with shock and disbelief. Some covered their mouths in horror, unable to tear their gaze away from the scene unfolding before them.

Time seemed to slow as Miracle tumbled backwards, the wind whipping past him in a dizzying whirl. The world spun in a blur of motion as he hurtled through the air, his heart pounding in his chest. With a sickening thud, he crashed onto the unforgiving ground below.

For a moment, there was only silence. Then, miraculously, Miracle stirred. With gritted teeth and sheer force of will, he dragged himself to his feet, every movement sending waves of pain coursing through his battered body. But he refused to give up. With one final surge of determination, he staggered forward, his eyes fixed on the distant platform.

Amidst the chaos, whispers of amazement and admiration spread like wildfire. "He's alive!" someone exclaimed, their voice tinged with awe. Others murmured in disbelief, unable to comprehend the sheer resilience displayed by the fallen contestant.

And as he rose to his feet, determination etched into every line of his weary face, the crowd erupted into cheers, their applause echoing across the vast expanse of the arena. He gritted his teeth and held on to the side of his stomach, a testament to the heavy pain he was bearing. He suddenly paused, and after a few seconds, he collapsed back to the ground; he passed out.

Miracle stood alone as the sole survivor of the treacherous fall, a testament to his remarkable resilience. The king, perplexed by the miraculous survival, spared no expense in providing him with the best medical care available. Little did they know, Miracle's survival would unveil a tale shrouded in mystery and magic.

Following the conclusion of the race, the king commended the warriors for their valiant efforts. He pledged to oversee Miracle's recovery until he was fully healed and ready to return to the land. Keeping his promise to Wealth of God, the king presented her with the gift she had requested and offered her the position of successor to the throne.

Though Followmehome harboured reservations about the proposition, he anticipated his daughter's rejection. However, to his dismay, Wealth of God saw it as an opportunity to forge her own path and establish her legacy. Believing that the Landers favoured males over females, she seized the chance to elevate her status and accepted the offer, pledging her allegiance to the king and the laws of the tree house.

Disheartened by his daughter's decision, Followmehome sought solace and counsel from his mother, Kala. Recognising the king's proposition as a ploy orchestrated by Warriorisborn and his chiefs to obtain the poison, she urged Followmehome to stand firm. Without the poison, she insisted, their plan would be rendered futile, and the true intentions behind the king's offer would be exposed.

Wealth of God saw herself sitting on that throne, the weight of leadership resting comfortably on her shoulders despite knowing her father's opposition and plan to destroy the tree house. She could feel the warmth of the golden crown, the gaze of admiration from her people. A smile tugged at her lips as she imagined issuing commands, her voice strong and unwavering.

Contentment settled in her heart as she embraced her decision. The rules of the tree house, once seen as rigid boundaries, now appeared as guiding principles she was eager to uphold. With determination etched on her face, she prepared to step into her new role, ready to shape her destiny and the future of the tree house.

Wealth of God's gaze lingered on the small, ominous bottle of poison. She understood its significance to both her father and the king. Her father's desire to possess it was clear, but she felt an even stronger resolve growing within her. Instead of allowing her father to claim it, she decided she would safeguard it herself.

She imagined the future moment when she would present it to the king, her hand steady, her eyes meeting his with confidence. The anticipation of striking the right bargain filled her with a sense of purpose. Determined to keep the poison out of her father's reach, she resolved to bide her time and leverage it wisely when the moment was right.

Warriorisborn was encircled by a cadre of fiercely loyal individuals, each willing to lay down their lives for his protection. These guardians, sharp of mind and steadfast of heart, formed an impenetrable shield around their king.

However, amidst this circle of trust, two stood apart. Alexandre and Lambert, harbouring a deep-seated hatred for Warriorisborn, had repeatedly conspired against him. Their acts of rebellion were carried out in the shadows, veiled in secrecy, ensuring the king remained oblivious to their treacherous schemes.

Charles and Muhammad, though good acquaintances of the king, often found themselves unnerved by his decisions. The fear these choices instilled in them was palpable, yet they maintained their loyalty, driven by their own ambitions. Only Cyril dared to speak the truth, his candour a rare commodity in the king's court. Despite their differences, the group of three men shared a common trait: an unquenchable thirst for power, willing to do whatever it took to ascend to the throne.

Wealth of God preferred to remain where power was tangible and measured, a stark contrast to the teachings she had grown up with. Before her father left the tree house, he imparted one final piece of wisdom; "Learn to discern the difference between strength and power." His words echoed in her mind as she navigated her new role, a reminder of the lesson she needed to embrace in order to truly lead.

Chapter Ten
The Awakening of Demetrious

Followmehome and the remaining Landers gathered their belongings, their movements deliberate and filled with a sense of finality. The race was over, and the once bustling tree house now felt like a distant memory. The towering branches and interwoven pathways that had been their battlegrounds stood silent and still.

As they prepared to depart, Followmehome cast a lingering glance around the tree house. Each step he took felt heavy with the weight of their experiences. The Landers, despite their weariness, moved with a quiet determination, ready to return to their homeland. They secured their packs, double-checked their provisions, and exchanged solemn nods, acknowledging the end of this phase.

Miracle, however, remained behind. His injury was severe, his body weakened from the harrowing race. The fall had taken a toll on him, and his recovery would be slow and arduous. The tree house, with its skilled healers and abundant resources, offered the best chance for his healing. He lay on a makeshift bed, his eyes half-closed, pain etched into his features.

Followmehome approached his son, kneeling beside him. The room was filled with the soft rustling of leaves and the earthy scent of the tree house, a serene contrast to the turmoil Miracle had endured. "Rest easy, Miracle," he said softly, his voice filled with a mixture of concern and encouragement.

"You are in good hands here. Heal well, and we will see each other soon."

Miracle managed a faint smile, his spirit unbroken despite his physical state. "I'll be strong, Father," he replied weakly. "Take care of everyone."

The resolve in Miracle's eyes touched Followmehome deeply. With a final pat on Miracle's shoulder, Followmehome rose, the weight of his duty pressing upon him. He joined the others, who were preparing for their descent from the tree house. The healers hovered nearby, their hands ready with poultices and herbs, their faces calm and reassuring.

The Landers began their descent, the sturdy ropes creaking softly under their weight. The air was thick with a sense of departure, mingled with the hope of a reunion once Miracle was restored to health. The canopy above swayed gently, casting dappled shadows on the ground below.

As Followmehome glanced back at the tree house, he saw Miracle's faint figure in the distance, held on both sides by two soldiers. He could already imagine how Miracle had threatened them to make him stand in order to pay honours to him. Followmehome felt a pang of worry, but also a surge of determination. The journey back to their homeland was just beginning, but the promise of returning for Miracle kept his spirits high. The path ahead was uncertain, but they moved forward with a sense of purpose and hope, leaving behind the towering tree house and its promise of healing for Miracle.

Wealth of God, now crowned as the king's successor, remained in the tree house. Her dream of residing in this majestic, intricate structure had come true, and she embraced her new role with fierce determination. The crown rested lightly on her head, a symbol of her newfound authority and the promise of a future she was eager to shape.

As she walked through the grand halls and among the towering branches, Wealth of God felt a deep sense of purpose. The tree house, once a place of challenge and uncertainty, now stood as her domain. The familiar sights and sounds had transformed in her eyes, no longer mere obstacles but opportunities for growth and leadership. The rustling leaves whispered tales of potential, and the sturdy trunks seemed to offer support for her burgeoning aspirations.

Her mind buzzed with plans and aspirations. She envisioned reforms, new alliances, and a brighter future for the inhabitants. With each step, she radiated confidence, her gaze steady and her spirit unyielding. The path ahead was daunting, but Wealth of God felt ready to face it head-on. The corridors, lined with the intricate carvings of the tree's history, now seemed to tell the story of her impending triumphs.

Standing on a high balcony, she looked out over the vast expanse of the tree house. The view symbolised the breadth of her new responsibilities. The sun dipped below the horizon, casting a warm, golden glow over the landscape. The leaves glimmered like gold coins, and the air was filled with the scent of blooming flowers. She felt a surge of pride and resolve.

"To a new era," she muttered to herself, clutching the edge of the balcony. The bark beneath her fingers was rough and grounding, a tactile reminder of the reality she now controlled. The tree house, under her guidance, was poised for transformation. She was ready to lead, to inspire, and to carve a legacy that would be remembered for generations to come. The distant sound of laughter and chatter from the inhabitants below filled her with a sense of community and responsibility.

The night began to fall, and the first stars appeared in the sky. They seemed to wink at her as if acknowledging her newfound role. She took a deep breath, the cool evening air filling her lungs with a sense of invigoration. Her heart beat with the rhythm of the tree house, strong and steady. Wealth of God was prepared to face whatever challenges lay ahead, her spirit fortified by the promise of a brighter tomorrow.

On the ominous fifth day after the conclusion of the hundredth Step of Horror race, the first Angel of Death made its chilling appearance. Demetrious, now transformed, emerged from the depths of the ocean with a ghastly white, scaly complexion. His arrival was like a harbinger of doom, a creature born from nightmares, bringing with him an air thick with dread.

His form, a grotesque amalgamation of man and beast, circled the tree house with a sinister grace. The grotesque sight of his dragon-like body sent shivers down the spines of all who caught sight of him. His pointed mouth and wing-like appendages exuded an aura of dread that permeated the air, casting long, dark shadows over the once peaceful tree house.

The scouts, upon witnessing this terrifying spectacle, were overcome with a primal fear unlike anything he had ever experienced. His heart pounded in his chest as he watched Demetrious glide effortlessly through the sky, his scales glinting ominously in the waning light. The scout's hands trembled as he turned to deliver the news, knowing the weight of the message he carried.

As Demetrious descended upon the platform, a palpable sense of impending doom hung heavy in the air. The ground seemed to quake beneath his landing, and a hush fell over the tree house. Onlookers, their faces pale and eyes wide with terror, could hardly breathe as they took in the sight of this otherworldly being. His presence was both malevolent and overpowering, filling the hearts of those who witnessed his arrival with an unshakeable fear.

The scout bolted through the grand halls of the tree house, his heart pounding in his chest. Sweat dripped down his brow as he skidded to a stop before the king's chamber. Without waiting for permission, he burst through the doors, his breath coming in ragged gasps.

"My king!" he exclaimed, his voice strained and trembling. "The Angel of Death has arrived. Demetrious has emerged from the ocean, and he's circling the tree house."

Warriorisborn looked up from his desk, his eyes narrowing. He rose slowly, the weight of the scout's words settling over him like a dark cloud. "Describe him," he commanded, his voice steady but tinged with an edge of urgency.

The scout swallowed hard, his throat dry. "He's monstrous, my king. A ghastly white, scaly creature with the form of a dragon. His presence is…it's unlike anything I've ever seen. He exudes an aura of pure dread."

Warriorisborn's face hardened, his jaw clenching as he absorbed the news. He turned to the window, his gaze fixed on the horizon as if he could already see the looming threat. The growing sense of foreboding gripped the tree house like a vice, tightening with each passing moment. The air in the chamber grew thick with tension, each breath a struggle against the encroaching fear.

"Prepare the guards," the king ordered, his voice low and resolute. "We must be ready for whatever comes next."

The scout nodded, bowing deeply before rushing out to carry out the king's orders. As the doors closed behind him, Warriorisborn stood alone in his chamber, the weight of his responsibilities pressing down on him. He knew that the arrival of Demetrious was only the beginning of the trials they would face. The tree house, once a sanctuary, now felt like a besieged fortress, its walls closing in under the shadow of the Angel of Death.

The king's eyes were hard, his mind racing with thoughts of strategy and survival. He felt the vice grip of foreboding tightening further, a stark reminder of the peril that now loomed over them all. As he prepared to face the coming storm, Warriorisborn steeled himself, ready to confront the darkness that threatened to engulf his kingdom.

The transformation of Demetrious into the fearsome Angel of Death was complete, and his presence heralded a new era of darkness. The inhabitants of the tree house, their nerves frayed and spirits shaken, braced themselves for the storm that was sure to come.

As night fell, the tree house stood in uneasy silence, the chilling echo of Demetrious's arrival lingering in the air, a stark reminder of the peril that now loomed over them. The once-vibrant and lively tree house was now shrouded in an oppressive atmosphere, its inhabitants moving with hushed whispers and cautious glances.

Groups of people huddled together in the main square, their faces pale and drawn with fear. Children clung to their parents, their wide eyes filled with a mixture of curiosity and terror. The elderly, with their years of wisdom and experience, wore expressions of grim determination, knowing all too well the weight of the darkness that had descended upon them.

"What will we do?" a woman whispered, her voice trembling as she clutched her young son to her chest. "How can we fight something like that?"

Her husband, his face etched with worry, shook his head slowly. "We must trust in the king," he said though his tone lacked conviction. "He will find a way to protect us."

For a fleeting moment, Demetrious lingered, casting a pall of unease over the gathered crowd. His grotesque form, illuminated by the dim light of the moon, was a haunting silhouette against the night sky. The people below, frozen in a mixture of awe and terror, watched with bated breath, unable to tear their eyes away from the nightmarish figure.

Then, with a sudden and unnerving agility, Demetrious vanished into the open expanse above. His movement was swift and fluid, like a shadow slipping through the fingers of light. The air seemed to ripple in his wake, and the oppressive weight of his presence lifted, if only slightly. As he soared upwards, the eerie glow of his scaly skin gradually faded, blending into the inky darkness of the night.

In a matter of moments, Demetrious had disappeared into the depths of the ocean below, leaving behind an eerie silence. The crowd, still reeling from the encounter, stood motionless, their ears straining to catch any sign of his return. The distant sound of crashing waves, once a soothing lullaby of nature, now seemed ominous—a harbinger of the darkness yet to come.

Warriorisborn, deep in slumber, missed the chilling spectacle, only awakening when summoned by Godhascome. The rest of the chiefs, however, bore witness to the horrifying scene, their faces drained of colour and their hearts pounding with dread. The crowd, stunned into silence, felt the tension in the air like a suffocating weight, their minds reeling with fear and uncertainty.

Godhascome, his face etched with urgency, entered the king's chamber and gently shook him awake. "My king, you must wake up," he said, his voice a mixture of respect and desperation. Warriorisborn groggily opened his eyes, disoriented and confused.

"What is it, Godhascome?" he mumbled, rubbing his eyes.

"Demetrious has appeared," Godhascome replied, his voice steady despite the gravity of his words. "He has transformed into an Angel of Death. The chiefs witnessed the entire event."

Warriorisborn's eyes widened as the gravity of the situation dawned on him. He quickly rose from his bed, his mind racing. "Take me to them," he commanded, his voice firm and resolute.

As they made their way to the main hall, the king could hear the hushed whispers of his people, the fear palpable in their voices. Mothers clutched their children tightly, and fathers exchanged worried glances. The young men, who had vowed to organise a defence, stood resolute but visibly shaken.

In the grand hall, the chiefs huddled together, their expressions a mixture of shock and horror. Their faces were ashen, and their eyes reflected the terror they had just witnessed. As Warriorisborn entered, all eyes turned to him, their hope resting on his shoulders.

"My king," one of the chiefs began, his voice trembling, "Demetrious…he has become something monstrous. We saw him with our own eyes. He is no longer the man we knew."

Warriorisborn took a deep breath, his face hardening with resolve. "So I hear," he said, his voice steady. "There's only one person that has sufficient knowledge about the solution to our current predicament." Turning to Godhascome, he said, "Summon Aza immediately. From what I can see, the people are stricken with fear. She is the only person in this tree house who can calm the people."

As whispers of terror rippled through the onlookers, Aza stepped forward at the king's command. With a voice that carried authority, she addressed the trembling crowd, her words cutting through the palpable atmosphere of fear.

"There are thousands more Angels of Death yet to be awakened," she proclaimed, her voice solemn and grave. Her words hung heavy in the air, a stark reminder of the imminent danger that loomed over them all.

The shock rippled through the gathered crowd like a wave, leaving some paralysed with fear, while others recoiled in horror. In the chaos that ensued, a few unfortunate souls succumbed to the overwhelming terror, their fear manifesting in a most undignified manner.

As the realisation of the Angels of Death sank in, the king's voice boomed over the panicked crowd, his words cutting through the chaos like a blade. "Seek shelter! Stay indoors!" he commanded, his tone firm and authoritative.

Guards were dispatched to patrol the perimeter of the tree house, their eyes scanning the darkness for any sign of the dreaded creatures.

With each passing moment, the tension in the air thickened, the silence broken only by the distant sound of footsteps and the rustle of leaves. Every shadow seemed to hold the promise of imminent danger, and the residents of the tree house huddled together, praying for the night to pass swiftly.

Aza, the blossom whisperer, had foreseen the impending arrival of the Angels of Death. In anticipation, she had nurtured hundreds of sapling trees infused with her secret enchantment, capable of thriving anywhere they were planted. However, unbeknownst to her, her chamber remained unguarded, allowing Alexandre and Lambert to uncover her secret before the king could be informed.

Shortly after, Demetrious swooped into a chamber teeming with soldiers, unleashing chaos and destruction in his wake. Despite their full alertness, the soldiers found themselves overwhelmed as Demetrious ruthlessly annihilated them. The soldiers, now on full alert, mobilised to hunt him down, devising a plan to capture the creature.

Godhascome stood before the gathered workers of the textile sector, his voice carrying authority and urgency. "We need a net," he declared, his eyes ablaze with determination. "A net strong enough to capture Demetrious."

The workers exchanged glances, understanding the gravity of the task at hand. They set to work immediately, selecting the finest and sturdiest materials the tree house had to offer. Each thread was woven with precision, the pattern intricate yet purposeful.

As the net took shape, Godhascome inspected it closely, ensuring that every knot was secure and every weave tight. "This must hold," he muttered to himself, the weight of their mission pressing down on him.

Finally, the net was ready, a testament to the skill and dedication of the workers. It gleamed in the light, a shimmering web of protection against the looming threat of Demetrious. The workers stood back, their faces flushed with pride at their creation.

With the net in place, they awaited Demetrious's next move, ready to spring into action at a moment's notice. The tension in the air was palpable, each breath drawn with anticipation. The fate of the tree house rested on their shoulders, and they were determined to succeed. With the net in place and their preparations complete, they awaited his next move.

Wealth of God stepped forward, her determination shining like a beacon amidst the gathering tension. "I will lead him down the Step of Horror," she declared, her voice steady despite the weight of her decision. She was hoping to trap him and gather more information about the Angels of Death.

Her bravery elicited murmurs of admiration from those gathered, their eyes reflecting both fear and respect for her resolve. Godhascome nodded in approval, acknowledging her courage with a solemn gaze.

Meanwhile, in the shadows, a team of skilled craftsmen worked in secrecy, carving out a hidden prison cell from the solid wood of the tree house. Their tools moved swiftly and silently, shaping the chamber with precision and care.

As the cell took shape, it remained hidden from prying eyes, its existence known only to a selected few. Each stone laid and each bar forged served as a testament to their dedication to securing Demetrious and conducting their studies in utmost secrecy.

With the net prepared and the prison cell ready, the stage was set for their plan to unfold. Wealth of God's bravery would lead the way, while the hidden cell stood as a silent sentinel, awaiting its captive.

Godhascome's plan bore fruit as Demetrious was successfully captured and swiftly imprisoned, concealed from view. Aza, sensing the opportune moment, sought out *the wizard* to unlock the usage of the metal cup. In a surprising revelation, she discovered that the cup not only controlled the beasts but also instilled fear in them, compelling them to submit to the bearer. Recognising the importance of this revelation, Aza chose to withhold this information from the king for the time being.

The king and his soldiers encircled the captive Angel of Death, their faces etched with a mix of curiosity and trepidation. As they locked eyes with him, they were struck by the unsettling blurriness that seemed to cloud his gaze, as if veiled by an otherworldly mist. His pupils, dilated with an eerie intensity, held a depth of darkness that sent shivers down their spines.

"Arrrgh!" he roared.

"Do. You. Understand. Me?" asked one of the soldiers, on the king's command.

"Nrambrigbragggggh!" the Angel of Death screamed back, leaving the questioner's face wallowed in saliva.

His voice echoed through the chamber like the anguished cries of a tormented soul, carrying with it an undercurrent of primal fury that seemed to seep into the very air they breathed.

Despite their efforts to glean insight from his words, they were met only with frustration and confusion. It was as if he existed in a realm beyond their comprehension, his thoughts and intentions shrouded in a cloak of enigma.

"Look into his eyes," the king commanded, again. "Tell me, what do you see?"

One of the soldiers, a seasoned warrior named Talon, stepped closer, peering into Demetrious's eyes. "It's like staring into the abyss, Your Majesty," Talon said, his voice trembling. "Time feels…warped like it's standing still and twisting all at once."

The first soldier, Gram, couldn't take his gaze off the creature. "It's as if we're looking into eternity itself," he murmured. "I can almost feel the weight of ages pressing down on me."

Demetrious's eyes flickered, and a guttural sound escaped his throat, a noise that sent chills down their spines. "Mmmmm."

"What other secrets do you think he holds?" the king asked, his voice barely above a whisper.

Talon shook his head. "I can't even begin to imagine, Sire. There's so much chaos in his presence, so much we don't understand."

Gram nodded in agreement. "It's terrifying to think what else might be hidden within him, waiting to be unleashed."

The king's gaze hardened as he looked at Demetrious. "We must uncover those secrets. For the sake of our people, we must understand what we are dealing with."

The soldiers exchanged uneasy glances, knowing that their task was far from over, and the true depths of Demetrious's being remained a mystery yet to be revealed.

The people were terrified of what was to come. They knew they could not survive an invasion of only two Angels of Death, let alone thousands. The air was thick with fear and uncertainty.

Aza, the blossom whisperer, approached the king with her usual calm but with a hint of urgency in her eyes. "Your Majesty, we must act swiftly," she advised. "We need to find new locations on land to grow the suckling of the mystery tree. It will grow tall in a few years, providing new homes for our people to escape the coming threat."

The king listened intently, his brow furrowed with concern. "But where do we start, Aza?" he asked. "We don't have much time."

Aza's eyes twinkled with a mixture of wisdom and mischief. "Seek Wealth of God," she said, her voice soft but firm. "She will know the way forward. Her insight will guide us through this dark time."

As she turned to leave, she laughed softly, the sound carrying a strange comfort. Leaning heavily on her walking stick, she limped away, leaving the king deep in thought.

Even though Warriorisborn had no clue on how to plant the tree root, he believed in Aza's words and did as he was told. He called Wealth of God to his private chamber, where he praised her for her courage in assisting with the capture of Demetrious.

"You have shown great bravery," he said, sitting on his throne. "Your actions have been invaluable to us."

Wealth of God bowed her head modestly. "Thank you, Your Majesty. I only did what needed to be done."

Warriorisborn leaned forward, his expression serious. "It is time to expand our kingdoms and find more locations for our people. The Angels of Death are coming, and we must be prepared. I need your wisdom and vision to guide us."

Wealth of God nodded, her eyes filled with determination. "I am ready, Your Majesty. We must act swiftly."

"Tell me," Warriorisborn said, "where would you choose to rule? What location do you believe would best serve our people?"

Without hesitation, Wealth of God replied, "Mount Ganjak. It is vast and magnificent, a place of great power and beauty. It would be an honour to rule there."

Warriorisborn smiled, pleased with her choice. "Mount Ganjak it shall be. Your wish is assured."

Wealth of God felt a surge of excitement. She was prepared for the coming of the Angels of Death, but now, with the king's support and a new domain to rule, she was ready to face the future with renewed strength and purpose.

Her heart throbbed in excitement—her dreams had begun unfolding before her eyes.

Chapter Eleven
Secrets, Betrayal and Shifting Alliances

Charles and Muhammad were uncritical by nature, harbouring numerous secrets they had never revealed to anyone. They knew that Gandoki was being coaxed by Alexandre and Lambert to murder Kala because they had overheard the discussion while the plan was being orchestrated. However, they decided to keep silent, fearing they might be struck down by lightning if they spoke up.

Among the secrets they kept were the truths about the suckling trees. They were aware that these trees would only grow with Aza's enchantment, a knowledge that gave them a silent sense of power and dread.

More so, Charles and Muhammad were well informed that Alexandre and Lambert, alongside Gandoki, had been planning to steal a few of the suckling trees and create their own kingdoms. They knew that if this plot were to unfold, someone would inevitably have to answer to the king.

Despite their own ambitions for wealth, Charles and Muhammad were wary of being caught in an act that would lead to interrogation by the king. They understood the stakes involved and the severe consequences that could follow. Their knowledge was both a burden and a shield, keeping them vigilant and cautious in a world where alliances could shift with the slightest whisper and ambitions could turn deadly.

To secure themselves a future, Charles and Muhammad stole Aza's enchantment, the one meticulously prepared to help grow the suckling trees anywhere in the world. They understood the immense value of this enchantment, recognising it as their key to unlocking vast doors of wealth. With this powerful secret in their possession, they felt a mix of trepidation and exhilaration, knowing that their actions could change the fate of kingdoms and their own destinies.

Before Wealth of God had her pivotal discussion with the king about ruling on Mount Ganjak, Aza the blossom whisperer summoned the king to her private chamber. The air inside was thick with the scent of exotic flowers, mingling with the faint aroma of burning herbs. The chamber was dimly lit, the flickering candlelight casting eerie shadows on the ancient tapestries that adorned the walls.

As Warriorisborn entered, Aza greeted him with a knowing smile, her eyes gleaming with the wisdom of centuries. "I will help you build an empire," she promised, her voice a mere whisper that carried the weight of her conviction. "I will make you the God of Land and Sea."

The king took a deep breath, feeling a mixture of anticipation and trepidation. He sat down, his attention fully on Aza as she began to speak. Her tone grew grave, and the atmosphere in the chamber seemed to darken with her words.

"It is time to build tentacles and enslave the Angels of Death before they multiply," she said. "You must get the cup and approach Demetrious. He will speak."

Warriorisborn listened intently, absorbing every word. Aza's voice was a blend of authority and mystery, each syllable carrying the weight of untold secrets. With a dramatic flourish, she opened a hidden door in her chamber, revealing a secret room filled with hundreds of suckling plants of the mystery trees. Each plant seemed to pulse with life, a testament to the ancient magic that nurtured them.

"The cup is the key to enslaving the Angels of Death, and the tree roots are your kingdom," Aza revealed. The king could see the flicker of determination in her eyes, the resolve of someone who had guarded these secrets for so long.

Despite her outward confidence, Aza harboured a deep-seated fear. The presence of *the wizard* was a constant source of intimidation for her. She knew her enchantment had been stolen, yet she had chosen not to report the incident to the king. Instead, she foresaw that more kingdoms would rise, necessitating more enchantments. She was content to let the thieves taste a mere fraction of the blossom whisperer's power, knowing they would soon realise the depth of their folly.

Aza's mind was already racing ahead, planning for the future. She had foreseen that she would eventually be overshadowed by the wizard even though she was the greatest witch to have ever lived. She knew the path ahead would be treacherous, but she was ready to face whatever challenges lay in wait, confident in her abilities and the power of her ancient magic.

As Warriorisborn pondered her words, the gravity of the situation weighed heavily on him. He could feel the enormity of the task ahead, but Aza's confidence bolstered his resolve. However, there was a crucial element he was unaware of—the suckling plants, so integral to his dominion, might not survive without Aza's secret enchantment. This hidden truth lingered in Aza's mind, a silent reminder of the precarious balance of power and magic upon which their plans depended.

The king, now more determined than ever, rose from his seat, his mind set on the path Aza had laid out. He knew that the road to becoming the God of Land and Sea was fraught with peril, but with Aza's guidance and the power of the ancient magic at his disposal, he felt ready to confront the challenges that lay ahead.

Warriorisborn called Wealth of God to his chamber, a room adorned with rich tapestries and the lingering scent of burning incense. The atmosphere was heavy with anticipation. As Wealth of God entered, the king's eyes gleamed with admiration.

"Your bravery in capturing Demetrious was remarkable," Warriorisborn began, his tone sincere. "I believe you have the strength and wisdom to lead our people in these uncertain times."

Wealth of God nodded, her eyes locked onto the king's, listening intently to his words.

"I have a proposal for you," Warriorisborn continued. "Would you like to build your own soldiers and establish a new tree house on Mount Ganjak? It's a grand location, fitting for someone of your valour."

Her eyes sparkled with intrigue and ambition. "Mount Ganjak is a magnificent place. It would be an honour to rule there and build a stronghold."

The king smiled, a sense of satisfaction evident in his expression. "Then it shall be done. But I need your help. Aza has revealed that the cup is essential to control the Angels of Death, to prevent them from multiplying and wreaking havoc. I need the poison bottle and the cup."

Wealth of God did not hesitate for a moment. "I agree," she said instantly, her voice steady and resolute. "I will provide the items as soon as possible."

Without delay, she left the chamber and soon returned with the poison bottle and the cup, presenting them to the king. Warriorisborn's face lit up with delight and pride at her promptness and dedication.

"I admire your courage," he said with a broad smile. "I shall make you a kingdom."

The king called upon Godhascome. The advisor entered swiftly, bowing deeply.

"Send a message to Followmehome," Warriorisborn instructed. "Tell him to visit me at once."

Godhascome bowed again and left to carry out the order. The king watched him go, his mind already turning to the preparations ahead. As the days turned into weeks and then months, the efforts to establish Wealth of God's new kingdom on Mount Ganjak and contain the Angels of Death progressed steadily. Warriorisborn remained resolute, knowing the future of his people depended on their actions in the coming days.

Meanwhile, Followmehome received the king's message with astonishment. "Why would the king demand my visit?" he wondered aloud, the message clutched in his hand.

Crown, overhearing his words, grew anxious. "I'm worried about Wealth of God and Miracle," she said, her eyes filled with concern. "I haven't seen them since they left for the tree house race. I need to see them again."

Followmehome nodded, understanding her worry. He called a meeting with his advisors to discuss the message. The room was filled with a tense atmosphere as they deliberated. After much discussion, they agreed it was wise for him to proceed with the journey, especially considering his children still resided in the tree house.

"It's settled, then," Followmehome announced, his voice firm with determination. "We will sail to the tree house with our family and crew."

Preparations began immediately. The bustling of activity filled their home as Crown's anxiety mixed with anticipation, hoping to reunite with her loved ones. Followmehome, though puzzled by the king's summons, felt a growing determination to face whatever awaited them in the tree house.

As the ship set sail, the salty sea air filled their lungs, and the horizon stretched out before them. Followmehome stood at the helm, his thoughts racing with possibilities. The journey ahead was fraught with uncertainty, but his resolve was unwavering. Crown stood beside him, her heart heavy with worry but also with hope, as they ventured towards an unknown future, driven by duty and the bonds of family.

Alexandre and Lambert knew the king had regained possession of the poison. They also knew that Aza had grown many suckling trees in her chamber.

Observing Gandoki's dissatisfaction with the king naming a successor, they saw an opportunity.

In hushed tones, Alexandre turned to Lambert. "We need to use Gandoki's anger to our advantage."

Lambert nodded, a glint of cunning in his eyes. "If we can coerce Gandoki into killing Kala, it will surely ignite a war between Warriorisborn and Followmehome."

Alexandre agreed. "This chaos will either topple the king or give us the perfect cover to escape with our stolen suckling trees and enchantments. We can then build our own kingdom, free from his rule."

With their plan in motion, Alexandre and Lambert approached Gandoki. "You deserve to be king," Alexandre whispered. "The current regime has no place for your rightful ambition."

Lambert leaned in, his voice dripping with deceit. "Kill Kala. Spark the conflict between Warriorisborn and Followmehome. In the ensuing chaos, we can seize our destinies."

Alexandre and Lambert decided to reveal a crucial secret to Gandoki, hoping to win his trust and further their plot.

"Gandoki," Alexandre continued, his voice low and conspiratorial, "there's something you need to know. The king threw you overboard when they were sailing to land. He said that he saw you as a threat to his kingdom, and nothing more."

Gandoki's eyes widened with a mixture of shock and anger. "And why are you telling me this now?" he demanded.

Lambert leaned in, adding, "We never mentioned this before because we were part of the crew. But there's more you should know. Aza has grown many suckling trees in her private chamber. With these trees and your rightful place, we can help you build your own kingdom."

Alexandre continued, "Yes! We can use these trees to our advantage. Together, we can create something powerful, something that will rival the king's rule."

Gandoki's expression shifted from shock to a cold determination. "Why would you help me? What's in it for you?"

"We seek the same thing," Lambert replied. "A new order, a chance to break free from the king's control. You have the potential to lead us into a new era. We only ask that you consider our proposition."

After a moment's silence, Gandoki nodded slowly. "Alright. Tell me more about these suckling trees."

With a shared understanding, Alexandre and Lambert detailed their knowledge, hoping to solidify Gandoki's allegiance and set their plan into motion.

Gandoki went and verified the information Alexandre and Lambert had shared; it was true. They needed him to steal the poison and murder Kala, knowing that if Followmehome discovered his mother was killed with the same poison his daughter traded back after the race, it might initiate conflict between the king and Followmehome, potentially evolving into a war between the tree house soldiers and the Landers.

Under the cloak of darkness, Gandoki moved stealthily through the halls of the tree house. Coaxed by Alexandre and Lambert, his heart pounded with a mix of fear and determination. He approached his father's chamber, his steps silent on the wooden floor. Taking a deep breath, he eased the door open and slipped inside.

The chamber was dimly lit by the faint glow of moonlight filtering through the window. Gandoki's eyes quickly adjusted to the shadows. He knew exactly where his father kept the poison—a small, intricately designed bottle hidden in a drawer beside the bed. With trembling hands, he opened the drawer and retrieved the bottle. For a moment, he hesitated, feeling the weight of his actions pressing down on him. But the voices of Alexandre and Lambert echoed in his mind, urging him on.

Carefully, Gandoki made his way to Kala's chamber. The corridors were eerily quiet, each creak of the floorboards amplified in the stillness of the night. When he reached her door, he paused, listening for any signs of movement. Hearing none, he entered.

Kala was asleep, her breathing soft and even. Gandoki's heart ached with guilt as he looked at her peaceful form. He approached the bedside table where the jar of root water sat. His hands shook as he uncorked the poison bottle and carefully let a single drop fall into the water. The liquid shimmered momentarily, then settled.

He quickly replaced the cork and slipped out of the room, his breath coming in quick, shallow gasps. Returning to his father's chamber, Gandoki replaced the poison bottle in its drawer, ensuring everything was exactly as he found it. He slipped out, the enormity of his actions weighing heavily on his shoulders.

Hours later, as the first light of dawn broke through the tree house, Kala stirred. Her throat was parched, and she reached for the jar of root water. Unbeknownst to her, death awaited in its depths. She took a sip, the cool liquid soothing her dry throat for a brief moment. Then, an intense heat spread through her body. She gasped, her eyes widening in horror as flames erupted from within her.

The room was instantly filled with the crackling roar of fire. Kala's scream couldn't pierce the morning air to draw the attention of anyone nearby. She died unnoticed. All that remained were the charred remnants of what once was.

A few months passed. Upon Followmehome's arrival, a big welcome party was held as usual. The air was filled with laughter, music, and the aroma of delicious food. Followmehome couldn't help but smile at the familiar faces and the warm greetings. The king soon appeared and escorted him to his private chamber.

"Welcome back, my friend," Warriorisborn said, embracing Followmehome. "We have much to discuss."

As the two leaders sat down, the atmosphere grew serious. They delved into matters of state, strategy, and the looming threat of the Angels of Death. Their conversation stretched long into the night, each word heavy with the weight of their responsibilities.

Meanwhile, Crown paced anxiously. Her heart ached with longing to see her son. She approached one of the king's advisors, her voice tinged with desperation. "Please, I must see my son. It has been too long."

The advisor shook his head sympathetically. "I'm sorry, but it can only happen on the king's orders."

Frustration bubbled within her. "Then I will seek out my daughter," she declared, determined to at least reunite with one of her children.

With renewed purpose, Crown made her way through the tree house, navigating the familiar paths that led to Wealth of God's quarters. Her mind raced with thoughts of their reunion, unaware of the changes time had wrought.

Wealth of God, aware of her family's arrival, ordered her personal guards to prevent any of them from entering her space. Her attitude shocked them; it was unfriendly and unexpected. They did not see it coming.

In her private quarters, Wealth of God paced, her mind swirling with the past and present. The weight of her new responsibilities as the king's successor was immense. She felt an urgent need to prove herself, to show she was worthy of the role. The discoveries she had made during the tree house race—whispers of doubt and betrayal from her own family—still haunted her. She had embraced a new ideology, believing that to lead effectively, she needed to detach from her past and focus solely on her future role.

As she heard the distant voices of her family trying to reach her, Wealth of God steeled herself. Their presence brought back memories she wished to forget, conflicts she needed to avoid. She believed that to fulfil her duties and build her future, she had to keep her family at a distance, at least for now.

The king said to Followmehome, "I need thousands of ships built within two years, and I will dispatch soldiers to assist in the construction."

He then asked, "What do you want in return?"

Followmehome, astonished by the king's demands, hesitated before replying. "Can you comply with my proposals?" he asked.

The king leaned forward, his gaze intense. "Speak."

Followmehome, angered by his daughter Wealth of God's decision to remain in the tree house and feeling the sting of disrespect—a grave taboo in his culture—made his demands clear. "I want the poison and for Miracle to be named your successor even though Wealth of God has already earned this position. I'm willing to make a bargain to overrule it."

The king's eyes narrowed. "Two thousand ships if you want me to switch my future heir."

Followmehome's mind raced, driven by a plan to break the bond between the king and his daughter. He feared the king, unaware of their kinship, might marry Wealth of God, committing incest. "I demand this agreement be put in writing and announced publicly."

The king clicked his fingers, and a servant brought forward the poison. "I promise Miracle will be announced as my heir in a fortnight."

Followmehome was shocked, wondering how quickly the king had regained possession of the poison. His thoughts turned to his daughter. He questioned the king about her whereabouts.

"Where is my daughter?" Followmehome demanded, his voice tinged with concern and frustration.

The king laughed, a sly smile playing on his lips. "She will rule a nation someday," he replied.

Right in front of Followmehome was the poison bottle. A bond was made, and an agreement was signed with the king. Despite his initial plan to teach his daughter a lesson, he was surprised at how much had changed in such a short time.

Stepping out of the king's chamber, he rushed to find his daughter. When he reached her chamber, he found his family waiting at the entrance, barricaded by soldiers. Determined, he approached them, his presence commanding respect, and no one dared to stop him.

Chapter Twelve
Web of Ambition

Inside, Wealth of God stood by the window, staring outside, guarded by her ladies. She turned as he entered.

"Father," she said, "I did not expect you so soon."

"Wealth of God," Followmehome said, his eyes softening as he looked at her, "a lot has happened. We need to talk."

She nodded, sensing the gravity in his voice. "Very well, Father. Let's talk."

"Wealth of God, is everything alright?" he asked, his voice full of concern.

She replied, "I am doing okay," but the look on her face betrayed her disinterest in speaking to her father. Her eyes were distant, her posture rigid.

Sensing her reluctance, Followmehome felt a pang of disappointment. He had hoped for a more meaningful reunion, but it was clear she had no intention of engaging with him. With a heavy heart, he turned and walked out.

Outside, his family waited, their faces a mix of anticipation and concern. "Let's go," Followmehome said, his voice tight with anger.

As they departed, Followmehome's mind was clouded with frustration. In his anger, he neglected to check on his mother, Kala, who had died in her chamber, her death still unnoticed by all.

Followmehome left the tree house, clutching the poison bottle. The agreement between him and the king weighed heavily on his mind. Exactly a fortnight later, the king honoured their pact. In a grand ceremony, Miracle was pronounced the successor, his ascension marking the fulfilment of the bargain made between the king and Followmehome.

Wealth of God sought absolute power, understanding the sway she could wield by aligning herself with the king's wishes. As she awaited a ship to set sail for land and plant a suckling plant on Mount Ganjak, she acquiesced to further demands, each one granted in turn, solidifying her influence and ambitions.

Warriorisborn requested the poison from Wealth of God. Surprisingly, she handed it over without hesitation. The king still perplexed invited her to his chamber for a chat. "Why didn't you hesitate to return those crucial items?"

"I have always believed in your wisdom and the future of this tree," Wealth of God replied calmly. "I trust that whatever you require of me serves a greater purpose for our people and our kingdom." Her words were measured, reflecting both loyalty and a subtle confidence that resonated with the king.

The king was struck by Wealth of God's intelligence and quick compliance. Intrigued, he decided to probe further, sensing a connection beyond mere loyalty. "Tell me," he asked carefully, "what was your grandmother's name?"

With calm assurance, Wealth of God replied, "Kala."

The king's breath caught in his throat. At that moment, realisation dawned upon him like a bolt of lightning. He felt goosebumps on his hands, in addition to the electrical feeling in his mind.

Followmehome was his…*son*, and Wealth of God, his *granddaughter?*

It all made sense now—the urgency for the poison bottle, the unwavering loyalty.

Aza the blossom whisperer's warning about hidden kinship echoed in his mind, now clearer than ever.

The king was now sceptical, unsure of whom to trust. The revelation of his kinship with Wealth of God and Followmehome complicated matters. As Wealth of God walked out after their conversation, she remained oblivious to the fact that her brother, Miracle, was the wizard who had unlocked the secret of the cup for Aza. However, the king was still unaware of the wizard's true potential. He was also oblivious to the fact that Miracle was a wizard.

Aza had been secretly visiting Miracle, the wizard, without his knowledge. Miracle possessed extraordinary powers, capable of making revelations even in his sleep. Aza, despite her formidable abilities, felt intimidated by his presence. His powers surpassed hers in ways she could not ignore, and it was through his subconscious revelations that she had unlocked the secret of the cup.

Warriorisborn called upon Godhascome. "I need to speak with the Angel of Death alone," he commanded.

Godhascome nodded and turned to the guards. "Everyone, clear the area. Move away from the cell," he ordered.

The guards hesitated for a moment, then followed his command, leaving the vicinity of Demetrious's cell. Warriorisborn stepped inside, the heavy door clanging shut behind him. He found Demetrious lying on the floor, exhausted and weakened from months without water.

"Demetrious," Warriorisborn began, his voice echoing in the dim cell. "I need to understand what you are and what you want."

Demetrious stirred slightly, lifting his head with great effort. His eyes, though weary, held a flicker of the same fire that had once terrorised the tree house.

Angels of Death need ocean water to sustain their abilities, as complete abstinence causes dehydration. However, they can be kept captive for a hundred years without water before they perish.

As the king approached the cell gate holding the metal cup, Demetrious rose and his eyes opened. Slowly, he began to change, transforming back into a human—but a grown adult. His skin had a pallor that seemed almost translucent, and his eyes, now a piercing silver, held an otherworldly glow. It was unbelievable; Demetrious himself was astonished. He could not remember what it felt like to be human; all he could utter was, "I feel…alive."

Warriorisborn was astonished by the power of the metal cup. His confidence grew; he knew he was in control and felt relieved.

"Listen," he ordered Demetrious, "I promise to redeem every Angel of Death if you remain loyal to me and join me in the battles to come."

The king had unlocked the full potential of the metal cup though he wasn't aware that the Angels of Death had to be served root water with the cup to fully agree to his command. To avoid uninvited visits from the five Angels of Death that would soon arise, he tricked Demetrious. "Help me keep them at bay until a meeting is scheduled," he promised, "and I will make you the head of the beasts."

However, the cup's true purpose was more complex. It was not only meant to serve a drink; it was designed to enslave beasts and make them cower. By flipping the middle round blockage metal, the cup would drain them of their powers. It would make them talk if commanded and could transform them into humans if the bearer professed though it could not enslave a werewolf.

Demetrious was not weak, nor was he convinced by the king's trick. He was bitter about the king's barbaric acts, yet he needed the full force of an Angel of Death to destroy humans and accomplish his plight. He agreed to the king's demands, planning to proceed with his own agenda. Though it was just a threat, the king knew his present kingdom would not survive if his plans failed, but still, he prevailed.

Warriorisborn met with Aza the blossom whisperer, who commended his tremendous efforts. "It's time to enslave Demetrious," she said. "Open the gate where he is kept and revive his sense of taste by giving him some root water using the metal cup."

The king hesitated, conscious of his safety. "I made a false threat to make Demetrious succumb to my terms," he explained.

Aza let out a loud laugh. "It takes courage to dine with the devil, and it takes more courage to make them drink and bow. What kind of king are you?" she asked. "You think you're smart, but you're only deceiving yourself. Demetrious would never succumb to your threats or promises if he hadn't drunk from the metal cup."

Warriorisborn's eyes widened. He left the chamber, promising to return, and arranged a second meeting with Demetrious. As he made his way to the prison cell, he knew he was taking a big risk. But he believed in the power of the metal cup he held and was ready to face the task.

Before approaching Demetrious, Warriorisborn figured out how to use the cup. The task seemed easier than he had anticipated. He reached the cell door and flipped the cup's mechanism. Before his very eyes, Demetrious turned into a human again. The king then opened the cell door and poured him some root water from the metal cup. Instantly, Demetrious became healthy and agile and transformed into a beast.

Though terrified, Warriorisborn was brave enough not to show fear. Demetrious bowed to the king, his two wings raised high above his head. The king invited him to walk along to his chamber.

They walked through the hallway, with Demetrious trailing behind the king. The guards, spotting Demetrious, were astonished and terrified by the king's newfound power.

As they continued down the hallway, the king abruptly turned to Demetrious. "We need to reassure my people of their safety," he declared. "I will call for an impromptu public event to celebrate your liberation."

Demetrious nodded, his eyes gleaming with a mixture of curiosity and latent hunger.

In her chamber, Aza the blossom whisperer sat with serene confidence. She had anticipated the king's next move. Her thoughts were focused on the hidden truths she held about the Angels of Death. She knew they needed to feed on humans to maintain their human form, and that destroying without feeding excited them in their beast form, providing them with a twisted sense of contentment. Yet she chose to withhold this information from the king. She smiled faintly, confident that he would come seeking answers when the time was right.

As the event began, the king addressed the gathered crowd. "People of our great kingdom, today we celebrate the liberation of Demetrious, an ally who will ensure our continued safety and strength!" His voice boomed with authority, but his eyes constantly darted to Demetrious, wary yet hopeful.

Aza watched from the shadows, her expression unchanging, as she waited for the inevitable moment when the king would need the knowledge only she possessed.

As the event progressed, the atmosphere was tense but festive. The crowd cheered, reassured by the king's confident words. However, amidst the celebration, Demetrious's eyes darted around, his urge for destruction growing uncontrollably.

Consumed by the atmosphere, he spotted a vulnerable man on the edge of the crowd. With a sudden, predatory swoop, Demetrious decapitated the man with a swift strike of his wings. Blood splattered, and the man's headless body fell to the ground like a piece of wood.

The crowd fell into an outright silence, their joy turned to shock and fear. It was the kind of fear that gripped one, such that one just stood paralysed by one's fear. Such was the crowd's astonishment. They gripped the hands or garments of a loved one nearby.

Demetrious, realising the gravity of his actions, bowed deeply before the king, his wings raised in a gesture of apology, wiping his blood-stained lips under the crowd's gobsmacked and distorted steeze.

Warriorisborn, for the first time, felt compelled to publicly address such a grave incident. He stepped forward, raising his hands to calm the crowd. "It was an error of command," he assured them, his voice steady despite the turmoil. "There is nothing to worry about."

The crowd remained silent—as if afraid that a single movement would cause any one of them to be the monster's next prey—their eyes fixed on the king and the monstrous figure beside him. Warriorisborn, maintaining his composure, turned and walked towards his chamber, with Demetrious following closely behind, his wings folded in submission.

As soon as he reached his chamber, the king immediately sent for Aza the blossom whisperer.

Aza arrived swiftly, her confidence unwavering. The king explained the atrocity committed by Demetrious, his voice laced with frustration and concern.

Aza listened intently, then replied, "The Angels of Death have a nature that demands human lives for their upkeep when they are above sea. This is a harsh reality we must manage carefully."

Her words hung in the air, the gravity of the situation settling in. Warriorisborn realised that controlling such a powerful ally would require more than just threats and promises.

Warriorisborn was bewildered, his mind racing with the implications of Aza's revelation. He directed his frustration towards her, "Why didn't you tell me this from the start, Aza?" he demanded, his voice edged with anger.

Aza, remaining composed, implored him to stay calm. "My king, there is a way out of this," she assured. "Send Demetrious back to the ocean. It will keep the others abased."

The king listened intently as Aza continued, "The first Angel of Death to rise is the most powerful. Since Demetrious drank from the cup with the middle mechanism intact, he will forever live as a beast, even if set free." However, the other Angels of Death will sense his weakness and try to dethrone him.

Warriorisborn's initial anger began to fade, replaced by a thrilling sense of control.

I hold the key to destroying humanity, he thought, marvelling at his newfound power.

Turning to Aza, he said, "You've given me invaluable advice. It's time to reward you. Make a wish."

Aza was taken aback. Despite being the mastermind behind much of the king's success, she had never been praised or compensated. Contemplating her options, she finally spoke, her voice steady but filled with determination. "My king, instead of a wish, I propose an option. Miracle must be killed, or I demand to follow Wealth of God and help her become prosperous on Mount Ganjak."

Warriorisborn was taken aback by the audacity of her demands. He couldn't agree to such a decision on the spot. "I need time to consider this," he replied, his mind ablaze with the implications.

Aza's proposal brought Warriorisborn's attention to the crippled boy, Miracle. The atmosphere in Warriorisborn's chamber was tense as he summoned

Godhascome. The air was thick with the scent of burning incense, a vain attempt to mask the stench of sweat and anxiety that permeated the room. Godhascome entered, his steps silent and his presence commanding respect. The king, pacing back and forth, finally stopped and faced him.

"Godhascome," Warriorisborn began, his voice strained. "I need your counsel. Aza has proposed something bold, and I must decide quickly."

Godhascome's eyes, filled with wisdom and contemplation, met the king's. "What does she propose, my king?"

"She demands the death of Miracle or to follow Wealth of God to Mount Ganjak," Warriorisborn replied, the weight of the decision evident in his tone.

Godhascome pondered for a moment, the flickering torch light casting shadows on his thoughtful face. "My king, there must be something intriguing about the boy for Aza to want him dead. With your wisdom, Sire, keep both" he finally advised. "Their contributions can serve you well in different ways."

Warriorisborn nodded, a plan forming in his mind. The pieces were in place, but the game was far from over. He needed to play this carefully, ensuring each move brought him closer to absolute control.

With his decision made, Warriorisborn called upon Aza. The scent of blooming flowers filled the air as she entered, a stark contrast to the musty chamber. She stood before him, her confidence unwavering.

"Aza," the king began, "I have decided. Miracle will dwell in the tree house, and you will be relieved of your duties once Wealth of God migrates to Mount Ganjak."

Aza inclined her head slightly, her eyes betraying a flicker of relief. "Until then, I shall follow your orders, my lord," she replied, her voice steady.

It was then that Aza revealed the truth about Miracle. "My king," she said, her tone cautious, "miracle is no ordinary boy. He is a wizard, capable of great power. He can profess hidden secrets and influence the minds of others."

Warriorisborn's eyes widened at this revelation. A wizard? This boy could be an asset or a threat. Either way, the king knew he had to keep Miracle close.

Aza, sensing the king's thoughts, continued, "I believe I have prepared you for the dangers that lie ahead. But sharing a territory with a wizard is not something I can do. I feel threatened by his presence."

The king nodded, understanding the delicate balance he had to maintain. The next morning, he decided to visit the crippled boy himself. As he approached

Miracle's quarters, the scent of fresh herbs filled the air, a sign that the boy was healing well.

Upon entering, Warriorisborn found Miracle sitting up, his eyes burning with defiance. "What kind of king are you?" Miracle spat, his voice harsh. "You made us race to our death, and yet they hail you. You're nothing but a coward."

One of the guards stepped forward, ready to silence the boy, but the king raised his hand to stop him. "Let him speak," Warriorisborn commanded. Turning to Miracle, he said, "you have the right to your anger. But tell me, what do you wish for?"

Miracle was taken aback by the king's reaction. He had expected punishment, not a question. "I seek nothing," he replied, his voice still defiant.

The king, recognising the boy's potential, ordered the guards, "Prepare a chamber for him next to mine. Treat him with the utmost hospitality."

As Miracle was escorted to his new quarters, he couldn't help but feel a mix of confusion and curiosity. Why was the king treating him with such kindness?

This was the beginning of Miracle's journey, a wizard who would soon play a pivotal role in the kingdom's fate. And as for Warriorisborn, he knew he was walking a fine line, balancing power and loyalty, deception and trust. The game was far from over, but he was ready for whatever came next.

Chapter Thirteen
Miracle the Wizard

The first night Miracle slept in his new chambers near the king, Aza sprayed an enchantment in his room. She felt it was time to reveal to the king how powerful the wizard was, now that her wish had been granted.

Aza proceeded to the king's chamber, her steps measured and purposeful. Upon reaching the entrance, she addressed the guard on duty. "I need to speak with the king urgently," she said, her voice carrying an undertone of urgency.

The guard nodded and quickly delivered Aza's message. The king, wide awake and curious about the sudden call, rose from his bed. He wrapped himself in his robe and stepped out of his chamber, his eyes sharp with curiosity.

"What is it, Aza?" the king asked, his voice steady.

Aza inclined her head slightly. "There is something you must see, my king. Follow me."

Without hesitation, the king followed Aza down the dimly lit corridor. The torches lining the walls cast long shadows, flickering with each step they took. The air was thick with anticipation as they made their way towards Miracle's chamber. The silence between them was heavy, each step echoing through the halls.

As they approached, the faint glow of flames became visible, flickering from the cracks around the door. The king's eyes widened in surprise and curiosity. Aza opened the door, and they were met with the sight of Miracle's room covered in flames, the air shimmering with heat and magic.

The king's gaze swept over the scene, mesmerised by the sight. The flames danced around the room without consuming it, an enchantment of pure power. Aza turned to the king, her eyes gleaming with anticipation.

"Ask the wizard any of your secrets," she instructed, her voice steady and confident.

The king, never having doubted Aza's abilities, stepped forward, ready to witness the full extent of the wizard's power.

Warriorisborn took a deep breath and approached the sleeping wizard. His mind raced with possibilities, but he settled on a question that had haunted him for years. Leaning in closer, he whispered, "What is the name of my mother?"

The room seemed to hold its breath. The flames crackled softly, casting eerie shadows on the walls. Miracle, still deep in his enchanted sleep, stirred slightly. His lips parted, and in a voice clear and unhesitant, he answered, "Eunice."

The king's heart skipped a beat. The name echoed in his mind, stirring memories long buried. He turned to Aza, his eyes wide with amazement and a newfound respect.

Aza met his gaze, her expression calm but knowing. "You see, my king," she said softly, "the wizard's power is immense. Use it wisely."

Warriorisborn nodded, the weight of his newfound knowledge settling upon him. He knew now that Miracle was not just a boy but a valuable asset, a key to unlocking the secrets of the past and possibly, the future.

The king could not believe what he had just witnessed. A smile slowly spread across his face, and he turned to Aza with a look of profound gratitude.

"You have truly brought me a gift beyond measure," he said, his voice filled with admiration.

Aza inclined her head slightly, her eyes gleaming with satisfaction. "Miracle is indeed a great wizard," she professed. "With him by your side, the sky's the limit."

Warriorisborn nodded, the gravity of Aza's words sinking in. He knew the power that lay within the boy could change the course of his reign.

However, Aza had her own motivations. Blossom Whisperers do not like to share domains with other witches or wizards. The thought of being outshined by the young wizard gnawed at her pride, prompting her to make such an unexpected wish from the king.

"This is why I made my request, my king," Aza continued, her tone more measured. "I cannot remain here with the wizard. Our powers clash, and I do not wish to be overshadowed."

The king, understanding her position, nodded. "Your wish will be honoured, Aza," he assured her. "But know that your contribution will always be valued."

Aza bowed gracefully, the flames around Miracle beginning to subside. "Thank you, my king," she replied. "I will continue to serve you until it is time for me to leave."

Warriorisborn turned back to the sleeping wizard, his mind racing with the possibilities that lay ahead. With Miracle's power and Aza's wisdom, his kingdom stood on the brink of unprecedented greatness. But he also knew that managing such powerful allies required careful strategy and unwavering resolve.

The following morning, Miracle woke up to the startling sight of the king standing right in front of him. His eyes widened in surprise, and his mind raced to grasp the reason for the royal visit.

"Why are you here?" Miracle asked, his tone impudent and direct. "Leave immediately."

The king was not angered by the boy's audacity. Instead, he smiled, appreciating the wizard's spirited nature. "I have no intention of leaving," Warriorisborn replied calmly. "I simply wish to ensure you are well taken care of."

With a nod, the king turned to the maids who had gathered outside the chamber. "Look after him and give him all he desires," he commanded.

The maids, well aware of the king's authority, bowed and complied without hesitation. As they moved to attend to Miracle's needs, the king gave one final glance at the boy, a mixture of curiosity and expectation in his eyes, before leaving the chamber.

Miracle watched the king depart, a flicker of confusion crossing his face. He had expected anger, perhaps even punishment, but instead, he was being treated with unexpected kindness and respect.

Meanwhile, Followmehome had begun preparations for building the king's ships. With the assistance of tree house soldiers, deployed to expedite the project, he laboured tirelessly. However, he chose not to involve the Landers, burdened by the guilt of losing two of his children to the king. Despite this, he had agreed to a bargain to construct thousands of ships.

The Landers were far from pleased with his decision. Whispers of dissent grew louder, questioning his competence. Many believed he was too fragile to rule, suggesting he might be better suited as an advisor, mocking him in his absence.

Followmehome, bearing the weight of their scorn, resolved to follow what he believed was the best course for the Landers. He couldn't afford to let his emotions cloud his judgement. The consequences of breaking the deal with the king were too dire to contemplate, and he knew the survival of his people hinged on fulfilling his end of the bargain.

After several arduous journeys, thousands of tree house soldiers were transported to the land to assist with the shipbuilding efforts. However, the Landers' growing resentment reached a boiling point. Their dissatisfaction led the chief and elders to convene a meeting and summon Followmehome for questioning.

The assembly was tense as Followmehome entered the room, the weight of their discontent palpable. Malcom, the eldest chief, a figure of authority and wisdom, spoke first, his voice firm yet tinged with frustration.

"Followmehome," he began, "we understand the necessity of this project, but the presence of so many tree house soldiers on our land has caused unrest among our people. They feel invaded, and their grievances cannot be ignored."

One of the elders, her eyes filled with concern, added, "We have received countless complaints. The people are unhappy, and they question your decision to exclude them from this vital task. They wonder if you still have their best interests at heart."

Followmehome, feeling the weight of their accusations, took a deep breath before responding. "I understand your concerns," he said, his voice steady but earnest. "The decision to rely on the tree house soldiers was not made lightly. I bear the guilt of losing two of my children to the king, and I believed this was the most efficient way to fulfil our end of the bargain without further endangering our people."

Malcom leaned forward, his gaze intense. "But the Landers feel alienated and undermined. They need to be part of this effort. We must find a way to integrate them into the project, to restore their faith in your leadership."

Nodding, Followmehome replied, "I will find a way to involve the Landers. We will work together to complete this task, ensuring their voices are heard and their concerns addressed. I am committed to our people's well-being, and I will not let emotions cloud my judgement. Together, we can achieve this without compromising our unity."

At some point during the heated meeting, one of the more outspoken elders, filled with frustration and anger, stood up and pointed an accusing finger at Followmehome. "You're nothing but a sycophant!" he shouted, his voice echoing through the room. "You have sold us all to the king! Two of your children are held captive, and you have done nothing about it. How can we trust you to lead us when you won't even fight for your own family?"

Murmurs of agreement spread through the assembly, the air thick with tension. The Landers, their faces etched with worry and doubt, exchanged glances, nodding in silent consensus. Malcom, though more measured in his approach, couldn't ignore the rising tide of discontent.

Another elder, his voice grave, addressed Followmehome. "The people fear you may not be the right leader at this point. They believe you have compromised our safety and sovereignty by submitting to the king's demands so readily."

Followmehome felt a deep pang of hurt but remained composed. He knew that defending his actions was crucial. "I understand your frustrations and fears," he began, his voice steady but strained. "I chose to comply with the king's demands to protect our people from further harm. The loss of my children weighs heavily on me, and I have not given up hope of their return."

But his words did little to quell the unrest. Another voice called out, "You may go on with your project, but we want you relieved of your duties. We need a leader who will stand firm against the king, not one who bends to his every whim."

The room fell silent, the demand hanging heavily in the air. Followmehome, feeling the weight of their disillusionment, took a deep breath. "If stepping down is what the people wish, I will respect your decision," he said quietly. "But know this: every action I have taken has been to ensure the safety and future of our land."

Malcom, sensing the gravity of the moment, rose to his feet. "We will deliberate on this matter and come to a decision. For now, continue with your project. The well-being of our Landers must remain our top priority."

Followmehome nodded, accepting their judgement.

Followmehome saw it coming. He agreed to the elders' decision without protest, knowing it was inevitable. He gathered his belongings and prepared to leave, a heavy heart weighing him down. Before departing, he bid a quiet farewell to his family, his eyes lingering on each of their faces. "Stay strong," he whispered to Crown, his wife, "and take care of our children."

He travelled to a distant region far from the Landers, where he could focus on constructing and building the king's ships. The journey was long and arduous, filled with moments of reflection and regret. He thought about the choices he had made and the sacrifices he had endured.

Upon reaching his destination, Followmehome wasted no time. He threw himself into the work, overseeing the construction with a diligence that left little room for personal sorrow. The tree house soldiers, loyal and industrious, followed his lead, and together they began the monumental task of building the fleet.

Days turned into weeks, and weeks into months. The distant land was harsh and unyielding, but Followmehome's resolve never wavered. He communicated with the king through messengers, ensuring that progress was steady and meeting expectations.

Yet, even in the midst of his relentless labour, the absence of his family and the estrangement from his people gnawed at him. He missed the familiar faces and the comforting routine of his old life. The weight of their disappointment and distrust was a constant burden.

In the evenings, after the day's work was done, Followmehome would sit alone, staring out at the horizon. He thought of Wealth of God and Miracle, wondering if they were safe if they understood his decisions. He hoped, silently and fervently, that one day he could return to his Landers, not as a broken leader but as a man who had fulfilled his promises.

His solitude in the new region brought a strange clarity. He realised that his journey was not just about building ships but about reclaiming his honour and proving his worth to those who had lost faith in him. And so, with every plank nailed and every sail raised, Followmehome worked not just for the king but for the hope of redemption and the dream of a united land once more.

Chapter Fourteen
Revelations and Burdens

Warriorisborn called upon Wealth of God, his expression serious and filled with purpose. As she entered his presence, he could see the curiosity and apprehension in her eyes.

"It's time," Warriorisborn said, his voice carrying the weight of the moment. "Time to present you with the gift I promised."

He called out Demetrious, the Angel of Death, holding the metal cup in his hand. The air around them seemed to grow colder as Demetrious appeared, his presence both awe-inspiring and terrifying.

Wealth of God looked at Warriorisborn, searching his eyes for an explanation. Why would he gift her the only Angel of Death enslaved to him?

Warriorisborn took a deep breath, ready to reveal his reasoning. "Wealth of God, you possess a strength and wisdom that few can match. In you, I see the potential for greatness."

He paused, watching her closely. "I know who you truly are. I know that you are my granddaughter."

Wealth of God's eyes widened in shock. She remembered Kala's words to her father, warning him not to let the king know about their relationship. Yet here it was, laid bare before her.

Warriorisborn continued, "Aza may have warned me to beware of my lost kin, but I believe in you. I trust you."

He paused, letting his words sink in before continuing. "But my decision is not solely based on our bond. I have a vision for our future, a kingdom where you will play a crucial role. By giving you Demetrious, I am not just bestowing a gift upon you; I am entrusting you with power and responsibility. This is not just about familial ties. It's about leadership, legacy, and the future of our realm."

Warriorisborn's eyes softened as he looked at Wealth of God. "I want to establish a kingdom where you are the ruler, where your strength and wisdom can guide our people. This is my way of empowering you, of showing my faith in your ability to lead. I understand the risks. You could revolt against me, use this power for your own ends. But I believe you will see the bigger picture. You will understand the importance of unity and the future we can build together."

He stepped closer to her, placing a hand on her shoulder. "This is a test of trust, of faith. I believe in you, Wealth of God. And I believe that together, we can create a kingdom that will stand the test of time."

Wealth of God felt the weight of his words, the depth of his trust and the responsibility he was placing on her shoulders. She understood the significance of this gift, not just as a token of power, but as a symbol of Warriorisborn's vision and faith in her.

Warriorisborn smiled, a mix of pride and hope in his eyes. "May you lead with wisdom and strength, my granddaughter. Together, we shall build a kingdom that will endure."

Suddenly, Demetrious emerged from his private chambers, his transformation both mesmerising and terrifying. His presence seemed to darken the room, shadows lengthening and deepening as he approached. His eyes glowed with an eerie, otherworldly light, and his form shifted between solid and ethereal as if he existed between two realms.

Wealth of God was terrified, her heart pounding in her chest. Every instinct screamed at her to flee, to escape the overwhelming presence of the Angel of Death. But before she could move, Warriorisborn's voice rang out, strong and reassuring.

"Do not be afraid," the king commanded, his voice cutting through the fear. "Demetrious will not harm you."

Wealth of God forced herself to stand her ground though every fibre of her being urged her to run. She looked at the king, seeking reassurance in his calm demeanour.

Warriorisborn continued, "As soon as the Tree Ganjak is ready, he will be yours to keep."

Demetrious stopped a few paces away, his form towering and menacing. The king turned his attention to the Angel of Death, his tone authoritative and unyielding.

"Demetrious," he commanded, "go into the sea and keep others abase until you are needed."

The Angel of Death bowed his head slightly in acknowledgement before his form began to shift once more. He moved with an ethereal grace, gliding towards the exit. As he passed Wealth of God, she could feel the chill emanating from him, a cold that seemed to pierce her very soul.

Without a word, Demetrious left the chamber, his presence lingering like a shadow. Wealth of God let out a breath she hadn't realised she was holding, her body trembling from the encounter.

Warriorisborn placed a reassuring hand on her shoulder. "You see, my granddaughter, the power you now possess is formidable, but it is also a responsibility. Demetrious will serve you, but you must wield his power wisely."

Wealth of God nodded, still shaken but more determined than ever. She understood the gravity of the gift she had been given and the expectations that came with it. The path ahead would be challenging, but she was ready to embrace her destiny and lead with the strength and wisdom her grandfather saw in her.

Wealth of God could not believe that the king had the power to enslave Demetrious. She was amazed at what she had witnessed, finally realising the extent of the king's power. Overwhelmed by the immense power she had acquired from the king, she awaited the ship that would take her to Mount Ganjak. In the meantime, she decided to visit her grandmother, Kala, in the lower section of the tree.

However, before visiting her grandmother, Wealth of God sensed a spark of admiration from Servant of Allah. Though she had been trained to suppress her emotions, she felt convinced that she needed a fearless soldier by her side to support her in times of uncertainty. His steady gaze and respectful demeanour hinted at an unspoken bond between them, one that could prove invaluable in the tumultuous times ahead.

On the other hand, Servant of Allah had never encountered a woman as brave and commanding as Wealth of God. Her strength and potential captivated him. Her unwavering resolve and formidable presence inspired him, making him believe that, together, they could achieve great things. As he observed her from a distance, his admiration grew, and he envisioned a future where they could rule Mount Ganjak together, their combined strengths and aspirations forging a powerful alliance.

Wealth of God had only seen her grandmother once before, a fleeting visit with her father when she was first brought to the tree house. That brief, secret encounter was shrouded in mystery and carried the weight of forbidden knowledge. Now, as she approached her grandmother's chamber alone, her heart pounded with a mix of trepidation and curiosity.

The entrance to the chamber loomed ahead, dark and uninviting. Wealth of God hesitated, recalling the faint, stern voice of her father warning her to keep this secret. She took a deep breath and stepped inside, the dim light from a few flickering torches casting eerie shadows on the stone walls. Each step echoed softly, amplifying the profound silence that filled the air.

The main room of the chamber was sparse and dusty, as though it had been abandoned for years. A few pieces of worn furniture lay scattered, covered in cobwebs. The air was thick with the scent of age and neglect, a stark contrast to the vibrant stories she had heard about her grandmother's wisdom and strength.

She cautiously moved deeper into the chamber, her eyes scanning for any sign of life. As she ventured further, she found an open door leading to a private room. The door creaked as she pushed it open, revealing a smaller, more intimate space.

Her breath caught in her throat as she stepped inside. In the centre of the room lay a dry, desiccated corpse. The sight was jarring, the skeletal figure a macabre testament to a life long gone. Wealth of God felt a wave of nausea and horror, her hand instinctively covering her mouth to stifle a gasp.

The private chamber was as stark as the main room. A small wooden chest, an ornate mirror, and a withered plant were the only remnants of a life that once was. The sight of the corpse, so shrunken and mummified, was a grotesque parody of the vibrant old wombat n she had hoped to meet. It was a harsh reminder of mortality, contrasting sharply with the image she had held in her mind.

As Wealth of God stood there, grappling with the shock and revulsion, a deep sorrow welled up within her. This was not the reunion she had imagined. She had hoped for guidance, wisdom, and perhaps a connection to her heritage. Instead, she was faced with a grim reality, a lifeless husk that spoke of abandonment and neglect.

Steeling herself, she approached the corpse, drawn by a strange compulsion to understand. As she leaned in closer, she noticed a faint glimmer on the skeletal hand—a ring, intricately carved and set with a dull gemstone. It was a poignant symbol of the life that had once been, a small reminder of the woman who had worn it.

Wealth of God took a step back, her mind racing. This discovery was unsettling, but it also kindled a fire within her. She resolved to learn more about her grandmother, to uncover the mysteries that had led to this desolate end. The journey ahead was uncertain, but she was determined to honour Kala's legacy and forge her own path with the strength and courage she had inherited.

Wealth of God stood in the dimly lit chamber, staring at the dry, lifeless body of her grandmother, Kala. Her mind raced with confusion and dread. The air was thick with the scent of decay, and she knew instinctively that this was not a natural death. In the tree house, death was rare and uncertain, making this discovery all the more unsettling. She began to brainstorm, piecing together the puzzle of who could have been capable of such an act. Her thoughts circled back to the king, the only one with access to the poison she suspected had been used.

Determined to uncover the truth, Wealth of God made her way back to the king's chamber. The corridors seemed longer and darker than usual, each step echoing her growing anxiety. As she approached the king's guards, they eyed her warily but allowed her passage. She entered the grand chamber, her heart pounding.

Chapter Fifteen
Secrets, Power and Destiny

The king sat upon his throne, his expression a mix of curiosity and irritation as he watched her approach. She took a deep breath, trying to steady her nerves. "My king," she began, her voice unwavering despite her inner turmoil, "I discovered Kala's body. It appears she was poisoned. Do you know anything about this?"

The king's eyes narrowed, and a flicker of anger crossed his face. "It is a coward's act for a king like me to kill without witnesses," he replied, his tone sharp. "The poison was given to your father as part of a bargain we made. No wonder your father wanted you removed as my successor. He perceived your boldness and was scared it might get you into trouble."

The king's anger was palpable, but so was his determination to address the situation. He immediately called for his advisors and commanded a thorough investigation. The king's soldiers and spies were dispatched to search for clues, scouring every corner of the tree house. Whispers and speculations spread rapidly, creating an atmosphere of tension and fear among the inhabitants.

Despite the king's initial fervour, as days turned into weeks with no definitive answers, the intensity of the search began to wane. The king, known for his ruthless authority, had previously made an example out of Seditious, and now, with an Angel of Death enslaved to him, he believed no one would dare challenge him. This conviction led him to apply limited pressure during the investigation, and gradually, the search quieted down, becoming a mere murmur in the background of daily life.

Wealth of God felt disrespected and deeply confused. The king's response had left her unsure of who to believe. The image of her grandmother's dried body haunted her thoughts, driving her to seek justice for the crime. She suspected her father or the king, but with the culprit still at large, her mind was a whirlwind of uncertainty.

Overwhelmed by her emotions, she sought comfort and clarity. She requested the company of Servant of Allah, hoping his presence would help her process her turbulent thoughts.

Servant of Allah was thrilled by her summons. He arrived at her chamber, prepared to attend to her every demand. Wealth of God, standing tall and resolute, clicked her fingers, and her maids promptly vanished from the room, leaving them alone.

With a slow, deliberate stride, she approached Servant of Allah. Her eyes never left his as she began to walk around him in a slow circle, her fingers lightly grazing his skin. The sensation sent shivers down his spine, and he could feel his heartbeat quicken.

"Undress," she commanded softly but firmly, her voice filled with authority and an underlying vulnerability that tugged at his heart. Servant of Allah complied without hesitation, removing his garments and lying down on his back, feeling the cool air against his skin.

Wealth of God stood over him, her expression a blend of determination and turmoil. She knelt beside him, her hands tracing patterns across his thigh. The intimacy of the moment was intense, but it was also a means for her to ground herself, to find a moment of peace amidst the chaos in her mind.

Her touch grew more assertive as she slowly stroked his body, igniting a fire within him. She guided him with a commanding presence, mounting him with a mixture of desperation and desire. Their union was wild and fierce, a physical manifestation of her inner turmoil and need for control. She rode him with fervour, releasing her pent-up emotions with every movement, her cries echoing through the chamber.

The next morning, Wealth of God awoke to find Servant of Allah still by her side. Surprised and somewhat unsettled, she roused him and ordered him to leave immediately.

Servant of Allah, feeling a mixture of satisfaction and frustration, reached out and held her neck gently. He pulled her close, giving her a lingering kiss that made her melt for a few brief seconds. But she quickly pushed him away, regaining her composure. He dressed and left, his mind already planning his next move.

Though he felt privileged to have been with the future queen, her dismissive behaviour left him feeling belittled. Determined to achieve his own ambitions, he returned to her chamber the next evening, this time with a clear purpose.

"May I have permission to propose a demand?" he asked, his tone respectful yet firm.

Wealth of God regarded him with a mix of curiosity and caution, wondering what this bold and enigmatic man would ask of her.

Servant of Allah overheard a conversation between the king and his right-hand man discussing the imminent announcement that Wealth of God would become the Queen of Ganjak. He realised this was his chance to bind himself to her greatness, even if it meant sacrificing his dignity.

Wealth of God told him to proceed with his demands, and thus he knelt before her and said with all the courage in the world, "Wealth of God, will you marry me? I swear to defend and protect you, even if it means using my very last breath to ascertain this."

Wealth of God was impressed.

"Stand upright," she said, authoritatively.

She walked towards him and grabbed his manhood right in the presence of her maids. They quickly averted their eyes.

"Get on your knees," she ordered, "and caress my private part with your tongue. I assure you, your proposal shall be granted if you can satisfy me."

Servant of Allah's eyes darted left and right, slightly embarrassed. Yet he could not resist. He fell to his knees and did as she had demanded despite the presence of her maids.

Minutes after, he was pulled up and kissed fervently by Wealth of God.

Wealth of God visited the king, her resolve evident in her stride. She informed him of her decision to choose a husband from among his soldiers, and then she presented Servant of Allah. As soon as Servant of Allah stepped forward, he went on his knees before the king and bowed deeply.

The king studied them both for a moment, recognising the strength and ambition that radiated from their union. He knew better than to put asunder such an incredible match.

"Godhascome," the king called, his voice echoing through the chamber. "Prepare the tree house for a feast."

Godhascome immediately set to work, carrying out the king's orders with efficiency and precision. News of the impending union spread quickly throughout the tree house, and excitement buzzed in the air. A day was set to seal their union, and preparations for the grand celebration began in earnest. The tree house was soon alive with activity, as everyone anticipated the day when Wealth of God and Servant of Allah would be united, marking a new chapter in their intertwined destinies.

The five Angels of Death would appear at any moment, and the king knew it was time to call upon Demetrious for an update about the beasts he kept restrained beneath the ocean. The king retrieved the metal cup and, speaking into it, he said, "Demetrious…Come right before me now!"

Seconds passed, and the tension in the air grew thick. Suddenly, a powerful surge disturbed the ocean's surface. With a deafening roar, Demetrious burst forth from the water, his immense wings beating with astonishing speed. He ascended rapidly, the spray of the sea trailing behind him like a comet's tail.

He flew through the treetop, breaking through the canopy with a thunderous rush, and landed on the round platform facing the king's chamber. His presence was formidable, a tangible aura of power and darkness surrounding him.

Demetrious stood tall, his eyes glowing with an eerie light as he awaited the king's command. The king, unfazed by the display, stepped forward, ready to address his formidable servant.

The king invited Demetrious into his chamber for a private discussion. Only Godhascome was present, standing quietly to the side, his presence a silent reminder of the gravity of the situation. The chamber, dimly lit by flickering torches, cast long shadows across the room, enhancing the solemnity of the moment.

The king's gaze was intense, his eyes boring into Demetrious with a mixture of curiosity and determination. "Demetrious," he began, his voice steady but carrying the weight of authority, "what are the intentions of the five Angels of Death?"

Demetrious, his form towering and ominous, met the king's gaze unflinchingly. His eyes glowed with an otherworldly light as he spoke, his voice resonating with an eerie calm.

"They have awakened, but they remain restrained. Their power simmers beneath the surface, awaiting the call to unleash their full wrath."

The king listened intently, his mind racing with the implications. He glanced briefly at Godhascome, who nodded almost imperceptibly, a silent acknowledgement of the seriousness of the matter.

Satisfied with the answer, yet knowing the situation required careful handling, the king gave his command. "Return to your post, Demetrious."

Without a word, Demetrious bowed slightly, then turned and exited the chamber. Within moments, he took flight once more, diving back into the ocean with the same breathtaking velocity, disappearing beneath the waves as swiftly as he had emerged. The king and Godhascome exchanged a glance, the weight of the impending events heavy in the air.

Two years had passed, and though the five Angels of Death had awakened, they had not yet sensed Demetrious's weakness, which had been exposed during this time. The people remained blissfully unaware that more Angels of Death had stirred from their slumber. They continued to place their faith in the king, their perceived almighty saviour, believing in his power to control the beasts.

However, what the people did not know was that their almighty saviour had made a pact with the devil. The king, who they trusted implicitly, had already signed a deed that would ultimately lead his own people to their doom. He was willing to sacrifice them, luring them towards a fate that could result in their extinction. Despite knowing the existence of the Angels of Death posed an existential threat to humanity, the king was prepared to follow through with his dark plan, keeping his true intentions hidden beneath a facade of benevolence and strength.

Followmehome could not deliver the ships on the expected date. The inexperience of the tree house soldiers and the lack of support from the Landers contributed to this failure. The late delivery of the ships enraged the king, who showed an unappreciative attitude towards Followmehome and refused to even look at the magnificent fleet of ships that had been intricately anchored to the tree roots.

Feeling disrespected by the king's reaction, Followmehome's sense of disappointment and frustration grew. Despite the effort and hard work that had gone into the project, his accomplishment was met with disdain. Without a word, he turned his back on the king's ingratitude and immediately departed the tree house, his heart heavy with the weight of unmet expectations and perceived injustice.

Before the arrival of the ships, Warriorisborn stood before the gathered people of the tree house, his presence commanding their undivided attention. He raised his hands, and a hush fell over the crowd.

"People of the tree house," he began, his voice resonating with authority, "I stand before you today to share a vision—a vision that stretches a hundred years into the future. Our tree house will not only survive, but it will thrive and expand, becoming the heart of a vast and powerful kingdom."

He paused, allowing his words to sink in. The people exchanged glances, a mixture of awe and curiosity in their eyes.

"We will see our influence spread far and wide. New kingdoms will rise under our rule, each one a testament to our strength and unity. Our prosperity will know no bounds. Safety will be assured for every one of you, as long as you remain loyal and steadfast."

Warriorisborn's gaze swept over the crowd, his eyes burning with determination. "I promise you, under my leadership, we will achieve greatness. The next hundred years will be a golden era for us all. Together, we will build a legacy that will be remembered for generations."

The people were astounded, their minds reeling from the enormity of his vision. They could scarcely believe that he intended to rule for such an extended period, yet no one dared to speak. The king's presence and power were palpable, and his promises, grandiose as they were, instilled a mixture of hope and fear in their hearts. The air was thick with a charged silence, as the future loomed large before them.

Followmehome was deeply disappointed and felt disrespected by the king's reaction upon delivering the fleet of ships. The king's dismissive attitude and refusal to acknowledge the magnificent vessels anchored to the tree roots fuelled a growing resolve in Followmehome. Realising it was time to settle the dispute with his people and reclaim his position, he became ready to wage war against the king if necessary.

As Followmehome prepared to set sail, he noticed an old man stumbling along the tree house entrance, appearing lost and vulnerable. Upon closer inspection, he realised the man was blind. Compassion stirred within him, and he decided to bring the old man aboard his ship.

The old man, it turned out, was a seer. He was the very same blind prophet who had foretold the bloodshed that would follow the construction of the tree house. He had been a revered figure, known for his accurate and often ominous predictions. Recently, the seer had sensed a shift in the air—a gathering storm of violence and betrayal, one that he knew he could not prevent but only escape. Fearing for his life, he had decided to flee the tree house.

Followmehome arrived on land with a new resolve and determination, one that speaks volumes of liberation.

Chapter Sixteen
Shadows of Destiny

Meanwhile, in front of the tree house, a fleet of ships stood ready to be boarded. The king, anticipating the journey ahead, called upon Wealth of God and granted her permission to proceed to Mount Ganjak. She was to be accompanied by Aza and Servant of Allah, along with three hundred soldiers and crew members. The scene was a flurry of activity as supplies were loaded and preparations finalised.

Wealth of God, with a regal bearing, boarded the lead ship, followed closely by her entourage. Aza, ever watchful, and Servant of Allah, steadfast and ready, took their positions by her side. The soldiers, disciplined and prepared, stood ready for whatever challenges lay ahead.

With everything in place, the ships unfurled their sails and set off from the shore, cutting through the water with purpose and determination. As they sailed towards land, a sense of anticipation filled the air, the journey ahead promising to shape the future of their world in ways none could yet foresee.

However, the five Angels of Death had been unleashed. Immediately, they sensed a weakness in Demetrious. Though they were uncertain if he had been enslaved, they were concerned about his leadership. His lack of aggression and the hint of deceit in his demeanour were troubling. Demetrious was acutely aware that, should they discover his servitude to the king, they could devour him. Yet he feigned strength in their presence, maintaining a facade of dominance while turmoil churned within him.

Recognising the imminent danger, Demetrious knew it was time to alert the king and seek a solution. He flew into the king's chamber with urgency, the air crackling with tension. His sudden arrival startled the guards, who quickly informed the king of his presence.

The king, holding the metal cup that bound Demetrious, emerged from his chamber. His eyes narrowed with suspicion and curiosity. "Demetrious," he said, his voice cold and commanding, "how dare you fly into my chamber without authorisation?"

Demetrious, his form towering and imposing, responded with a low, rumbling voice that carried the weight of his predicament. "My king, I risk my life to warn you of an impending threat," he began, his words laced with urgency.

The king's gaze hardened. "Speak further," he ordered, gripping the cup tighter.

"The five Angels of Death have awakened," Demetrious continued. "They demand easy access to the tree house. If their demands are not met, they will take my life, freeing themselves from the depths of the ocean. They have sensed my vulnerability and will act on it."

The king's mind raced. He knew he could control the Angels with the metal cup, but defeating them required the poison, which was no longer in his possession. Without it, he needed to tread carefully and act with cunning. The existence of more beasts could not be revealed to his people just yet.

"Demetrious," the king said after a moment of contemplation, "I need one more year to make the necessary arrangements. We cannot afford haste in this matter."

Demetrious bowed his head slightly, acknowledging the king's command. "As you wish, my king," he replied, his voice tinged with both relief and apprehension. He knew the king's delay was a temporary reprieve, but it was better than immediate death.

With a mighty flap of his wings, Demetrious took off, soaring back towards the ocean to deliver the king's message, as though it were his. The five Angels of Death, sensing his return, awaited his report with growing impatience.

Meanwhile, the king pondered his next move. He knew the blossom whisperer had never mentioned that Demetrious could make a bargain if his life was at stake. This revelation unsettled him, but he also saw an opportunity to strategize and outmanoeuvre the impending threat. He needed to buy time, rally his resources, and find a way to reclaim the poison or devise another means to subdue the Angels.

In the days that followed, the king summoned his most trusted advisors, including Godhascome, to discuss the situation. He shared the news with them, careful to keep the details secret from the broader populace. They began to formulate a plan, understanding that their survival hinged on their ability to outthink and outmanoeuvre the formidable Angels of Death.

As Demetrious relayed the king's message to the Angels, he felt their collective disdain but also their begrudging acceptance. They communicated their agreement through a series of menacing roars and silent, mental exchanges. The Angels of Death in their beast form don't communicate with their mouths, except Demetrious who drank from the metal cup with its middle mechanism intact. They would give the king one more year, but they would not be patient forever.

Back in the tree house, the tension was palpable. The king, knowing he had only bought a brief respite, worked tirelessly to strengthen his position. The stage was set for a confrontation that would test the limits of his power and cunning, and the fate of the tree house and its inhabitants hung precariously in the balance.

***

Followmehome disembarked from the ship, guiding the old blind man with a steady hand as they walked towards the ocean bank. The old man's frail frame was evident, and his steps were tentative, but he moved with a quiet dignity that spoke volumes of his inner strength.

As they approached the shoreline, one of Followmehome's sons spotted them and raced to the scene. "Father!" he called out, his voice filled with a mix of relief and curiosity. He took the old man's other arm, helping him walk with more ease. "Who is this?" he asked, glancing at the blind man with concern.

"A man in need of our help," Followmehome replied. "He was alone and helpless. We must look after him."

The journey to their home was slow but steady. Followmehome's son held the old man upright, supporting him as they progressed. The old man, despite his blindness, seemed to sense the surroundings with an uncanny awareness.

When they finally reached home, Followmehome's wife hurried out to meet them. Her eyes widened in surprise at the sight of the old blind man. "Who is this, Followmehome?" she asked, her voice gentle but filled with concern.

"A stranger in need of care," Followmehome replied. "We must ensure he is comfortable and looked after until he regains his strength."

Without hesitation, his wife took the old man's arm and guided him inside. She prepared a place for him to rest, ensuring he was comfortable. Over the next few days, she tended to his needs, providing food, water, and gentle care. The old man's health began to improve though his blindness remained.

The family did not know the old man's background or the depth of his wisdom. They only knew he needed their help, and they were determined to provide it. Followmehome's wife would sit by his side, talking to him and sharing stories of their life on land. The old man listened intently, occasionally offering a kind word or a nod of understanding.

As the days turned into weeks, the old man grew stronger. His presence became a quiet but steadying force in their household. He rarely spoke of his past, but his words held a depth of knowledge that hinted at experiences far beyond the ordinary.

Warriorisborn paced his chamber, lost in thought, his mind racing with the news from Demetrious. The urgency to retrieve the poison bottle gnawed at him. As the sun dipped below the horizon and darkness enveloped the tree house, he made a decision.

He moved stealthily through the corridors, his footsteps echoing softly. Reaching the wizard's chamber, he hesitated for a moment before entering. The room was dimly lit, the only light coming from a flickering candle by the bedside where the wizard lay in a deep sleep.

Warriorisborn approached the sleeping wizard, leaning in close. "Wizard," he whispered urgently, "I need your counsel. How can I reclaim the poison bottle?"

The wizard remained still, his breathing slow and steady. Then, in a voice thick with sleep, he began to murmur, "Force…only through force…the poison can be reclaimed…"

Warriorisborn listened intently, his eyes narrowing as he absorbed the wizard's words. "Are you certain?" he pressed though he knew the wizard could not hear him.

The wizard continued, his voice a low, slurred murmur, "I unlock secrets of the past…cannot project the future…but force…is the only way…"

Warriorisborn nodded to himself, the wizard's sleep-talking confirming his suspicions. He placed a hand on the young boy's shoulder, a silent gesture of gratitude.

"Thank you, Wizard," he whispered softly though he knew he couldn't hear him.

With a final nod, Warriorisborn turned and left the chamber, the weight of the wizard's words heavy on his mind as he prepared for what lay ahead.

Followmehome did not anticipate what was to come. Busy mending the trust issues he had with his people, he decided it was time to share the truth. Gathering the chiefs and elders, he stood before them, his expression earnest.

"My people," he began, "I know I have lost your trust. But I implore you to hear me out." He took a deep breath, his voice steady but filled with urgency. "The bargain I made with the king was not out of weakness or betrayal, but necessity. The poison is valuable beyond measure, a tool of immense power."

The chiefs murmured among themselves, scepticism evident in their eyes. Followmehome raised a hand to quiet them.

"Warriorisborn seeks to invade our land," he continued. "His ambitions know no bounds, and his power grows daily. The poison, if used wisely, can be our safeguard. My intention was never to submit to him but to protect our people, to ensure we have a weapon to counter his aggression."

He paused, allowing his words to sink in. "I ask for your patience and your trust. Everything I have done has been in the interest of our survival, of safeguarding our future."

The chiefs exchanged glances, their expressions softening. After a moment of quiet deliberation among the leaders, one of them stepped forward.

"We understand now," the elder said, his voice firm. "Your actions were driven by a desire to protect us. We reinstated you as our leader because we believe in your vision and your dedication to our cause."

Followmehome felt a wave of relief wash over him. He nodded, gratitude evident in his eyes. "Thank you," he said sincerely. "Together, we will face whatever comes our way and ensure the safety of our land and our people."

The chiefs cheered, their faith in their leader restored, and the bond between them stronger than ever.

Warriorisborn knew it was time to make Followmehome adhere to his command. He summoned Godhascome and gave him a stern look. "It's time to humble the Landers," he said, his voice cold and commanding. "Take your men and bring Followmehome to his knees."

Godhascome nodded, his expression resolute. "It will be done, my king."

Godhascome and his soldiers sailed and marched into the Landers' domain with purpose. The air was thick with tension as they approached Followmehome's dwelling. Godhascome's voice boomed as he demanded, "Bring me Followmehome!"

Followmehome emerged from his chamber, his expression a mix of determination and wariness. He was not alone; his advisors flanked him, their faces set in grim lines. "Welcome, Godhascome," Followmehome said, his tone guarded. "What brings you here?"

Godhascome's eyes scanned the room, noting the presence of the advisors. He knew there would be no private conversation. "I'm here under the king's orders," he declared. "Followmehome, you are to submit to his command."

Followmehome stood tall, his resolve unwavering. "I will not be intimidated," he said firmly. "We will discuss this matter as a council."

But Godhascome had other plans. He gestured to his soldiers, who moved swiftly to seize Crown, his wife. The Landers were caught off guard, unprepared to face the soldiers of the tree house. Crown was dragged away, struggling against her captors. She screamed and cursed but to no avail.

"Leave her out of this!" Followemehome roared in disbelief, but he was immediately deterred from making any moves in interjection.

"This is just a taste of what is to come if you defy the king," Godhascome warned, his voice dripping with menace. "Submit, or more will suffer."

Followmehome's heart burned with humiliation and rage, but he kept his composure. He remembered the wisdom of his teachings: "He who is slow to anger is better than the mighty, and he who rules his spirit can conquer the city."

Followmehome felt humiliated in front of his people. This made three of his family members currently in the possession of the king. His steeze was on the line, but he was going to best the situation, maintaining it.

The chiefs gathered in a tense meeting, the cruel actions of the king's soldiers fresh in their minds. Followmehome addressed them, his voice steady. "We have witnessed the king's ruthlessness," he said. "But we must remain united and strong. I ask for your trust in my leadership. We won't let go of the poison to redeem our people. We'd find other ways instead."

The leaders murmured among themselves, weighing their options. Finally, one of them spoke up. "We agree, Followmehome. Lead us and make the decisions you believe are right."

Followmehome stood firm in the face of the king's threats. He was resolute, refusing to yield or bargain, even if it meant risking Crown's life. His determination to defend his people was unwavering.

As he pondered his next move, he recalled the words of the old man he had rescued; "Do not be a pawn; you are also a king. Act like one." The memory of those words steeled his resolve, reminding him of his true strength and leadership. Followmehome knew he had to stand his ground and lead his people with courage and wisdom, no matter the cost.

***

Wealth of God, accompanied by Aza the blossom whisperer and a contingent of soldiers, reached the land. Servant of Allah, the commander of the soldiers, instructed them to remain vigilant as they disembarked from the ship and moved into the jungle.

"We must be cautious," Servant of Allah said, his voice low and firm. "Stay alert and follow Wealth of God's lead."

Wealth of God nodded, her eyes scanning the dense foliage ahead. "Follow me," she commanded, her tone decisive. She led them along a narrow, winding path that veered away from the usual routes to avoid being noticed by the Landers.

As they advanced deeper into the jungle, Servant of Allah suddenly halted, his eyes narrowing as he spotted a movement in the underbrush. A black baby jaguar wandered into the path, its sleek fur glistening in the filtered sunlight.

"Hold," Servant of Allah commanded, raising a hand. The soldiers came to a stop, alert and ready.

Wealth of God stepped forward, her gaze following Servant of Allah's pointed finger. "A baby jaguar," she murmured, a smile playing at the corners of her lips. "How extraordinary."

"What shall we do, my lady?" asked Servant of Allah.

"We'll capture it," Wealth of God decided with a glint of excitement in her eyes. "It will make a fine pet."

With careful precision, a couple of soldiers moved forward, gently corralling the young jaguar without startling it. The animal, though wary, allowed itself to be approached, perhaps sensing no immediate threat.

Once the jaguar was securely held, Wealth of God knelt beside it, stroking its smooth, black fur. "I'll call you Jacko," she said softly. She reached into her satchel and pulled out a small vial of root water. "Here, drink this," she coaxed, holding the vial to the jaguar's mouth. Jacko lapped at the liquid, its eyes meeting hers with a mixture of curiosity and trust.

Standing up, Wealth of God handed Jacko over to one of the soldiers to carry. "Let's continue," she commanded. "We have a long way to go."

As they resumed their journey, the presence of Jacko seemed to invigorate Wealth of God. She walked with renewed purpose, leading her entourage through the jungle towards Mount Ganjak. The soldiers remained vigilant, ever alert to the dangers that might lurk in the shadows.

Back at the tree house, the year was nearly over, and the king grew increasingly impatient. Holding the metal cup, he summoned Demetrious. After a few tense minutes, Demetrious arrived.

"You must swim to land and kill one of the Landers in front of their people," the king commanded, his eyes blazing with anger. "Followmehome refuses to bargain, so we will force his hand."

Demetrious nodded to the king's orders. Warriorisborn perceived the unwillingness to bargain from Followmehome, and he felt since he was reluctant, it was time to impose force to regain the possession of the poison.

However, Followmehome knew it was impossible to rescue Crown from captivity, but he was determined to secure the rest from getting captured, so he went to a secluded place and devised a plan.

Demetrious reached the land, where the Landers were going about their daily tasks. As he emerged, his presence caused an immediate stir. The people had never seen such a terrifying creature, and they gathered in fear and curiosity.

Demetrious stood calm and seemingly harmless, waiting for enough witnesses to gather. When the leaders arrived to see what the commotion was about, Demetrious sprang into action. With a sudden, brutal attack, he decapitated one of the Landers, ripping out his heart. Holding the heart in his right hand, he dove back into the sea.

The Landers were left in shock and terror, unable to comprehend what they had just witnessed as they scattered, taking to their heels.

Followmehome retreated to his chamber with his advisors and sons. "I have overheard talk of this creature," he said, his voice grave. "They are called the Angels of Death."

The population of the Landers had grown significantly, and Followmehome knew they needed to take measures to stay concealed from the Angels of Death and the king of the Tree House. Gathering everyone, he laid out his plan to ensure their safety, which required dividing the Landers into four groups.

He addressed his fellow leaders, "We must protect our people from the impending threats. We need strong leaders to guide each group. Who among you will stand against the beasts and the king?"

The room fell silent. None of the leaders were bold enough to accept the task. Just as Followmehome was about to speak again, his sons stepped forward.

"I will," declared Mighty, the eldest, stepping to the front. "I pledge to guide and defend the jungle against the Angels of Death and the king." His voice was resolute, and a murmur of admiration spread through the crowd. This moment marked the beginning of Mighty the Jungle King.

Moses, the second son, rose next. "I, too, will lead," he said. "I will guide my followers against the king and the Angels of Death. I promise to build the biggest ship ever seen and become the guardian of the sea." His confidence earned him the title Moses the Sea King.

Followmehome's third son, Monkey, stood up. "I pledge to lead and defend the Landers against the king and the Angels of Death. I will follow our father and protect our people." The determination in his voice was palpable.

Finally, Magnus, the fourth son, stepped forward. "I pledge to remain on land and scout for attacks. I will ensure the safety of our people from any threat." His swift movements and sharp gaze earned him the title Magnus the Messenger.

Followmehome looked at his sons with pride. "You have shown great courage. Together, we will ensure our people's safety and prosperity."

The leaders and Landers were amazed by the courage of the sons and quickly embraced the plan. The four groups were formed, each led by a brave and dedicated son of Followmehome. With their new leaders, the Landers felt a renewed sense of hope and unity, ready to face whatever challenges lay ahead.

The next day, Followmehome called a public town meeting. The Landers gathered, eager to hear the latest developments and the outcome of the leaders' meeting.

Followmehome stood tall before them and began, "My people, today I bring you news of our future. We have devised a plan to ensure our safety and prosperity. I present to you your new leaders, my sons."

He gestured to his eldest, who stepped forward. "Mighty the Jungle King, my first son. He is a strong and fearless warrior, a proven team leader, and a true jungle monster in his love for the wild." Mighty stood with pride, his presence commanding respect.

Next, Followmehome continued, reintroducing his second son, next. "Moses the Sea King, my second son. Though soft-hearted, beneath his gentle exterior lies a ruthless mind. He despises bullies and will always stand against them." Moses nodded solemnly, his eyes burning with determination.

Then, Followmehome turned to his fourth son. "Magnus the Messenger, known for his speed and agility. He is the perfect leader for our scouts and messengers." Magnus, quick and alert, flashed a confident smile.

Finally, Followmehome addressed the crowd about his third son. "Monkey will join me in protecting the women and children in the Moon Cave. Though his bravery may not be as outwardly displayed, he is every bit as fierce."

The Landers listened intently, their confidence growing with each introduction. Followmehome continued, "We will divide into four groups. A large proportion of our boys will follow Mighty into the jungle. Another large group will join Moses on his ocean adventure, sailing on the biggest ship ever seen, called the Sea King."

He paused, looking at the remaining Landers. "Those who stay will follow Magnus the Messenger. These are our strongest, pledging to work day and night to secure us from any intrusion." He handed out the iron glasses, retrieved from the race, as a sign of respect and honour.

The Landers were pleased with the plans. They began to organise themselves into four groups, each led by one of Followmehome's sons. The unity and hope among the Landers were palpable as they prepared to face whatever challenges lay ahead, confident in their new leaders and the path forward.

Magnus the Messenger drew his fierce character from his sister. They spent most of their time together growing up, and she trained him physically and mentally to fear neither the past nor the future. Three tribal marks adorned his face, drawn with his own iron glass, a remembrance of the beast he encountered while exploring the jungle at night, alone while others slept. Because of his nocturnal adventures, they called him the Night Owl.

Meanwhile, Wealth of God, accompanied by Servant of Allah and Aza, the blossom whisperer, reached the top of Mount Ganjak. The soldiers waited a few miles away, acting under the command of Servant of Allah. Aza handed Wealth of God a jar containing an enchantment mixed with root water. With this, Wealth of God climbed the mountain to its peak and proceeded to complete her mission.

Reaching the peak at midnight, Wealth of God dug a hole at the centre of Mount Ganjak, pouring the root water mixed with Aza's enchantments into it.

She then planted the suckling tree. After completing her task, she lay on the ground to rest until daybreak. When she awoke, she discovered seven baby ravens in a nest just a few inches from where she lay. Delighted by the beautiful creatures, though unaware of their usefulness, she decided to present them to the king upon her return, while keeping Jacko the jaguar for herself. She carefully picked up the ravens and returned to her people.

Back at the Landers' settlement, Mighty and his men ventured into the jungle. Moses had started building a ship that'd aid in security watch, and Followmehome, along with Monkey and the remaining Landers, headed into the cave he had discovered fifteen years ago, known as the Moon Cave—the cave that gave rise to Monkey the Werewolf.

Chapter Seventeen
The Moon Cave

The Moon Cave was a massive rock formation, concealing an expansive network of chambers beneath it. These interconnected rooms, capable of housing several thousand people, had been carved out over centuries. The cave's entrance was narrow, allowing only one person to enter at a time, providing a natural barrier against intruders. Ancient markings on the walls and remnants of past inhabitants hinted at a long-lost civilisation that once thrived within its depths.

A river flowed through the heart of the cave, its clear waters winding around the rooms and providing a vital resource for the cave's former dwellers. Followmehome had spent years exploring the Moon Cave, piecing together its history from scattered artefacts and cryptic symbols. He believed that the cave had been a refuge for a sophisticated society, its design a testament to their ingenuity and desire for protection.

Despite his discoveries, Followmehome knew there was much more to learn. The Moon Cave had been meticulously designed, not just as a home but as a fortress, shielding its inhabitants from external threats. The secrets of the Moon Cave's construction and the true extent of its purpose remained shrouded in mystery, beckoning to those who sought to uncover its ancient stories.

Therefore, no one could comprehend how the rooms were carved out with such precision or how the river was ingeniously constructed to flow through the cave. The true number of people who lived there at the time remained an enigma, lost to the ages.

For women and children, the Moon Cave was a sanctuary, a place of safety and solace. They could move freely within its vast chambers, secure in the knowledge that the cave offered them protection from the outside world. However, for men, the cave held a darker secret.

There was a particular plant that thrived within the cave, a strange and ancient species that did not require sunlight to grow. Its roots intertwined with the cave's foundation, drawing sustenance from the mineral-rich soil and the river's waters. This plant bore fruit, small and unassuming in appearance, yet it possessed a mysterious and transformative power.

If a man consumed the fruit, it would trigger a profound change within him. The transformation was unpredictable and varied from one individual to another. Some men experienced a surge of strength and agility, becoming formidable protectors of the cave. Others, however, were not so fortunate. The fruit could induce madness, distort their minds, and turn them into unpredictable and dangerous beings.

The women and children, aware of this peril, learnt to identify the plant and avoid its fruit, ensuring their continued safety. The plant's presence added another layer of mystery to the Moon Cave, its origins and purpose as enigmatic as the cave itself. The cave's history was a tapestry of secrets and wonders, waiting to be unravelled by those brave enough to venture into its depths.

Followmehome and the rest of the Landers, most of whom were women and children, reached the Moon Cave as dusk approached. The sheer size and mystery of the massive rock instilled a sense of fear among them; no one knew what lay beneath its imposing facade.

Determined to ensure their safety, Followmehome took the lead, venturing into the cave's narrow entrance. The old blind man, assisted by Monkey, followed closely. Monkey held him gently, guiding him through the confined space with careful precision. One by one, the rest of the group slipped through the entrance, hearts pounding with trepidation.

As they emerged into the vast interior of the cave, the last light of day faded, casting long shadows across the ancient walls. The immense chambers of the Moon Cave gradually revealed themselves, their scale both awe-inspiring and daunting. The air was cool and carried a faint, earthy scent. Everyone had made it through just in time, now safe within the mysterious depths of the Moon Cave.

The old man directed Followmehome to walk to the river and drink from its waters. His voice, though frail, carried an urgency that commanded attention. "Do not let anyone eat the fruit," he warned, describing its appearance as it had appeared in his vision: "It is small, with a deep crimson hue, and it emits a faint, sweet fragrance. Its skin is smooth, yet a single touch can leave a trace of its colour on your fingers. This fruit grows in clusters on a vine that twists and winds through the cave, thriving in the shadows where sunlight cannot reach."

Followmehome walked to the river, a journey that took nearly a day. The darkness was oppressive, and each step felt like a blind leap into the unknown. The sound of water grew louder with each passing hour, guiding him forward. The air was cool and damp, the scent of fresh water mingling with the musty smell of the cave.

Finally, he reached the river. Its gentle current glimmered faintly in the darkness, a welcoming sight after the long and arduous journey. Kneeling beside the water, he cupped his hands and drank deeply. The water was crisp and invigorating, flooding his senses with a newfound clarity.

As he drank, a strange sensation washed over him. His vision, once clouded by darkness, began to clear. He blinked, astonished, as the cave around him came into focus. He could see through the dark as if a veil had been lifted from his eyes. The intricate patterns on the rock walls, the subtle glint of minerals, and the path back to the entrance were all visible now.

Following the old man's instructions, he scanned the surroundings and noticed ancient lamps hanging along the walls. Their ornate designs hinted at a long-forgotten craftsmanship. Hesitantly, he reached out and touched one of the lamps. As soon as his fingers made contact, a brilliant light flared to life. The illumination spread rapidly, each lamp igniting in quick succession as if by magic.

The once dark and foreboding cave was now bathed in a warm, golden glow. The lamps revealed the true grandeur of the Moon Cave, its vast chambers and intricate passages illuminated in all their splendour. The air seemed to hum with an ancient energy, the light casting dancing shadows on the walls.

Followmehome marvelled at the transformation. The path back to his companions was now clear; the journey that had taken hours reduced to a swift walk. He filled his water pouch, the river's water sparkling under the newfound light, and set off back to the entrance.

The return was swift, his steps sure and confident. The cave, once a maze of shadows, was now a familiar terrain. As he approached the entrance chamber, the sounds of anxious whispers reached his ears. His companions were huddled together, their faces drawn with worry.

People were starting to panic. Their voices rose in anxious whispers, and the darkness seemed to close in around them, heavy and suffocating. One of the chiefs, a tall man with a stern expression, stood up and made his way towards the entrance, his intentions clear. He was just about to step out into the darkness when a sound echoed through the cave, a distant rumble that grew louder, coming from the direction they had entered.

"Wait!" someone called out, pointing towards the entrance.

Everyone turned to look. In the distance, a faint glow appeared, steadily growing brighter. It was not the cold, pale light of the moon or stars but a warm, flickering light that moved with purpose. The sight of it sent a ripple of hope through the group.

"It's fire!" a woman exclaimed, her voice filled with relief and wonder.

The glow intensified, spreading rapidly across the cave walls. Lamps, unseen before, began to ignite one by one, the flames racing through the darkness with astonishing speed. Within moments, the entire inner part of the rock was bathed in a golden light. The transformation was breathtaking.

The immense chambers of the Moon Cave were revealed in all their splendour. The light danced off the ancient walls, highlighting the intricate carvings and the natural beauty of the rock formations. The river, previously a faint murmur in the background, now sparkled as it wound its way through the cave.

People gasped in amazement, their fear melting away in the warm glow. Children clung to their mothers, wide-eyed and mesmerised by the sudden illumination. The chief, who had been ready to leave, now stood frozen, his stern expression softened by the wonder before him.

"Look!" someone cried, pointing towards the centre of the cave.

Followmehome emerged from the shadows, his face lit by the golden light of the lamps. He carried a water pouch, its surface glistening with droplets. His steps were sure and confident, his eyes no longer straining against the darkness.

"He has returned!" the same voice exclaimed, this time with joy and relief.

Followmehome raised his hand, signalling for silence. He approached the group, the old seer beside him, who had guided him through the journey. The seer's face was serene, his blindness now seeming less a disability and more a mark of his inner sight.

"The river's water has given us sight in this darkness," Followmehome explained, his voice strong and clear. "The lamps were waiting to be lit, and now they show us the way. But heed the seer's warning: there is a fruit here, small and crimson, with a sweet fragrance. Do not eat it. It is dangerous."

The people nodded, their fear replaced by trust and respect for Followmehome and the seer. The chief, who had been so ready to leave, now stood humbled, his faith in their leaders restored.

The cave, once a place of shadows and fear, was now a sanctuary of light and hope. The journey was far from over, but for the first time, the Landers felt a sense of purpose and unity. The Moon Cave had revealed its secrets, and with it, a path forward for those who sought refuge within its ancient walls.

Yet, despite Followmehome's assurances, some still cast doubtful glances toward the old man. Their mistrust lingered, a silent reminder of the prejudice that clouded the judgement of men, as was also true.

Monkey's stomach growled with hunger, and he did his best to hide his discomfort from the others. He wandered away from the group, his eyes catching sight of a dark room ahead. In the dim light, he saw a small mouse scurrying across the floor and what appeared to be fruit growing in the shadows.

Driven by his hunger, Monkey decided to taste one of the fruits. "Delicious," he whispered to himself, savouring the sweet, tangy flavour. He sat down and began to eat more, filling his belly with what looked like reddish mushrooms that tasted like berries.

While Monkey was satisfying his hunger, his father was deep in conversation with the seer, aside from the crowd, and had asked the seer to re-describe the forbidden fruit to him, of which the old seer was now doing in great, vivid detail. "The fruit is the colour of blood," the seer said, "and sweet in the mouth, to its victim. It is dangerous and must not be eaten."

Monkey, now finished with his meal, felt a brief moment of satisfaction. As he was about to rejoin the group, he overheard the seer's voice describing the forbidden fruit. His stomach dropped, and a cold sweat broke out across his skin. The words echoed in his mind: deep crimson hue, sweet fragrance, smooth skin. The realisation hit him like a punch to the gut.

He had just eaten the forbidden fruit…

Panic surged through him, twisting his insides. His heart pounded painfully in his chest, and his breathing grew rapid and shallow. A wave of guilt and fear washed over him, so intense it nearly brought him to his knees. His vision blurred with unshed tears, and a deep sense of shame engulfed him.

How could he have been so foolish?

He felt certain that his mistake would lead to his death.

Desperate and terrified, Monkey sprinted back to his father and the seer. His voice trembled as he cried out, "I have eaten the forbidden fruit, Father. It is as sweet as they say. What will become of me?" The words tore from his throat, a raw plea for reassurance or salvation.

The seer looked at him with sorrowful eyes. "You are now a werewolf, Monkey," he replied. "Every full moon, you will be cast out of the cave because you will transform. You must not be angered, for when you return after the full moon, it will be painful. No creature, not even the Angel of Death, can kill Monkey the werewolf, except for one thing which I cannot reveal."

Monkey's father, Followmehome, looked at his son with a mix of fear and sorrow.

The transformation had begun. Monkey's limbs contorted, muscles bulging and shifting under his skin. He suddenly felt his vision sharpen, and his senses heightening beyond human capacity. Fur sprouted along his arms, and his face elongated into a snout. He dropped to all fours, a primal scream escaping his lips as the change completed.

It was a great howl, indeed.

The group, hearing the anguished cry, turned towards the source of the sound, startled.

"Who brought in a dog, Mama?" a young boy who had first discovered the source of the noise asked, tugging at his mother's dress.

Horror spread across their faces as they saw the transformation. The chief stepped forward, his face grim. "We must find a way to contain him, to protect ourselves and the others."

The crowd took several steps behind the chief, even tripping on each other, here and there. Their fate was now pressing hard on them. Might the Moon Cave have been the best decision?

It was as if the words of the seer still echoed in the cave like a sombre reminder of the ancient curse that had claimed yet…another victim.

Monkey the werewolf was locked up in a room to ensure he wreaks no havoc. After a few days been locked up, he transformed back into a human. However, the people feared him.

Chapter Eighteen
The Ravens

Warriorisborn had been anxiously awaiting feedback from Followmehome, but time was running out. He knew he had to make a decision, but uncertainty gnawed at him. His mind raced through the possibilities, each one fraught with potential peril.

Feeling the weight of responsibility and the pressure of the moment, Warriorisborn pulled out the metal cup, its surface cold and reassuringly solid in his hand. Taking a deep breath, he called out, "Demetrius!" His voice echoed through the tree house, carrying his desperation and resolve.

As the sound faded, Warriorisborn's heart pounded in his chest. He had taken the first step, but what would come next? Demetrius emerged from the ocean, his powerful form cutting through the waves. In his hand, he held the heart he had ripped out of the Lander he had slain, its blood still dripping into the sea. The sight was both terrifying and awe-inspiring.

The king watched from the shore, his eyes gleaming with a mix of satisfaction and anticipation. A grim smile spread across his face as Demetrius approached. "You have done well," the king said, his voice a low rumble of approval.

Demetrius, standing tall and unyielding, awaited the king's next command. The king continued, "Bring me the five Angels of Death. Only then can we bargain for your life to be spared from execution."

The weight of the task was immense, but Demetrius knew there was no turning back. The fate of the king—and perhaps much more—hung in the balance.

Demetrius dove into the ocean, following the king's command. After a few moments, he soared back, not alone this time, but with the five Angels of Death: Rawana, Samael, Satan, Seth, and Chernobog.

In the tree house, the sight of Demetrius on the platform conversing with the king had become familiar. However, the presence of six Angels of Death was unprecedented. As they landed on the platform, the king emerged, clutching the metal cup in his hand. In an instant, the Angels of Death transformed into human form, all except Demetrius, who remained unchanged.

The king stepped forward, his voice firm and commanding. "I will make five of you leaders," he promised, "if you agree to keep the rest of the Angels trapped in the ocean. You will live as humans in the tree house, feeding on humans once a day, and you must always obey the king's orders."

The Angels of Death nodded in agreement. Turning to Demetrius, the king decreed, "You shall be enslaved to Wealth of God for eternity." Demetrius accepted his fate with a solemn nod.

The king then unlocked the metal in the middle of the cup and removed it. Taking a tiny rope, he threaded it through a small lever in the metal's centre. "Bend your head," he instructed Demetrius, securing the metal plate on his back as a seal of their agreement. "Until this plate is removed, you cannot be freed."

The king took the ornate cup, its intricate designs glinting in the dim light of his chamber. He carefully filled it with root water, a liquid shimmering with an otherworldly glow. Raising the cup to his lips, he drank deeply, feeling the potent liquid course through his veins. With a solemn expression, he handed the cup to the Angels of Death who stood before him, their dark, ominous figures towering in the candlelit room.

One by one, each Angel of Death took the cup, their skeletal hands gripping the delicate metal as they drank in turn. As the last angel sipped, a palpable energy filled the room, sealing their bond with the king. The air grew thick with a sense of impending power and doom. The king's eyes gleamed with satisfaction.

The king then provided them with a chamber in the tree house, a place to reside while fulfilling their new roles.

Turning his attention to Demetrius, the king spoke with a commanding tone, "Return to the sea, Demetrius. Await my call. Your time will come again."

Demetrius bowed deeply, his dark wings folding around him as he exited the room. The king watched him leave, contemplating the power he held within his grasp.

He knew that the key to controlling the Angels of Death lay in the cup. Its middle part, if detached, would bind the rest of the Angels to the depths of the sea, an eternal prison unless the cup was reassembled. The intricate mechanisms of the cup, however, had remained a mystery until the king sought the aid of Miracle, the wizard.

Miracle's chamber, a place of enigmatic wisdom and arcane knowledge, had become the king's refuge whenever confusion clouded his mind. Miracle, in his slumber, was an unparalleled advisor. The king would often visit him during his deep sleep, listening to the wizard's sleep-talking, which revealed secrets and ancient lore that were otherwise unattainable.

On one such visit, Miracle had spoken of the cup in his sleep. "The cup…it binds them…detachment is the key…reassembly the only freedom…" The king had listened intently, piecing together the cryptic messages. Miracle's slumbering words guided him to unlock the puzzles that had eluded many for centuries.

With Miracle's unconscious guidance, the king had deciphered the cup's mechanisms, understanding how its parts interacted with the magical forces binding the Angels of Death. This knowledge, coupled with the wizard's sorcery, made Miracle an indispensable ally, even if he was unaware of his own contributions while asleep.

In the dim light of his chamber, the king held the cup, his fingers tracing its patterns. The power to command the Angels of Death was now his, thanks to the wisdom imparted by a sleeping wizard. The king's lips curled into a satisfied smile as he placed the cup back on its pedestal, its mysteries now his to control.

Wealth of God and the rest returned home after a very hectic journey, and she was welcomed by the king's guard. Exhaustion clung to her every step, but the sight of the towering tree house brought a sense of relief. As she approached, the guards' stern faces softened, recognising her. They led her to the king's chamber, where he awaited her return.

The king, seated on his intricately carved throne, radiated an air of calm authority. His eyes sparkled with curiosity as Wealth of God entered. Bowing respectfully, she began, "My king, the journey was arduous but fruitful." She then presented a small cage containing seven baby ravens, their feathers a deep, lustrous black.

The king's eyes widened with delight. "Seven baby ravens," he exclaimed, reaching out to stroke their tiny heads. "I know exactly what to make of them!" He quickly summoned a servant, who brought forth a jug of root water. The king fed the ravens himself, his hands gentle and deliberate.

Wealth of God, encouraged by the king's mood, ventured, "My king, may I keep Jacko as a pet?" The king's brow furrowed momentarily. "Who is Jacko?" he inquired.

She carefully drew a small, spotted baby jaguar from her bag. "I found him on my way to Mountain Ganjak." The king glanced at the jaguar but his attention swiftly returned to the ravens. With a dismissive wave and a joyful smile, he said, "Do as you wish."

As Wealth of God turned to leave, the king called after her, "Wait." He reached for the metal cup, a sacred artefact filled with potent spirit. Drinking deeply, he then spoke into the cup, his voice imbued with a rare cheerfulness. "It is time to fulfil my promise," he announced.

After finishing the spirit, he called out, "Demetrius!" Moments later, a whoosh of air filled the chamber as Demetrius, the formidable Angel of Death, flew in and landed gracefully on the platform.

The king addressed Wealth of God with a solemn tone, "As long as the metal remains intact on his neck, you can control Demetrius with your mind. He will obey your every command, except for one—he cannot harm the cupbearer, which is I."

The king's voice echoed conspiratorially, in his mind: *There is only one way to become the bearer of the metal cup, but that secret remains mine alone, unlocked with the aid of Miracle, the wizard.*

Wealth of God's eyes gleamed with a newfound power. She commanded, "Demetrius, bow before me." Instantly, Demetrius knelt, his wings folded submissively. "Now, behead that soldier," she instructed, her mind exerting its will.

In a flash, Demetrius leapt and, with a swift motion of his wings, decapitated the soldier. Wealth of God gasped, astonished by the speed and precision.

The king's laughter echoed through the chamber. "You see? His loyalty is absolute." Wealth of God, regaining her composure, ordered, "Demetrius, return to the sea and rest." Without a word, Demetrius vanished, leaving behind a gust of wind.

The chamber buzzed with awe as courtiers murmured praises for the king. Summoning Aza, the blossom whisperer, the king entrusted her with the ravens. "Prepare them for the duty that lies ahead," he instructed.

Aza, with her gentle touch, nurtured the ravens for months, training them diligently. When the time came, the king sent his first message to Followmehome using one of the ravens. He attached a small scroll to its leg, whispering words of urgency and direction.

The raven soared across the sky, guided by an innate sense of purpose. It found Followmehome deep within the Moon Cave. The bird's presence was unexpected, and its arrival brought an air of mystique. Carefully, Followmehome untied the scroll and read the king's message, his brow furrowing at the proposition.

To reply, Followmehome wrote his response on the same scroll, reattaching it to the raven's leg. He whispered a silent prayer, hoping the bird would find its way back. Remarkably, after three days, the raven returned to the king, carrying Followmehome's refusal.

The king, reading the reply, sighed. "Followmehome insists he is not interested in any bargain that demands the poison." A contemplative silence fell over the room as the king pondered his next move.

The raven was sent back to Followmehome with a grim warning about the potential outcome of his rejection. As the bird circled above, it seemed to speak, delivering a message from the tree house king. Followmehome blinked in disbelief, thinking he was hallucinating. He approached the seer, his voice trembling with confusion.

"The raven...it spoke to me. I must be losing my mind," Followmehome muttered.

The seer, with a knowing glint in his eye, reassured him. "No, Followmehome. It is a raven, a messenger. You must capture one for yourself, but only one."

The following morning, the raven returned, its eyes piercing as it delivered another message. Followmehome's heart sank as he listened to the dire threat. "Your wife will be fed to the Angel of Death if you do not come to terms with the king," the raven croaked, its voice echoing with the weight of the threat.

Determined to take control, Followmehome captured the raven as soon as it finished speaking. He brought it to the seer, who instructed him with a grave tone. "Feed it some water from the Moon Cave and lock it up for a few days. This will bind it to you, and it will no longer leave the cave. The raven will recognise you as its new master."

Chapter Nineteen
Crown

Three days passed, and Followmehome's anxiety grew with each hour. Finally, the seer spoke, "The raven is yours now. It will not leave until you send it a message. You can use it to communicate with the king or anyone you wish. All you need to do is hold the raven, speak your message, and release it into the air."

Followmehome felt a mix of relief and trepidation as he approached the raven. Its eyes, now familiar, seemed to acknowledge him.

The raven, now bound to Followmehome, flew with purpose, carrying his words across the vast expanse to the king. This small victory gave Followmehome a glimmer of hope amid the looming threat, knowing that he had the means to protect his loved ones and defy the king's ominous ultimatum.

The king waited anxiously for two weeks, but his raven had not returned. Growing increasingly worried, he sought out Miracle the wizard under the cover of night. Miracle, powerful and wise, could only offer grim news. "Your raven has been captured," he revealed. "Its location is hidden from me, and as powerful as I am, I cannot find where Followmehome is keeping it."

Disturbed by this revelation, the king sought answers from the blossom whisperer, but she too could provide no explanation. The king's frustration grew, gnawing at him as days passed without any sign of his raven.

Meanwhile, Followmehome decided to use the raven to communicate with his sons. He held the bird, speaking his message with the authority of a father and a leader. The raven, bound to Followmehome, carried his words swiftly. His sons received the message immediately, recognising the voice of their father. They knew exactly what to do and sent their feedback promptly.

To ensure his raven could be distinguished from others, Followmehome made a unique mark. He burned the middle part of the raven's head, creating a bold patch that would make it easily recognisable. They named it the 'Bold Raven'.

In the depths of the night, the king returned to Miracle, who could only reveal his wisdom while asleep. Even in slumber, Miracle's body remained powerful, and he spoke willingly yet unknowingly. The king listened to the sleep-talking wizard, hoping to glean any hidden knowledge. But no answers came.

Followmehome's sons received Bold Raven, recognising its new identity instantly. They knew it was their father's messenger and followed his instructions meticulously. As Bold Raven flew back to Followmehome, it carried not just messages but a new sense of hope and determination for the family.

The king's frustration mounted with each passing day, but Followmehome and his family found solace in their newfound communication. Bold Raven became a symbol of their resilience and connection, a beacon in their struggle against the king's ominous threats.

Warriorisborn sent out another raven to Followmehome, demanding to know the whereabouts of his raven. Followmehome's reply was terse and defiant: "It is mine now!"

The wizard, Miracle, despite his immense power, had a critical limitation—he could only perceive past events, not foresee the future. However, his abilities allowed him to uncover secrets that lay beyond human comprehension—and even that was only possible when he was drugged to sleep, or genuinely asleep at night. The king's power was incomplete, and he longed for Miracle to possess the gift of foresight.

As the king sat on his throne, gently caressing his temple with his long fingers, a bulb suddenly clicked in his mind. His mind flashed back to many years ago when an old blind man rumoured to see the future. His brows went up.

Speaking aloud to no one in particular, he said, "That man's mystical ability might be just the bridge to fill in the gap!"

The king sat on his ornate throne, the golden accents gleaming under the dim torchlight. His fingers drummed impatiently on the armrest as he summoned his guards. The air in the chamber was thick with tension, a palpable undercurrent of unease rippling through the gathered servants.

"Bring the old blind man to me at once," the king commanded, his voice cold and imperious.

The guards exchanged uneasy glances before one stepped forward, clearing his throat nervously. "Your Majesty, we…we cannot find him."

The king's eyes narrowed dangerously. "What do you mean you cannot find him?" he demanded, his voice rising with each word. "Search the grounds! Leave no stone unturned!"

The guards hastened to obey, their footsteps echoing through the halls as they spread out in a frantic search. The king rose from his throne, pacing back and forth, his mind a whirlwind of thoughts. After what felt like an eternity, the captain of the guard returned, his face pale and tense.

"Sire," the captain began, his voice trembling, "we have discovered that Followmehome took the old blind man with him when he left."

Fury consumed the king. He felt Followmehome was not only defying him but also usurping what rightfully belonged to him. His fists clenched and unclenched as he stormed from the throne room, his mind consumed by rage.

"He thinks he can take what is mine?" the king muttered to himself, his voice a low, dangerous growl. "He will learn the price of his insolence."

The stone corridors echoed with the king's heavy footsteps. His face, a mask of rage, was contorted with anger. Guards and servants scattered out of his way, avoiding his burning gaze. The iron door of Crown's cell stood cold and unyielding, yet it trembled under the force of the king's wrath as he threw it open.

Inside, Crown recoiled at the sight of the furious monarch. Her chains clinked as she tried to back away, but there was nowhere to go. The king's eyes, once sharp with intelligence, now blazed with a mad fervour. Without a word, he seized her arm, dragging her from the cell, and handing her to one of his guards.

He retrieved his cup and said, his voice a low, dangerous rumble: "Seth, come."

Crown's pleas for mercy filled the air, but the king was deaf to her cries. Seth, the Angel of Death, arrived, his dark presence filling the corridor with a palpable dread. The king shoved Crown towards him.

"Feed on her," the king ordered, his voice cold and devoid of compassion.

Seth's eyes glinted with hunger as he reached out for Crown. Her screams echoed through the tree house, a chilling testament to the king's merciless resolve. The guards and servants could only watch in horror, powerless to intervene.

Meanwhile, Followmehome, oblivious to the horror unfolding in the tree house, continued to fortify his position. The Bold Raven perched nearby, a symbol of his newfound strength and resilience. The old blind man sat in the shadows, offering silent counsel. They were bound together by a shared destiny, ready to face whatever challenges the king would hurl their way.

The next morning, the king summoned Godhascome to his chamber. The air was still thick with the remnants of the previous night's turmoil, a haunting silence that seemed to echo the cries that had filled the tree house.

Godhascome entered the chamber, his face a mask of calm. The king, still seething from the events of the night, did not wait for formalities.

"Godhascome," he began, his voice laced with grim satisfaction, "I fed Crown to Seth, the Angel of Death. She paid for the defiance of Followmehome."

Godhascome's expression tightened, a flicker of dismay crossing his features. He bowed his head slightly, concealing his true feelings. "Your Majesty, you have made your decision," he said carefully. "But I must confess, I am not pleased with this alliance with the Angels of Death."

The king's eyes flashed with irritation. "You question my judgement?"

"Never, Sire," Godhascome replied quickly, choosing his words with care. "But I worry about the long-term consequences of such a pact. The Angels of Death are powerful and unpredictable."

The king stood from his throne, his anger barely contained. "Do not forget your place, Godhascome. The pact was necessary to secure our dominance. Followmehome has defied me for the last time, and Crown's fate will serve as a warning to all who dare oppose me."

Godhascome bowed his head deeper, hiding his clenched fists. "I understand, Your Majesty. I will support your decisions, as always."

The king turned away, staring out of the window, his mind already plotting his next move. "See that you do," he muttered. "Now go, and ensure the preparations for the next phase are underway."

Godhascome left the chamber, his heart heavy with the weight of his unspoken objections. As he walked through the corridors, he couldn't shake the image of Crown's fate from his mind. The alliance with the Angels of Death was a dark path, one that could lead to untold destruction.

In the dim light of the tree house, Godhascome found a quiet corner to gather his thoughts. He knew he had to tread carefully, to find a way to mitigate the king's reckless decisions without drawing his ire.

The sound of the king's laughter from the chamber echoed in his ears, a chilling reminder of the darkness that now held sway over their world.

Godhascome resolved to find a way to counterbalance the king's fury with wisdom and caution, even if it meant acting in secret.

All the while, most of the prisoners of the tree house had been fed to the five Angels of Death to fulfil the king's dark bargains. The king began to realise that people would soon grow suspicious of his pact if there were no more prisoners left to offer. The notion gnawed at him, pushing him to a chilling conclusion; he needed more prisoners to maintain his alliance, not fewer.

In the dim glow of his chamber, the king pondered his next move. His eyes flickered with a sinister idea. He would create new laws, turning even the slightest mistakes into crimes punishable by imprisonment. This way, he could ensure a constant stream of prisoners without arousing suspicion about his true intentions.

The next day, the king summoned Godhascome to his side. "We must act swiftly," he commanded, his voice cold and unyielding. "Announce the new laws. Every minor infraction will now be met with a prison sentence. We need to fill the dungeons, not the oceans." He handed Godhascome a hand-written copy of the law.

Godhascome hesitated, a frown creasing his brow, as his eyes danced across the page. "Your Majesty, are you sure this is wise? The people may fear you, but such drastic measures could lead to serious unrest."

The king's gaze hardened. "Do not question me. Make the announcement."

Bowing reluctantly, Godhascome obeyed. He called a gathering in the central courtyard, the people of the tree house assembling with apprehensive whispers. As Godhascome stood before them, his heart was heavy with the burden of the king's commands.

"By order of the king," he began, his voice steady despite the turmoil inside, "new laws will take effect immediately. Any infraction, no matter how minor, will be punishable by imprisonment. The following offences and their respective sentences are hereby enacted…"

He listed the offences, each one met with growing disbelief and fear from the crowd. Talking back to an elder, forgetting to water the communal garden, even the simple act of accidentally dropping food—each carried the weight of a prison sentence.

Murmurs of fear and outrage rippled through the assembly. The people's faces were a mix of shock, fear and simmering anger. Whispers of dissent began to spread, but no one dared to voice them aloud.

"The king has spoken," Godhascome concluded, his voice carrying a note of finality. "These laws are for the safety and order of our tree house. Disobedience will not be tolerated."

As the crowd dispersed, the weight of the new laws settled over the tree house like a suffocating blanket. People moved with caution, their eyes constantly darting around, fearful of making the slightest mistake. The atmosphere grew tense, a palpable sense of dread hanging in the air.

Chapter Twenty
The Ambush

Within a short period of time, thousands of people were arrested and locked up in prisons. Despite their best efforts to avoid breaking the new laws, it seemed almost impossible not to fall afoul of the king's draconian rules. The tree house had become a place of constant vigilance, with fear permeating every corner. The king had placed watchers in every nook and cranny, ensuring that no offender escaped his grasp.

Each day, more people were taken from their homes, their cries echoing through the tree house as they were dragged to the dungeons. The prisons swelled with the unjustly condemned, their faces marked with despair and confusion. Families were torn apart, friends turned on one another in paranoia, and a dark cloud of dread settled over the community.

The king watched this all unfold with a cold satisfaction. His plan was working perfectly. The prisoners were reserved as a grim menu to sustain the Angels of Death, buying Warriorisborn more time to figure out his ultimate plans.

One evening, the king stood on the balcony of his chamber, gazing out over the tree house. The sight of his people living in fear and desperation filled him with a twisted sense of accomplishment. He turned to Godhascome, who stood beside him, his face a mask of forced neutrality.

"Look at them," the king said, his voice low and triumphant. "They scurry like mice, trying to avoid the traps I've set. But they cannot escape. The Angels of Death will be fed, and I will buy us the time we need."

Godhascome nodded slowly, his heart heavy with the knowledge of the suffering below. "Yes, Your Majesty. But how long can this continue? The people are growing desperate. This fear cannot sustain them forever."

The king smirked, his eyes gleaming with a dangerous light. "They will do as I command. And as long as the Angels of Death are appeased, they will keep their end of the bargain. We need only maintain control until I have the answers I seek."

Down below, in the cramped and dark cells of the dungeons, the prisoners huddled together, sharing whispers of hope and resistance.

The king was desperate. His mind raced with thoughts of how to regain control and power. He summoned thousands of his soldiers, placing them under the command of Servant of Allah, and issued a single, critical mission: go to the land, arrest Followmehome, and bring back both the poison and the raven he had taken.

With the king's orders ringing in their ears, Servant of Allah and ten thousand tree house soldiers set out in ten grand ships, their sails billowing against the sky. The journey was arduous, taking several months. The soldiers endured storms, hunger, and fatigue, their resolve hardening with each passing day. Finally, they touched the ocean bank, their eyes set on the vast land before them.

Magnus the Messenger, always vigilant, had been tracking their progress. As the soldiers disembarked and began to organise, Magnus quickly dispatched his followers into small, covert groups. Their mission was to take the message of the impending danger to his brothers and father. With a few trusted allies, Magnus stayed behind, watching the soldiers' every move from the cover of the dense jungle foliage.

The soldiers, led by Servant of Allah, moved cautiously through the jungle, their formation a disciplined straight line. They trekked deep into the wilderness, their eyes scanning for any signs of the Landers. The once-vibrant home of the Landers now stood deserted, an eerie silence hanging in the air. They moved stealthily, stepping over roots and ducking under low-hanging branches, but no trace of the Landers could be found.

Servant of Allah, determined and relentless, paused to assess their situation. "Spread out," he commanded, his voice low and authoritative. "We must find them. Leave no stone unturned."

The soldiers fanned out, their eyes sharp, their movements careful. Yet the jungle seemed to conspire against them, every rustle and shadow playing tricks on their senses. They weren't seasoned warriors, as far as the land was concerned, and the depth and complexity of the jungle were unlike any battlefield they had faced.

Meanwhile, Magnus' followers moved with purpose, their steps quick and silent. They knew the land well, weaving through the underbrush with the grace of those born to it. Each group had a specific destination, a person to warn and a message to deliver. Their task was to ensure that Followmehome and the others were prepared for the confrontation that was surely coming.

Back with the soldiers, frustration began to mount. "It's like they vanished into thin air," one soldier muttered to another, swatting at a persistent mosquito.

Servant of Allah's eyes narrowed. "They are here somewhere. Keep looking."

Hours turned into days, and the search grew more desperate. The soldiers were relentless, but the jungle's secrets were well-guarded. Every hidden path, every concealed shelter seemed to elude them. The Landers had vanished, leaving the soldiers with nothing but the haunting stillness of the jungle.

Magnus, watching from the shadows, knew the time was drawing near. He signalled to his companions, and they retreated further into the jungle, ready to regroup and strategize. The message had been sent, and now it was a waiting game. They knew the jungle well, and with Followmehome's guidance, they had prepared for this day.

The soldiers, weary but undeterred, continued their search, unaware that they were being watched. The jungle was a labyrinth, and they were its uninvited guests. The king's orders were clear, but the path to fulfilling them was shrouded in mystery and danger.

Mighty had constructed an intricate underground hideout in the heart of the jungle. The entrance was hidden beneath thick foliage, and only those who knew its location could find it. From above, the hideout was almost invisible, blending seamlessly with the dense jungle canopy. High above, some of his followers perched silently on the branches of towering trees, their eyes trained on the paths below, waiting for any sign of the enemy.

As the tree house soldiers, led by Servant of Allah, marched into the jungle in a single file, they were unaware of the danger lurking around them. The jungle was eerily quiet, the usual cacophony of wildlife replaced by an unsettling silence. The soldiers glanced around nervously, their hands tightening around their weapons.

Suddenly, a shrill whistle echoed through the trees. It was the signal. Mighty and his followers sprang into action with precision and ferocity. Arrows rained down from the treetops, finding their marks with deadly accuracy. The soldiers barely had time to react before Mighty's men, faces painted with war paint, emerged from their hiding spots and engaged them in fierce combat.

"Push forward!" Mighty roared, his voice cutting through the chaos. He wielded his iron glass with unmatched skill, cutting down soldiers with swift, lethal strikes. Beside him, Magnus the Messenger moved with a deadly grace, his twin blades flashing in the dappled sunlight.

The battle was intense but brief. The tree house soldiers, disoriented and outmatched, fell quickly. Within minutes, the jungle floor was littered with their bodies. Only Servant of Allah and seven others managed to break free from the melee. They ran towards the ocean, their breath ragged and their hearts pounding.

"We need to get to the water!" shouted one of the surviving soldiers, panic evident in his voice.

"They're right behind us!" another cried, glancing back at the pursuing warriors.

Reaching the shoreline, they dove into the ocean, the cool water a stark contrast to the heat of the battle. They swam with all their remaining strength, the salty water stinging their wounds. Behind them, the victorious cries of Mighty's men echoed, a haunting reminder of their narrow escape.

Servant of Allah and his remaining men, exhausted and desperate, swam to the nearest bank, seeking refuge. They were not accustomed to swimming, and the journey pushed their endurance to its limits. Just as hope seemed to fade, they spotted a giant ship heading in their direction.

The news of their plight had reached Moses, the Sea King. He had built a colossal ship, capable of holding up to two million people without impacting its speed. It was the largest ship ever seen. The ship moved swiftly towards them, a beacon of hope in the vast ocean.

Moses's crew quickly spotted the struggling men in the ocean. With swift efficiency, they captured Servant of Allah and the seven others who had escaped Mighty's ambush. Recognising Moses, Servant of Allah's heart sank, knowing the dire situation they were in. Exhausted but alive, they were hauled aboard the magnificent vessel, their faces etched with relief and fatigue.

Moses surveyed the captives with a calculating gaze. "Release one," he ordered, his voice calm yet commanding. "He will return to the king and relay what he has seen." He pointed to Akika. "You, go back and deliver the message."

Akika, though weary, nodded, understanding the gravity of the task. Moses's ship sailed a few miles closer to the tree house before Akika was lowered into the water. He swam with all his remaining strength, propelled by a mix of fear and duty.

Akika was a resilient soldier though not among the elite. He had a knack for surviving battles with minimal injuries, earning him an iron glass used to defend himself in numerous wars alongside Servant of Allah. Some accused him of cunningly avoiding danger, but in truth, he was a skilled and courageous fighter, an unsung hero in the shadows.

As Akika approached the tree house, scouts had already spotted the massive ship in the distance and reported it to the king. The description of the ship intrigued Warriorisborn, who momentarily hoped it carried Followmehome.

Upon reaching the tree house, Akika was escorted to the king's chamber. Warriorisborn's eyes narrowed as he looked at Akika. "Speak," he commanded.

Akika, still catching his breath, began, "My lord, we were ambushed by an unknown force in the jungle. Many of our men were killed. We tried to escape, but Moses—one of Followmehome's sons whom his crew called the Sea King—captured us. He spared me to deliver a message and warn you."

The king's face darkened. "Warn me? Of what?"

"Of the strength and unity of your enemies," Akika replied. "They are formidable and working together."

Warriorisborn's excitement immediately soured. He drew closer to Akika and inclined his chin with his right hand. "How can I trust you?"

Akika stood tall. "I have always been loyal, my lord. I have no reason to deceive you."

The king pondered for a moment before speaking. "You will be kept in a cell until I decide your fate. Guards, take him away."

As Akika was led away, the king's mind raced. The news of powerful, united enemies was troubling. He realised he needed to strategize carefully to face the growing threats. The guards locked Akika in a cell, his fate uncertain. His message had been delivered, and now, the king's next move was beyond his control.

Akika paced the confines of his cell, his face twisted in anger and disbelief. He had always been loyal and had fought fiercely in the king's battles, yet here he was, locked away like a common criminal. The injustice gnawed at him. He clenched his fists, his thoughts a tumult of betrayal and frustration.

Chapter Twenty-One
More Conspirations

In the throne room, the king sat brooding, his mind weighed down by the news of the devastating ambush. Ten thousand soldiers gone, just like that. The loss was a blow not only to his forces but to his pride. He rubbed his temples, trying to concoct a plan to salvage the situation.

Wealth of God, with an anxious expression, burst into the room, her breath coming in short, sharp bursts. "My lord," she began urgently, her voice shaking slightly, "I have just heard about the ambush and the capture of Servant of Allah. We must do something!"

The king's eyes flickered with interest and a hint of amusement at her distress. He leaned forward, his sharp gaze assessing her. "What is it you propose, Wealth of God?" he asked, his tone deceptively calm.

"We need to reconnect with my family," she said, her voice steadying but still filled with desperation. "A family reunion is necessary. Perhaps we can negotiate for the release of Servant of Allah and understand what has happened."

The king paused, a sly smile forming on his lips. This could be the opportunity he needed. While outwardly showing approval, his mind raced with conspiratorial thoughts. If Wealth of God could reunite with her family, it would be the perfect chance to plant someone within her entourage. Someone who could infiltrate Followmehome's chamber and, if possible, steal the poison that had caused so much trouble.

"Very well," the king said, his tone measured. "I see the wisdom in your suggestion. We shall arrange for your journey immediately."

Wealth of God's eyes widened in surprise at the king's swift agreement, but she nodded gratefully. "Thank you, my lord. I will prepare."

As she left the room, the king summoned one of his young most trusted soldiers, a shadowy figure named Requin. "Requin," he said, his voice low and urgent, "I have a task for you. Wealth of God is planning a reunion with her family. You will accompany her, under the guise of protection, but your true mission is to infiltrate Followmehome's inner circle. I need you to find and retrieve the poison, by any means necessary."

Requin bowed deeply, his eyes gleaming with understanding. "It will be done, my lord."

As Requin departed, the king leaned back on his throne, a sense of satisfaction settling over him. His plan was set in motion. While Wealth of God prepared for what she thought would be a peaceful family reunion, the king knew this could be his chance to turn the tide in his favour.

Meanwhile, in his cell, Akika finally slumped against the wall, the weight of his anger giving way to exhaustion. He didn't know what the future held, but he vowed silently that he would find a way to prove his loyalty once more. For now, he would bide his time and wait for the right moment to reclaim his honour.

The next day, the preparations for Wealth of God's journey were underway. The king watched from his balcony, his eyes cold and calculating. He saw Requin blending seamlessly with the guards, his presence unnoticed by most. The king smirked. Soon, very soon, he hoped to turn the tables on Followmehome and regain the upper hand in this dangerous game.

Wealth of God was worried about her husband's capture, she did not even think a bit of her mother rotten in the tree house cell, not knowing she'd been fed to the Angel of Death. At this point, she was blinded by the kinship of her grandfather, she felt maybe it was time to make it known to her brothers that the king of the tree house was her grandfather.

Wealth of God paced her chambers, her heart heavy with worry for her husband, Servant of Allah. The news of his capture had struck her like a physical blow, leaving her reeling with a mixture of fear and desperation. Her thoughts were consumed by his plight, so much so that she had almost forgotten about her mother, rotting in a cell somewhere in the tree house, not knowing that she had already been fed to the Angels of Death.

Her mind raced, trying to find a way to save her husband. As she sat down, she thought about her family, about the ties that bound them and the secrets that had been kept. Her grandfather, the king of the tree house, had always been a shadowy figure in her life, a powerful presence that she had never fully understood. Maybe, just maybe, it was time to reveal the truth to her brothers.

They deserved to know who their grandfather was, and perhaps, this knowledge could help them in these dire times.

As a kind gesture, the king presented Wealth of God with one of the Ravens. She accepted it with a mixture of surprise and gratitude, bowing her head in appreciation. "Thank you, my lord," she murmured, her voice thick with emotion.

Holding the raven close, Wealth of God felt a glimmer of hope. This gift was not just a token of the king's favour but also a symbol of potential communication and alliance. She knew she needed a loyal servant to accompany her on this journey. Servant of Allah was held captive, and she couldn't predict what awaited her at her father's domain.

As she prepared to leave, a wave of guilt washed over her. Memories of her last encounter with her father, Followmehome, flooded her mind. She had been distant, cold, and dismissive. Her pride had clouded her judgement, and now, for the first time, she felt a pang of guilt for her attitude. Tears welled up in her eyes as she thought about the rift between them.

She stood in her chambers, the raven perched on her shoulder, as she tried to compose herself. The weight of her emotions was almost too much to bear. She needed to make amends, not just for her husband's sake but for her own conscience.

On the other hand, to avoid being apprehended, Wealth of God called upon Demetrius. Emerging from the ocean, his dark presence sent shivers through the air. "It is time for us to go on a journey," she commanded.

Before departing, she made her way to the cell where her mother had been held. To her shock, the cell was empty. She knew of the deal the king had made with the Angels of Death, and a cold dread settled in her stomach. Her mother's absence spoke volumes. Holding back her fury, she maintained a calm facade as she boarded the ship alongside Demetrius, Jacko, and her raven perched on her right shoulder.

As the ship sailed towards land, Wealth of God felt a maelstrom of emotions. Her thoughts kept drifting back to the king and his ruthless bargain. Her mother, gone without a trace, was a stark reminder of the king's merciless nature. Her eyes hardened as she stared at the horizon, the weight of her mission pressing down on her.

On the ship, the crew worked silently, sensing the tension in the air. Demetrius, with his dark wings folded, stood vigilant. Jacko, the baby jaguar, prowled restlessly, picking up on Wealth of God's unease. The raven, ever watchful, shifted its gaze between the crew members and the vast expanse of the sea.

Meanwhile, back in the tree house, the blossom whisperer returned, seething with anger over the king's deal with the Angels of Death. She stormed into the king's chamber, her face flushed with rage.

"My king," she began, trying to control her temper, "the deal you made with the five Angels of Death while I was away was reckless. You have misused the wizard's power. Patience could have saved us from this disaster."

The king, seated on his throne, looked up with a weary expression. "We had no choice. The threats were growing, and we needed their power."

The blossom whisperer shook her head, frustration evident in her eyes. "You have invited more chaos upon us. We must seek new locations to plant new homes. More Angels of Death will surely arise, and with the dwindling number of prisoners, we cannot sustain this balance."

The king sighed, the weight of his decisions bearing down on him. "Very well. We shall begin preparations to find new locations. Also, at the current mortality rate, the race of Steps of Horror race shall end today."

Chapter Twenty-Two
Gandoki's Mission (1)

Warriorisborn called upon Gandoki, his son, and asked if he could go on a journey to find suitable locations for planting new homes. Gandoki, a cunning individual with a cruel mindset, stood before his father, his eyes gleaming with ambition and shrewdness. His intellect was formidable, surpassing even that of Warriorisborn, but he had mastered the art of controlling and maintaining his irrational tendencies as he awaited his opportunity.

"Gandoki, my son," Warriorisborn began, his voice resonating with authority and a hint of desperation. "I need you to undertake a crucial mission. Seek out fertile locations for us to plant new homes, places where we can rebuild and strengthen our forces."

Gandoki's face remained impassive, but his mind was already calculating the potential benefits of this task. "And what do I receive in return for this perilous journey, Father?" he asked, his tone measured and deliberate.

The king eyed his son warily, sensing the gravity of the request about to be made. "What is it you desire?" he inquired, his voice carrying a mix of curiosity and caution.

Gandoki's lips curled into a faint smile as he made his demand. "I wish to be the Cup Bearer," he stated, his eyes locking onto his father's with unwavering resolve.

Warriorisborn's eyes widened in disbelief. The audacity of Gandoki's demand was staggering. The cup was not just an artefact; it was a symbol of immense power and control. "The Cup Bearer?" he echoed, his voice tinged with incredulity. "Do you understand the magnitude of what you are asking?"

Gandoki nodded, his expression unchanging. "I do, Father. And I believe I am worthy of such a responsibility. Grant me this wish upon the completion of my task, and I will find the locations you seek."

The king considered his son's request, his mind racing with the implications. He knew the cup's true nature—that it could not be wielded by anyone except him unless it was fully assembled. This knowledge gave him a sense of security, yet he could not help but admire Gandoki's boldness.

"Very well," Warriorisborn agreed, his voice firm despite the swirling doubts. "Prove yourself worthy by completing this mission, and I will grant your wish."

Gandoki's smile widened, a rare display of emotion. "Thank you, Father. I will not disappoint you."

With a final nod, Warriorisborn dismissed his son, watching as Gandoki left the chamber, his mind already plotting the steps to achieve his goal. The king knew he had taken a significant risk, but he also recognised the potential for greatness in his son. As Gandoki's figure disappeared from sight, Warriorisborn couldn't shake the feeling that this journey would change everything.

The king, Warriorisborn, at this point made several decisions on his own, without consulting his right-hand man or the blossom whisperer. He acted based on the cryptic words he heard from the wizard Miracle most of the time. The constant threat of the Angels of Death arising and the Landers being in possession of the poison weighed heavily on his mind. As he aged, the king found himself willing to abandon both the tree house and the metal cup, contemplating a solitary life in a distant location if things went south. A future he envisioned as a faint lantern light in the dark, uncertain but quietly calling him.

Gandoki, eager to prove himself and fulfil his father's command, picked a few warriors and crew members for his voyage. His chosen men were loyal, skilled, and ready for the challenges ahead. As he prepared for departure, the atmosphere in the tree house was tense but hopeful.

After the abduction of Servant of Allah during the war led by Mighty the Jungle King, a lot of iron glassware was secured from the dead soldiers of the tree house. Followmehome and the Landers expressed their gratitude for the tremendous act, as conveyed by Magnus the Messenger.

"To our fallen heroes," Magnus intoned solemnly, raising a goblet of wine as he addressed the gathering. "Their sacrifice will never be forgotten."

The crowd, gathered in the great hall, echoed his sentiment. Goblets clinked, and a murmur of reverence filled the room. Followmehome stood at the front, his expression a mixture of pride and sorrow. He took the stage next, his voice steady and filled with emotion.

"We have secured a significant victory, but it has come at a great cost," Followmehome began, his eyes scanning the faces of those gathered. "The bravery of our soldiers and the aid of our allies have brought us to this moment. Let us honour their memory and their sacrifice."

Cheers erupted as he finished, the crowd raising their goblets high. The celebration was both a homage to the lost and a testament to their resilience.

Warriorisborn retreated to his chamber, his hand resting on the metal cup. He took a deep breath and raised it to his lips, drinking deeply of the potent spirit within. The room seemed to blur around him as the effects of the drink took hold, and he spoke aloud to himself, a rare moment of vulnerability.

"If this fails, I will leave it all behind," he murmured, his voice barely a whisper. "The tree house, the cup, everything. I will find a place where I can live in peace."

As Gandoki's ship sailed into the distance, Warriorisborn knew that the future of the tree house hung in the balance. The decisions he had made, the risks he had taken, would soon bear their consequences. And whether for better or worse, the course of their destiny was now set in motion.

Aza, the blossom whisperer, approached the king after Gandoki's departure. Her steps were light but deliberate, her presence commanding attention. Warriorisborn, still contemplating the future and the challenges ahead, looked up as she neared.

"The werewolf is awakened," Aza announced, her voice steady and filled with a quiet urgency.

The king frowned, puzzled. "Why is this werewolf so important, Aza?"

She stepped closer, her eyes locking with his. "You must be aware, my king. The werewolf is the only creature that can devour up to thousand Angels of Death in one full moon. This is how powerful it is."

The king's expression shifted from curiosity to astonishment. "A creature with such power…But it must have a weakness."

Aza nodded. "Yes, its limitation is swimming. It cannot traverse water, making it vulnerable in that regard."

The king began to pace, his mind racing with this new information. "If it cannot swim, then it cannot come from the sea. It must be somewhere within the tree house or nearby."

He stopped and looked out over his kingdom, the towering trees and dense foliage providing a deceptive sense of security. "But where could such a creature be hiding?" he mused aloud.

Aza stepped up beside him, her gaze following his.

***

Wealth of God stood on the deck of her ship, the cool sea breeze whipping through her hair as she sailed towards land. She looked over her right shoulder and saw a colossal ship approaching. Her eyes widened in disbelief at its sheer size, an enormous vessel that dwarfed her own.

The ship was so immense it seemed capable of crushing her vessel in mere seconds. She could do nothing but watch in awe and trepidation. As the ship drew closer, it suddenly halted, towering over them like a giant sentinel. Relief and surprise washed over her as she recognised the figure standing on the deck of the massive ship—it was her brother, Moses.

"Moses!" she called out, her voice carrying across the water.

Moses smiled down at his sister. "Wealth of God, what brings you to these waters?" he asked, his voice warm and welcoming.

She explained her purpose, detailing the urgency of her visit to the land. Moses listened intently, his expression growing more serious. Despite the family's rift, he could not turn his back on his sister. He nodded resolutely. "You may proceed with me, sister."

With Moses' ship now accompanying them, Wealth of God felt a renewed sense of determination. They sailed together towards land, the imposing presence of Moses' ship a comforting shield against any potential threats.

Meanwhile, back in the tree house, Warriorisborn was deep in thought. At this point, he was convinced that the blind seer was with Followmehome. It dawned on Warriorisborn that Followmehome possessed many things that rightfully belonged to him—things he believed had been taken without authorisation. Among these were the seer and the raven, valuable assets that he was determined to reclaim.

"It's time to confront the Landers," Warriorisborn muttered to himself, a fire igniting in his eyes.

He summoned Godhascome, his most trusted advisor, to devise a plan. "We must tread carefully but with conviction," Warriorisborn said. "The seer and the raven are crucial to our cause, and Followmehome must answer for his theft."

Godhascome nodded, his mind already working on strategies to outmanoeuvre the Landers. "We need to gather our forces and prepare for a calculated strike. We cannot afford to act rashly."

As the two men delved into their plans, the atmosphere in the tree house grew tense with anticipation. The stakes were higher than ever, and the path ahead was fraught with peril. But with careful planning and unwavering resolve, Warriorisborn was determined to reclaim what was his and secure the future of his kingdom.

Wealth of God was spotted by Magnus the Messenger and his men from afar, guided by Moses, the Sea King. Without hesitation, Magnus dispatched his followers to deliver the news to his father, Followmehome, and his brothers, Mighty and the others.

As Wealth of God made it to the shore, she disembarked from her ship, accompanied by Demetrius and Jacko, with her raven perched on her right shoulder. Moses, having ensured his sister's safe arrival, headed back to the sea. As she stepped onto the sandy beach, she was met by Magnus and his men.

Magnus's eyes widened as he saw Demetrius by her side. The presence of Demetrius sent a shiver down his spine. The last time Demetrius had appeared, he had flown in from nowhere and ripped out the heart of a Lander in a brutal and shocking display of power. The memory of that atrocity still haunted the Landers, leaving a lingering sense of fear and dread.

Demetrius, with his dark wings and towering presence, was a figure of sheer terror. His eyes gleamed with an unearthly light, and his aura exuded menace. The Landers had never forgotten the day he had unleashed his wrath upon them, leaving a trail of death and destruction in his wake. The sight of him now, standing protectively beside Wealth of God, was enough to make Magnus and his men pause in their tracks, their hearts pounding with a mixture of fear and awe.

Chapter Twenty-Three
Gandoki's Mission (2)

Magnus was a man known for his stoicism, and so he could not easily trust that Wealth of God was not acting under the king's command, after being with him for so many years. "You must all be in shackles before any discussion can take place," he declared, his eyes cold and unyielding.

Wealth of God sighed and raised her hands in surrender. "I've come of my own will," she said, her voice steady but filled with determination. "I demand to speak to Father."

Magnus' jaw tightened, but he nodded curtly. Wealth of God, Demetrius, Jacko, and the rest of the crew were escorted by Magnus and his men to the old, deserted Landers' domain. The once-vibrant settlement was now overgrown with ivy, its wooden structures creaking with age and neglect. The air was thick with the scent of damp earth and decaying leaves. Shadows danced ominously in the flickering torchlight as they made their way through the crumbling village.

"Move along," one of the guards barked, pushing Demetrius and Jacko toward a decrepit building.

Wealth of God glanced over her shoulder, watching as Demetrius was shoved into a dark room. His towering figure disappeared into the shadows, and the door slammed shut behind him with a resounding thud. Jacko growled lowly, his eyes reflecting the torchlight, before he, too, was locked away. The other crew members were similarly forced into different rooms, their protests silenced by the guards' stern commands.

Magnus turned to her, his expression stony. "You'll stay here," he said, nodding to a small, musty room nearby.

Wealth of God stepped inside, the wooden floorboards creaking beneath her feet. The room was bare, save for a rickety wooden chair and a table covered in dust. Cobwebs clung to the corners of the ceiling, and a single, grimy window let in a sliver of moonlight.

As the door closed behind her with a heavy thud, silence enveloped her. She could hear the distant hoot of an owl and the occasional rustle of nocturnal creatures outside. The room felt oppressive, the walls seeming to close in on her.

She sat on the chair, her hands trembling slightly. The dim light cast long shadows, making the room feel even more desolate. She stood and paced the room, her footsteps stirring up little clouds of dust. Every creak and groan of the old building made her heart race.

Her mind was a whirlwind of anxiety and anticipation. She couldn't stop thinking about her father's possible reaction, Magnus's distrust, and the immense task that lay ahead. She kept replaying her planned conversation with her father, in her mind, trying to anticipate every possible outcome.

As the night wore on, Wealth of God finally sank back into the chair, exhaustion pulling at her eyelids. But sleep would not come. She stared at the grimy window, watching the sky slowly lighten as dawn approached. The weight of her mission pressed heavily on her shoulders, and the first light of dawn found her still wide awake, her eyes red and weary but her resolve unbroken.

The next morning, Followmehome arrived, accompanied by Monkey, and guided by Magnus and his men. Wealth of God stood as her father entered, her eyes meeting his with a mixture of hope and fear.

"Why have you come?" Followmehome asked, his voice stern but edged with curiosity.

Wealth of God's composure broke, and she burst into tears. She wept openly, something her father hadn't seen in ages. Followmehome's stern expression softened. He walked towards her and took her hands, pulling her into a comforting embrace.

"Father," she choked out between sobs, "Mother is dead. The king is furious because you refused to bargain for the poison. And…the Angels of Death are coming."

Followmehome's face hardened, but he couldn't ignore the raw emotion in his daughter's voice. He believed she had come in peace. "Tell me everything," he said gently.

Wealth of God wiped her tears and continued, "The tree house on Mount Ganjak—it's a perfect hiding place for the war that lies ahead. We need to unite and carve into the tree to protect ourselves."

Followmehome's eyes widened in surprise. "Mount Ganjak? I have never heard of any tree house there. How did it come into existence?"

Wealth of God took a deep breath, steadying herself. "It was built in secret by me, with the king's permission. He gave me complete domination over there. The tree house at Mount Ganjak is my kingdom, earned out of loyalty to the king."

Followmehome pondered her words, then called for an emergency meeting with his sons and the chiefs. Magnus and Mighty the Jungle King were sceptical.

Mighty crossed his arms over his chest, glaring at Wealth of God. "Why should we trust you?" he demanded. "What about the Angel of Death that accompanied you?"

Wealth of God took a deep breath. "The metal collar around his neck keeps him in check. I control him. There are still thousands of Angels of Death awakening beneath the ocean, besides the five that have chambers in the tree house and feed on humans every night."

Her family exchanged uneasy glances, unsure whether to believe her. "I can prove it," Wealth of God said. She closed her eyes, her face becoming a mask of concentration.

Inside his cell, Demetrius stirred. Responding to her mental command, he escaped and flew to their location. Moments later, he landed and bowed before her family.

Magnus's eyes widened in shock, and Mighty took a step back, his suspicion momentarily forgotten. The display of control and power was undeniable.

"Perhaps we should listen," Followmehome said, his voice carrying the weight of reluctant admiration.

He turned to the assembled chiefs and elders, explaining the tree house on Mount Ganjak. "Wealth of God has revealed a hidden sanctuary. It is deep within the forest on Mount Ganjak, camouflaged by the dense foliage. This tree house, unknown to many, can serve as our stronghold against the Angels of Death."

The chiefs and elders murmured amongst themselves, absorbing this new information. Magnus and Mighty remained sceptical but intrigued.

"We need to carve into the tree on Mount Ganjak," Wealth of God continued. "It's our best chance to defend against the Angels of Death."

Followmehome turned to his sons and the chiefs. "We have no choice but to trust her," he said. "Prepare for the journey to Mount Ganjak. Our survival depends on it."

As the family began to mobilise, Wealth of God felt a sense of hope. She had taken the first step towards mending the rift with her family and securing their future against the impending threat.

A year had passed, and Gandoki's search for a suitable location on the sea had yielded nothing. The vast expanse of water stretched endlessly, the horizon mocking him with its emptiness. His frustration grew with each passing day until he could no longer bear the fruitless endeavour. Desperation gnawed at him, and he made a decision that could change everything: he would head towards land.

As the days inched closer to the full moon, a sense of anticipation filled the air. The crew buzzed with excitement, their spirits lifted by the promise of a successful mission. Gandoki stood at the bow of the ship, the wind whipping through his hair, his eyes fixed on the distant shoreline. The silver crescent of the moon hung low in the sky, promising to light their way when they arrived.

"We'll make it by the full moon," Gandoki announced to his crew, his voice brimming with determination. "The moonlight will guide us and reveal what we've been searching for."

The men cheered, their enthusiasm infectious. They worked with renewed vigour, the promise of land revitalising their weary bodies.

As night fell on the final day of their voyage, the moon began its ascent, casting a silvery glow over the dark waters. Gandoki stood at the helm, his eyes scanning the horizon. The land came into view, a dark silhouette against the shimmering sea.

"There it is!" a crew member shouted, pointing towards the approaching shore.

The ship glided smoothly towards land, the moonlight illuminating their path. As they drew closer, the landscape began to take shape—rugged cliffs, dense forests, and a hint of something more, something that seemed almost mythical.

Gandoki's heart pounded in his chest. He had heard tales of this land from the king, stories that seemed too fantastical to be true. But now, as they approached, he felt a strange sense of déjà vu, as if the legends were coming to life before his very eyes.

The ship anchored just off the coast, and Gandoki and his men disembarked. They set foot on the rocky shore, the cool night air filled with the sounds of the forest. The moonlight cast eerie shadows, creating an otherworldly atmosphere.

"Let's move inland," Gandoki ordered, his voice steady but filled with anticipation.

The crew followed him, their footsteps crunching on the gravel path. The forest seemed to come alive around them, the rustling leaves and distant calls of nocturnal creatures creating a symphony of sounds.

As they ventured deeper into the forest, the moonlight filtered through the canopy, casting dappled patterns on the forest floor. Gandoki could feel a sense of purpose growing within him. This was no ordinary land; it was a place of secrets and ancient power. The truth is that he spent all of his life in the tree house and had never really ventured to land. The one time when he would have, well…he woke up to find himself overboard and had to struggle to keep afloat while he watched his father's ship sail away.

He dispersed the thought immediately, gritting his teeth.

But what seemed to be a fairytale to the king became true…

As the hours dwindled towards the full moon, a heavy tension hung in the air. Followmehome gently shook Monkey awake in the deepening twilight of the woods. Monkey stirred, a groan escaping his lips, as he rubbed his eyes, feeling a gnawing discomfort spreading through his body.

"Come on, son," Followmehome said softly, but with an undertone of urgency. "It's time."

Monkey winced, clutching his stomach. "I don't feel right, Father," he admitted, his voice strained.

"I know," Followmehome replied, his eyes filled with a mix of sorrow and determination. "We have to get you ready. Remember what the seer said."

Monkey nodded weakly, allowing his father to guide him deeper into the woods. The forest around them seemed to hold its breath, the leaves rustling with a faint, ominous whisper.

They reached an ancient tree, its gnarled branches stretching out like skeletal fingers. Followmehome began to tie Monkey to the trunk, the rough bark pressing against his back. Monkey's discomfort intensified, his muscles twitching involuntarily.

"Why do we have to do this, Father?" Monkey asked, his voice tinged with desperation.

"It's for your own good," Followmehome replied, his hands steady but his heart aching. "You need to remember who you are. Remember your own."

With the final knot secured, Followmehome stepped back, his face etched with worry. The moon was beginning to rise, its silver light casting long shadows across the forest floor.

"Stay strong, son," Followmehome whispered, his voice barely audible over the sound of the wind. "I'll be back when it's over."

He turned and hurriedly walked away, each step feeling like a weight on his soul. He couldn't bear to look back, knowing the transformation his son was about to endure. It was a necessary evil, a consequence of the past, but it didn't make it any easier.

Alone in the clearing, Monkey's breathing grew ragged as the full moon inched higher into the sky. His body convulsed, the pain intensifying, but he clung to his father's words. The seer's instructions were clear, and he had to face this alone.

The forest around him seemed to come alive, the shadows deepening, and the air growing colder. The moon's light bathed Monkey in an ethereal glow, and he felt the change begin. He closed his eyes, trying to hold on to his humanity as long as he could.

The moon, now fully risen, cast a silver glow over the landscape, its light dancing on the restless waves and illuminating the dense jungle ahead. The air was thick with tension, a palpable force pressing down on Gandoki and his men as they made their way inland. Each step was accompanied by the soft crunch of sand transitioning into the damp, earthy smell of the jungle floor. The silence around them was almost oppressive, broken only by the distant call of a nocturnal bird and the rustle of unseen creatures in the underbrush.

Chapter Twenty-Four
The Werewolf

Deep within the jungle, Mighty the Jungle King and Magnus the Messenger remained vigilant, fully aware of the approaching intruders. They knew the dangers that lurked in the forest under the full moon, especially with Monkey having transformed into a werewolf. For this reason, they and their people were in secret hiding, avoiding the deadly predator that roamed their territory.

Gandoki, leading a thousand soldiers and crew members, pressed forward into the jungle. The rustling leaves and distant animal calls heightened their senses, keeping them on edge. As they advanced, a sudden movement caught their attention. What seemed like a giant dog darted through the trees, a shadow among the shadows. The men tensed, their eyes scanning the darkness.

"Stay alert," Gandoki whispered, his voice barely audible over the sounds of the night. "We don't know what we're dealing with here."

Before they could react, Monkey, now a fully transformed werewolf, lunged from the underbrush. His massive form was a blur of fur and fangs, and he fell upon Gandoki's soldiers with savage ferocity. Screams pierced the night as the werewolf tore through their ranks, a whirlwind of claws and blood.

Panic spread like wildfire among the men. "Fall back!" Gandoki shouted, but his voice was drowned out by the chaos.

The jungle became a scene of carnage as Monkey continued his relentless attack, his snarls mingling with the cries of the dying.

Gandoki fought desperately, slashing at the werewolf with his sword, but it was like striking a stone wall. Monkey's eyes, glowing with a primal fury, locked onto him. With a roar, the werewolf knocked Gandoki aside, sending him sprawling to the ground.

Realising the battle was lost, Gandoki scrambled to his feet. "Retreat!" he bellowed, his voice hoarse. He and the few surviving men turned and fled, the sounds of slaughter echoing behind them. They ran through the jungle, branches whipping at their faces, until they reached the ocean's edge.

Without hesitation, Gandoki and a few of his men took to their heels. Luckily, they made it back to the sea and dove into the water, the cold shock momentarily numbing their fear. They swam with all their might, putting as much distance as possible between them and the massacre on the shore. Exhausted and gasping for breath, they finally surfaced, looking back at the jungle now shrouded in a deadly quiet.

The full moon hung high in the sky, casting a haunting reflection on the water. Gandoki's heart pounded as he realised the extent of their loss. Nearly all their soldiers and crew members had been slaughtered that night. As he floated in the ocean, the weight of his failure pressed heavily on him. The jungle, with its lurking werewolf, had proven too formidable an adversary.

"We need to regroup," Gandoki said to his remaining men, his voice grim. "This isn't over. But for now, we survive."

The following morning, Mighty and Magnus emerged from their hiding places, stepping cautiously into the jungle's clearing. The sight that greeted them was beyond their wildest expectations. Bodies lay strewn across the forest floor, the ground soaked with blood. They exchanged a grim look, knowing exactly who had caused this massacre.

"Mighty, look at this," Magnus said, pointing to a fallen soldier's uniform. "These are the soldiers of the Tree House."

Mighty's brow furrowed. "This is a serious turn of events. We need to inform Followmehome immediately."

They quickly made their way back to their hidden camp, where Followmehome and his children were waiting. As they reported what they had seen, a heavy silence fell over the group. The implications were clear: Gandoki and his men had been decimated, and the king would soon learn of this disaster.

Followmehome sighed deeply. "We must act swiftly. The king will retaliate once he knows. It's time to move faster with Wealth of God's plan."

Wealth of God stepped forward, her face determined. "We must prepare the Tree House on Mount Gunjak. It's our best chance to fortify against the coming onslaught."

Mighty, with his broad shoulders and fierce eyes, nodded in agreement. "We need all the strength we can muster. I will lead our men."

Followmehome looked at his assembled children and followers. "Wealth of God, Mighty, Magnus—let's move forward with the plan. We will need every able-bodied person to help."

The call to arms was issued, and soon about twenty thousand men, each equipped with iron glass, gathered. They were resolute, understanding the gravity of the situation. The volunteers stood ready, a mix of determination and anxiety on their faces.

Wealth of God addressed the crowd, her voice steady. "We have no time to lose. Together, we will carve a new sanctuary on Mount Gunjak. This will be our fortress against the king's wrath."

***

As the number of prisoners in the Tree House dwindled, whispers and rumours began to circulate among the people. They speculated about the seemingly endless capacity of the Tree House prison, which had managed to hold thousands of prisoners in a short span of time and still seemed to have room for more. The mystery of its vastness gnawed at their curiosity and fuelled their growing unease.

In the throne room, the king paced back and forth, his mind preoccupied with the delicate balance he was trying to maintain. He had found a method to keep the Tree House's population in check and to ensure the Angels of Death were fed, but the unrest among the people was becoming increasingly difficult to ignore. The absence of Gandoki and Wealth of God only added to the tension.

One morning, as he looked out over his domain, the king saw a gathering of people around the king's chamber. Their faces were etched with anger and fear, and their voices rose in a chorus of demands. They needed answers. They were being held back by the guards.

The king clenched his fists, his mind racing for a solution. He needed to assert his authority and quell this burgeoning rebellion. He summoned the five Angels of Death who lived disguised as humans within his realm. They entered the throne room, their eyes gleaming with an otherworldly light as they bowed before him.

"Transform into your beast forms," the king commanded, his voice cold and resolute. "Show the people the power that keeps them in check. Scare them back into submission."

The Angels of Death bowed lower, their forms beginning to shift and contort. Their human facades melted away, revealing monstrous shapes with glowing eyes and gnarled claws. The air around them grew heavy with an oppressive sense of dread.

"Go," the king ordered, "and ensure they remember who holds the true power here."

The transformed beasts stormed out of the throne room, their footsteps shaking the ground. As they approached the protesting crowd, the people fell silent, their eyes widening in terror. The Angels of Death roared, a sound that reverberated through the air and sent chills down the spines of those gathered.

Immediately, the people began to scatter, their defiance dissolving into panic. The sight of the monstrous Angels of Death, with their menacing presence, was enough to break their will. They fled in all directions, seeking safety from the terrifying creatures.

From his vantage point, the king watched as order was restored through fear. He knew this was only a temporary measure, but for now, it was enough. The protests ceased, and the people were reminded of the power he wielded, both through his own might and through the beasts he controlled.

As the Angels of Death returned to their human forms and the crowd dispersed, the king allowed himself a brief moment of satisfaction. He had bought himself more time, but he knew the true test would come with the return of Gandoki and Wealth of God. Until then, he would maintain his grip on the Tree House with an iron fist, ensuring that no one dared to challenge his authority again.

After months at sea, Gandoki finally made it back to the Tree House though he was the only one who survived. The others had been lost to the sea waves, having lost hope and fearing the king's reaction. They decided to end it all by suicide than death at the hands of the Angels of Death.

As Gandoki stumbled onto the tree house, bedraggled and weary, the king saw him and immediately knew something had gone wrong.

The king's face darkened with disappointment. "What happened, Gandoki?" he demanded, his voice heavy with expectation.

Gandoki, covered in shame, bowed his head. "My lord, we encountered great adversity," he began, his voice trembling. "We were attacked…by a werewolf."

The mention of the werewolf caught the king's full attention. He rose from his seat, eyes wide with a mixture of curiosity and fear. "A werewolf? Describe it. Tell me about its power and strength."

Gandoki nodded, swallowing hard. "My lord, the creature was incredibly powerful. It slaughtered a thousand of our soldiers in a single night. Its speed was unmatched, and it had the terrifying ability to become invisible during its attacks."

The king's eyes narrowed as he listened, the story of the werewolf reminding him of the warnings from Aza, the blossom whisperer. He decided it was time to pay her a visit.

Aza received the king in her humble abode, her eyes filled with the weight of unspoken knowledge. "Aza," the king said, "I need your counsel. We have encountered a werewolf, and it has decimated my forces."

Aza nodded knowingly. "Werewolves only turn on the full moon," she said. "You must find out who transforms and ensure they are dealt with. The werewolf could very well be the end of you in battle."

The king mulled over her words, his mind heavy with the need for action. He had been awaiting Wealth of God's return for a long period. Also, no words from Requin. Growing impatient and desperate for war, he needed Demetrius's metal plate to unlock more Angels of Death and wage war against the Landers. He summoned Akika and ordered him to travel with ten thousand soldiers.

Years passed, and still, the king awaited Wealth of God's return. He began to suspect that she might have been coaxed by her family. With Servant of Allah held captive, he needed someone he could trust to wage war against the Landers and retrieve the metal plate from Demetrius's neck.

The king called upon Akika once more. "Akika, you must sail to the land and do whatever it takes to retrieve the metal plate from Demetrius's neck," the king commanded.

Akika, delighted by the task, bowed deeply. "I will not fail you, my lord," he promised.

Impressed by Akika's courage, the king allowed him to make a wish. Akika, knowing this was an opportunity, chose his words carefully. "I only ask for ten thousand soldiers to carry out this task, and perhaps, a wish to be granted upon my return."

The king nodded, providing him with the soldiers and promising to grant his wish upon his successful return. Akika departed with the troops the next morning.

Knowing the importance of the preparation, Akika planned to approach the Landers with a façade of peace, intending to discuss matters with Wealth of God to avoid chaos. However, he was prepared for conflict if necessary.

Meanwhile, Wealth of God, alongside her brother Mighty and his warriors, was already on Mount Ganjak. They were diligently carving into the tree and building the structure, following the advice given by Followmehome. The anticipation of the coming war weighed heavily on them all as they prepared for the inevitable conflict.

Chapter Twenty-Five
Akika's Agreement

A few months passed, and even though the Landers knew the king might wage war after the atrocity committed by Monkey the werewolf, most of their warriors had moved to Mount Ganjak to build themselves home because they all knew the king would retaliate especially when he noticed Wealth of God had committed treason.

Fortunately for Akika, even though he sailed with ten thousand soldiers, he was not spotted by Moses the Sea King, which would have distracted his plight.

Magnus the Messenger stood on a high cliff, his sharp eyes scanning the horizon. As the morning mist began to lift, he spotted an unexpected sight—a fleet of ships, their sails billowing as they approached from an unusual direction. His heart skipped a beat, recognising the insignia of the Tree House. This was no ordinary arrival.

"Warriors, to arms!" Magnus bellowed, his voice echoing through the dense forest. "Send word to the tribe and prepare for their arrival!"

Swift-footed messengers darted off in all directions, their urgency palpable. Magnus watched them disappear into the undergrowth before turning to his trusted men. "We must confront them. Follow me."

With determined strides, Magnus led Mafo the Saint, Tapa the Charmer, Emmanuel, and Makado the Ruthless down the winding path towards the shore. The air was thick with tension, the forest unusually quiet, as if it too sensed the impending conflict.

As they broke through the treeline, the ships were already moored, and soldiers of the Tree House were disembarking in disciplined rows. At the forefront stood a tall, imposing figure exuding an air of arrogance.

"You there!" Magnus called out, stepping forward with his men flanking him. "State your business. Why have you come to our land?"

The leader of the Tree House soldiers, his eyes gleaming with cockiness, responded with a smirk. "We come with a message and a mission. We seek Wealth of God."

Magnus felt a shiver of unease but stood firm. "You are outnumbered here. Explain yourselves."

The leader's smirk widened. "We come in peace if our demands are met. Deliver Wealth of God to us, and no harm will come to you or your people."

Magnus took a step closer, eyes blazing with defiance. "Wealth of God is under our protection. We will not hand her over without understanding your true intentions."

In a swift, calculated move, the Tree House leader gestured, and Magnus felt the cold steel of swords at his neck. His men were similarly subdued, their weapons stripped away by the efficient Tree House soldiers.

"You have no choice," the leader said coldly. "You and your men will be held until Wealth of God is brought to us."

Bound and under guard, Magnus and his men were led away, the reality of their capture sinking in. They were taken to a makeshift camp within the forest, where they were secured to sturdy posts. The leader approached Magnus, his expression one of grim satisfaction.

"Rest assured, no harm will come to you if our terms are met," he said. "We only seek what is rightfully ours."

Wealth of God received the urgent message from Magnus, carried swiftly by the raven. As she listened to the raven's urgent croaking, her face tightened with determination. She spoke directly to the raven, her voice clear and resolute. "Tell my father that the Tree House army has encamped in our deserted homes. Should we wage war against them?" The raven cawed in acknowledgement and took flight, disappearing into the night.

The reply came swiftly, the raven returning with Followmehome's words. "Meet with their leader and ask why they have come. Avoid immediate aggression." Wealth of God nodded, understanding the gravity of her father's advice.

Gathering her resolve, she prepared to descend from Mount Ganjak. Her brother, Mighty, his warriors, and their formidable allies—Jacko, now a fully grown jaguar, and Demetrious—stood ready by her side. The air was thick with tension as they made their way down the mountain, their steps quiet and purposeful.

In the dense forest near the deserted homes, Wealth of God and her group moved with stealth and precision. The sounds of the forest—the rustling leaves, the distant calls of nocturnal creatures—seemed amplified in the stillness of the night.

"Mighty," she whispered, "we need to approach with caution. Let's not provoke them unless necessary."

A few days had passed, and the journey was arduous. Wealth of God, Demetrious, Jacko, and a few loyal men finally arrived at their homeland, now occupied by Akika and his troops. The sight was sobering—once-familiar grounds now trampled under the weight of enemy boots.

Wealth of God, with Demetrious by her side and Jacko prowling protectively, approached the Tree House soldiers cautiously. The air was thick with tension, every step forward measured and deliberate.

"We come in peace," Wealth of God announced, her voice steady though her eyes were sharp and vigilant. Demetrious stood tall, his presence formidable, and Jacko's silent, feline grace added a layer of intimidation.

Mighty, trusting in his sister's diplomatic skills, had positioned his warriors strategically in the surrounding forest. Hidden among the trees, they watched over her, ready to spring into action at the slightest sign of danger. His eyes never left Wealth of God as she advanced, his heart pounding with the weight of responsibility.

"Stay alert," Mighty whispered to his men. "Watch for her signal. We move only if she's in trouble."

Wealth of God and her small entourage halted a short distance from the soldiers. Akika, standing tall and exuding confidence, stepped forward. His smirk was a thin veil over his true intentions.

"Welcome, Wealth of God!" Akika's voice carried an air of mockery.

Wealth of God, guarded by Demetrious and Jacko, approached Akika with measured steps. The tension was palpable, and the atmosphere crackled with the weight of impending decisions. Akika stood tall, his eyes gleaming with determination. He was aware of the significance of Wealth of God's relationship with the king, yet he remained undeterred. His loyalty to the king and his desire for recognition drove him to complete his mission at any cost.

As Wealth of God drew nearer, her gaze met Akika's unwaveringly. She knew the stakes. The metal plate on Demetrious' neck was both a shackle and a shield. Without it, Demetrious' loyalty and ferocity were uncertain. The king's demand to retrieve the plate meant only one thing: he sought to enslave more Angels of Death for his war against the Landers.

Akika, with a voice edged with authority, spoke first. "Wealth of God, you understand why I am here. I will take Demetrious into custody. In exchange, I will release your brother, Magnus."

Wealth of God's heart pounded, but she maintained her composure. "And what of Servant of Allah? He is your superior, held captive as well. Do you not wish to bargain for his release?"

Akika's eyes narrowed, a flicker of impatience crossing his face. "Servant of Allah is not my concern. My task is clear: retrieve the metal plate. That is my only priority."

Demetrious growled softly, a reminder of his presence and power. Jacko, ever watchful, mirrored his mistress's tension. Wealth of God took a deep breath, considering her options. She knew that conceding to Akika's demand might spell disaster, but refusing could endanger her brother and ignite a war.

"Very well," she said, her voice steady but firm. "I will remove the metal plate from Demetrious, but he remains under my care. In return, you will release Magnus and his men, and I will guarantee you safe passage back to the Tree House."

Akika raised an eyebrow, a smirk playing on his lips. "And why should I trust you? What assurance do I have that you will honour this agreement?"

Wealth of God stepped closer, her eyes flashing with determination. "You have my word. And remember, Akika, Moses the Sea King is on his way. His ship can crush your fleet to pieces. Defy my demands, and you will not leave these shores alive."

For a moment, Akika wavered, the weight of her words sinking in. He glanced at Demetrious, then back at Wealth of God. "Very well," he conceded though his tone was laced with reluctance. "Remove the plate. But know this: any trickery and our agreement is void."

Akika knew of Moses the Sea King, the legendary figure who had once freed him instead of Servant of Allah. This act of mercy had catapulted Akika into his current position of power, and for that, he felt a grudging sense of gratitude. As Wealth of God drew nearer, Akika couldn't help but recall the immense ship of Moses, capable of crushing fleets with ease. He realised that defying her demands could spell disaster.

"Akika," Wealth of God began, her voice strong and unwavering, "I will remove the metal plate from Demetrious' neck, but he remains under my care. In return, you will release Magnus and his men. I will ensure your safe passage back to the Tree House."

Akika studied her, his mind racing. He knew that honouring this agreement was not just a matter of strategy but also a matter of survival. The memory of Moses' ship, a floating fortress of unrivalled power, loomed large in his mind. With a nod, he signalled his agreement. "Very well," he replied, his voice measured but carrying a hint of the gravity he felt.

Wealth of God gestured for Demetrious to kneel. The massive figure complied, lowering himself before her with a growl of anticipation. She reached out, her fingers deftly working to unfasten the intricate metal plate that had bound Demetrious to her will. The soldiers of the Tree House watched intently, their breaths held as the plate came free.

Akika took the metal plate from Wealth of God, his fingers brushing against its cold surface. He felt a surge of power, but also a reminder of the responsibility that came with it. As he held the plate, the distant sound of waves grew louder.

Suddenly, the enormous ship of Moses appeared on the horizon, its silhouette dominating the sea. The Tree House soldiers murmured in awe, their eyes widening at the sight of the formidable vessel.

Moses, standing tall at the helm, guided the ship with a commanding presence. Akika, seeing the ship up close, felt a rush of relief. He silently thanked the fates for guiding him to accept Wealth of God's terms. Had he chosen otherwise, the arrival of Moses' ship could have spelt their doom.

"Magnus and the others will be released," Akika declared, his voice carrying across the tense gathering. "You have my word."

The captured men were brought forward, their faces etched with relief and gratitude as they rejoined Wealth of God's side. Magnus, though battered, stood tall, his eyes filled with a renewed determination.

Wealth of God turned to Akika, a hint of a smile playing on her lips. "You've made a wise choice, Akika. Go now, and take your men with you. We honour our agreements."

Akika nodded, a mix of respect and acknowledgement in his gaze. "I owe my life to Moses once, and now I owe my safe passage to you," he said, his voice sincere. "We will depart immediately."

As Akika and his soldiers retreated towards their ships, the immense vessel of Moses loomed ever closer. Akika felt a deep sense of humility and gratitude, knowing that his decision had averted a potential catastrophe.

Chapter Twenty-Six
The Right-Hand Man

Moses the Sea King stood at the helm of his mighty ship, scanning the horizon with a mixture of anticipation and anger. Akika's fleet had managed to avoid his watchful eye, and now they were preparing to depart. His heart burned with the desire to unleash his wrath upon them, to crush their ships and send their men to the ocean's depths.

He stepped down from the ship, his powerful strides carrying him towards the shore where Wealth of God and her companions waited. His jaw clenched as he approached, his eyes narrowing at the sight of Akika's soldiers preparing for departure.

Wealth of God, standing tall and resolute, turned to meet her brother's gaze. "Moses," she began, her voice calm but firm, "we've come to an agreement with Akika. We've traded the metal plate on Demetrious' neck for Magnus' release and safe passage back to their land."

Moses stopped in his tracks, his anger momentarily giving way to shock. "An agreement?" he echoed, struggling to keep his voice steady. "You made a deal with them?"

"Yes," she replied, her eyes unwavering. "It was the best course of action to ensure our people's safety and to buy us time. We cannot afford to lose more lives."

Moses glanced at Demetrious, who knelt beside Wealth of God, the metal plate now removed from his neck. The former captive rose slowly, flexing his shoulders as he adjusted to his newfound freedom. The soldiers around them watched in silence, the tension palpable.

"You are free now," Wealth of God said, her voice steady.

"You can return to the ocean and live your life as you wish."

Demetrious shook his head, his expression resolute. "No, Wealth of God. I do not wish to return to the ocean, at least not permanently. You have freed me, and I swear by the ocean's depths, I will not feed on the Landers. I owe my life to you and your people."

Wealth of God studied him, her eyes searching for any sign of deceit, but she saw only sincerity in his gaze. "What do you propose, Demetrious?" she asked.

"Allow me to reside on land," Demetrious pleaded. "I can dive into the sea whenever I need, but I wish to stay and support the Landers in any battles that lie ahead. I vow to protect them, as you have protected me."

For a moment, there was silence. Then, with a slow, deliberate nod, Wealth of God agreed. "Very well, Demetrious. You may stay. But remember your vow. Any betrayal will be met with swift retribution."

Demetrious bowed deeply to her, his massive form radiating both strength and humility. "Thank you, Wealth of God. I will honour my vow to you and your people."

With that, he turned and walked towards the ocean, the waves crashing against the shore in a rhythmic symphony. He paused at the water's edge, casting one last glance back at Wealth of God and her companions, before diving gracefully into the depths. The water swallowed him, but the promise of his loyalty lingered in the air.

Wealth of God watched him disappear beneath the waves, a sense of cautious hope stirring within her. She turned to her brother Mighty, who had been silently observing the exchange.

"Do you trust him?" Mighty asked, his voice low.

"I do," she replied. "For now, we must. We need every ally we can get in the battles to come."

Mighty nodded, his expression thoughtful. "Then let us prepare. The king will not wait, and neither should we."

After several months at sea, Akika finally returned to the Tree House with exactly ten thousand men and the precious metal plate. When he presented the plate to the king, there was a moment of stunned silence in the royal chamber. The king's eyes widened in disbelief, and then his face broke into a broad, approving smile.

"Incredible," the king murmured, taking the plate from Akika's hands. "You have surpassed all expectations, Akika. Your bravery and resourcefulness are unmatched. As promised, I am prepared to grant you any request. Name your desire."

Akika had dreamed of this moment his entire life. He had rehearsed his words countless times, visualising his rise to power. Even though Godhascome, the king's current right-hand man, stood in the chamber, Akika's determination did not waver.

Taking a deep breath, Akika stepped forward, his eyes locked with the king's. "Your Majesty, my greatest desire is to serve you as your most trusted advisor, your right hand. I have proven my loyalty and my capability. Allow me to stand by your side, to help lead and protect our people."

Godhascome's expression darkened, but he remained silent, knowing this moment was not his to contest. The king's smile faded as he considered Akika's request, the weight of the decision visible on his face.

"You ask for a great honour, Akika," the king said slowly. "To be my right hand is a position of immense responsibility and power. But you have proven your worth. Your bravery has brought us the means to strengthen our forces."

The king glanced at Godhascome, then back at Akika. "Very well. From this day forth, you shall be my right hand. Serve me faithfully, and together, we will lead our people to greatness."

Akika bowed deeply, a mix of triumph and humility in his expression. "Thank you, Your Majesty. I will not fail you."

As Akika rose, the king gestured for him to step forward, placing a hand on his shoulder. "Let us prepare for what lies ahead. With this plate, we can awaken more Angels of Death and ensure our dominance. We have much work to do."

Godhascome clenched his fists at his sides, but he maintained his composure. The chamber buzzed with a renewed sense of purpose, the air thick with anticipation.

Akika had achieved his dream, but he knew that his real work was only just beginning. He would need to prove his worth every day, to stay vigilant and loyal. The path to power was fraught with peril, but Akika was ready for the challenges ahead.

The king knew that promoting Akika would mean finding a way to honour Godhascome appropriately. If he were to grant Akika's wish, Godhascome's loyalty needed to be ensured and his contributions rewarded. With a thoughtful nod, the king called upon Aza the blossom whisperer.

"Aza," the king commanded, "bring forth a suckling tree."

Aza bowed gracefully and left the chamber. Moments later, she returned, carrying a small, vibrant tree with roots cradled in rich soil.

The king took the tree from her and turned to Godhascome. "You have served me faithfully, Godhascome, and your loyalty does not go unnoticed. As I elevate Akika, it is only fitting that you, too, are rewarded for your dedication. I present to you this suckling tree as the foundation of your own kingdom. Build an army of soldiers who will abide by the rules of the Tree House, and ensure our legacy endures."

Godhascome's eyes widened in surprise and gratitude. He stepped forward and knelt before the king, his voice filled with emotion. "Thank you, Your Majesty. I am honoured by your generosity and trust. I swear to serve you and uphold your commands with unwavering loyalty."

The king placed the suckling tree in Godhascome's hands, a symbol of his new beginning. "Rise, Godhascome, and take this gift. May your kingdom flourish and your soldiers be strong. Together, we will fortify our dominion and secure our future."

Godhascome rose, clutching the tree to his chest, a mixture of pride and determination on his face. He understood the significance of this gift—it was a chance to build something lasting, a testament to his service and a new chapter in his life.

The chamber buzzed with renewed energy as the king's advisors and soldiers watched the ceremony. Akika stood beside the king, knowing his own path to power had been secured but also aware of the responsibility that now rested on his shoulders.

As Godhascome exited the chamber, the suckling tree in hand, he couldn't help but feel a profound sense of purpose. He would build his kingdom, create an army loyal to the Tree House, and continue to serve the king with all his might.

The king, now flanked by his newly appointed right-hand man and a trusted advisor with his own burgeoning kingdom, felt a sense of accomplishment. The pieces were falling into place, and with the power of the metal plate, they would awaken more Angels of Death, preparing for the battles that lay ahead.

Alexandre and Lambert stood at the edge of the king's chamber, their expressions darkening as they watched the king admire the metal plate Akika had presented. The realisation of the impending danger settled heavily on their minds. With both the metal cup and the metal plate, the king now possessed the complete mechanism to release more Angels of Death.

As the king bestowed a kingdom upon Godhascome, Alexandre and Lambert exchanged uneasy glances. The implications were clear: with an army of Angels of Death, the king's power would be unparalleled, and the Tree House would be forever under his iron rule.

Once the ceremony concluded and the chamber began to empty, Alexandre pulled Lambert aside into a secluded alcove. "We cannot stay here," he whispered urgently. "The king is becoming too powerful. If he releases more Angels of Death, the Tree House will be plunged into chaos."

Lambert nodded, his face grim. "I've been thinking the same. We need to act quickly. We'll take a few suckling plants and leave, soon enough. We can start our own kingdom, far from the king's reach."

Gandoki stood at another angle of the grand hall, watching Akika bask in the king's praise. The sight of the metal plate, symbolising Akika's triumph, filled him with a deep sense of shame. He had returned empty-handed, a stark contrast to Akika's success. The weight of his failure to the Tree House pressed heavily on his shoulders.

Determined to redeem himself, Gandoki sought out Alexandre and Lambert. He found them in a secluded corner of the garden, discussing their plans in hushed tones. Their expressions brightened as he approached though their eyes held a glint of calculation.

"We need to talk," Gandoki said, his voice filled with resolve. "I can't stay here and face my father's disappointment any longer. I am willing to do whatever it takes to leave the tree house with you both."

Alexandre and Lambert exchanged a quick glance, their minds racing. They knew Gandoki's presence could complicate their escape, but they also saw an opportunity. "Of course, Gandoki," Alexandre said smoothly, giving a bow. "We were just discussing our plans. There's a way you can help."

Gandoki's eyes lit up with hope. "Anything. Just tell me what to do."

"We need suckling plants for our new kingdom," Lambert explained. "Five, to be exact. They're kept in Aza's chamber. If you can steal them and bring them to us, we can all leave this place behind."

Gandoki nodded eagerly. "Consider it done."

As Gandoki hurried off, Alexandre turned to Lambert. "He doesn't know we're planning to leave him behind, does he?"

Lambert shook his head. "No. He thinks he's coming with us. We'll use him to get the plants and then ditch him. The king will look for him, not us."

Late that night, Gandoki crept into Aza's chamber, his heart pounding in his chest. The soft glow of the suckling plants illuminated the room. He carefully dug up five of them, wrapping their roots in cloth. His hands trembled with a mix of fear and excitement as he secured the precious cargo.

With the plants in hand, he made his way back to Alexandre and Lambert's hideout. They greeted him with smiles, their eyes gleaming with triumph.

"You did it," Alexandre said, clapping Gandoki on the back. "You've secured our future."

Gandoki's chest swelled with pride. "What's next?"

"Rest," Lambert said, his tone reassuring. "We'll move the plants to a safe place and finalise our plans. You've done your part."

Gandoki nodded, exhaustion washing over him. "I'll be ready."

As Gandoki returned to his chamber and drifted off to sleep, Alexandre and Lambert quietly discussed the final details of their plan.

Charles and Muhammad, ever the shadowy figures with an uncanny knack for knowing secrets, were already aware of Alexandre and Lambert's plan to elope with the stolen suckling trees. Their mysterious sources of information were as impenetrable as ever, but their knowledge gave them a distinct advantage. Recognising an opportunity, they decided it was time to make a strategic bargain.

In the dimly lit confines of their secluded hideout, Charles and Muhammad discussed their next move.

"We have the information, and we have leverage," Charles said, his eyes glinting with cunning. "It's time to call in our contact. Anonymous will know how to broker this deal."

Muhammad nodded, his expression equally calculating. "Yes, but we must tread carefully. We need to ensure we get what we want without giving away too much. A portion of Aza's enchantment should be enough to secure the suckling."

Chapter Twenty-Seven
Negotiations

Anonymous was an enigma to one and all. He was reclusive, yet powerful. He was the metaphor of the saying: *There is power in the mysterious and the unknown.*

For Mohammed, the first meeting with Anonymous had left an indelible mark on his soul. Mohammed had always been cautious, valuing knowledge and wisdom as powerful allies in a world fraught with danger. The encounter that cemented his trust in Anonymous occurred during a particularly tumultuous period, a time known as the secret purge. The king, driven by paranoia and the whisperings of his advisors, had ordered the silent elimination of anyone suspected of disloyalty or harbouring rebellious thoughts.

Mohammed, then a rising figure in the Tree House, had unknowingly attracted the king's suspicion. One evening, as he went about his duties, he felt a growing sense of unease. It was a subtle shift in the air, an almost imperceptible tension that clung to the corridors of power. That night, under the cover of darkness, a hooded figure appeared at his door. The hooded figure said: "Come with me. Now."

He was led to a hidden chamber beneath the great tree filled with so many turns and twists that it was almost impossible to recall the route.

In the cool, musty air of that secret sanctuary, Mohammed found himself face-to-face with Anonymous for the first time. The chamber was dimly lit by flickering candles, their light casting long shadows on the stone walls. Anonymous stood at the centre, cloaked in his usual garb, his face partially obscured. Despite the mystery surrounding him, there was an undeniable aura of authority and calm about him.

"Do you know why you're here?" Anonymous asked, his voice a quiet murmur that seemed to echo in the confined space.

Mohammed shook his head, his heart pounding. "No, but I have a feeling it's important."

Anonymous nodded, his eyes piercing through the dim light. "The king's men come for you tonight," he began, his tone measured and steady. "But there is a way to turn the situation to your advantage. Remain in your quarters, but do not resist when they arrive."

There was something in Anonymous' demeanour—an unwavering confidence and an almost paternal concern—that compelled Mohammed to trust him. It wasn't just the words he spoke but the way he carried himself, the certainty in his gaze. Mohammed felt a strange sense of reassurance, as though he were a child seeking comfort from a protective figure. Anonymous exuded an air of infallibility, a quiet strength that made one feel safe even in the face of imminent danger.

Following Anonymous' advice, Mohammed had waited in his quarters, heart pounding, as the king's guards burst in. They had bound him and brought him before the king, who accused him of treason. But Mohammed, calm and prepared thanks to Anonymous' guidance, had eloquently defended himself, exposing the 'false accusations' and shifting the suspicion onto his accusers. The king, impressed by Mohammed's composure and argument, had not only spared his life but also promoted him, recognising his value and loyalty.

That night, as Mohammed lay in his chambers, reflecting on the day's events, he felt an overwhelming gratitude towards Anonymous. He had seen the depths of power and cunning, and it had saved his life. In his mind, Anonymous became more than just a mysterious benefactor; he became a beacon of hope and a symbol of ultimate wisdom. The reverence he felt was akin to a child's awe of a hero, a figure who embodied safety and guidance in a perilous world.

Before leaving Anonymous' chamber, back then, he recalled asking only one question.

"Why are you helping me?"

Anonymous stared at him for a brief moment before saying, "You're meant for something great. Your moves…Well, I've been observing them for a while. It's been the most stealthy and well-planned, so far. I can't let your talent die. I know it'll be worth the save, someday."

Now, with the Tree House again on the brink of chaos and the threat of the king unleashing the Angels of Death looming, Mohammed knew he needed Anonymous' wisdom once more. The stakes were higher than ever. The fate of the Tree House hung in the balance, and Mohammed felt a heavy responsibility to navigate this treacherous path with the utmost caution. He recalled the calm, steady voice that had once guided him to safety, and a deep-seated trust welled up within him. Mohammed knew that, no matter the peril, Anonymous would have the knowledge and foresight to lead him through the darkness.

With each step he took towards Anonymous' hidden sanctuary, Mohammed's resolve grew stronger. He could still picture the shadowy figure standing in that dimly lit chamber, a bastion of strength and wisdom amidst the chaos. The memory of Anonymous' guidance was a beacon, a reminder that even in the darkest of times, there was hope and a way forward. And so, with a heart full of trust and a mind steeled by determination, Mohammed prepared to seek counsel from the one person he believed could save them all.

Anonymous, despite the king's ruling, was always ever ready to stay hidden, avoiding any encounter with the socialites. Known for his wisdom and resourcefulness, Anonymous had established himself as a powerful figure within the Tree House, operating from the shadows and always keeping a low profile. His hidden sanctuary, a dark, secret chamber beneath the great tree, was where he conducted his clandestine meetings and orchestrated his plans.

Aware of all the plans unfolding at the top, Anonymous had his finger on the pulse of the Tree House's intricate politics and power struggles.

Muhammed and Charles moved quietly through the labyrinthine passages of the Tree House, their footsteps barely making a sound on the wooden floors. The air was thick with tension and the scent of aged wood. They finally reached the entrance to Anonymous' hidden chamber, a place shrouded in darkness and secrecy.

Inside, the chamber was dimly lit by a few flickering candles, casting long shadows on the walls. The air was cool and damp, a stark contrast to the bustling activity above. Anonymous sat at a wooden table, his face partially obscured by the shadows. He looked up as they entered, his eyes keen and perceptive.

"We managed to steal the enchantments from Aza's chamber," Muhammed began, his voice a low murmur. "Charles and I took them while she was away. The thing is…Alexander and Lambert have also stolen five suckling trees. We intend to trade a few portions of the enchantments for three of those trees. However, we need your guidance to ensure they agree to our terms without resistance."

Anonymous listened intently, his fingers steepled under his chin. The flickering candlelight did nothing at all to accentuate the expression on his face. His back was to it so his face was mostly shade. He remained silent for a moment, processing the information.

Finally, Anonymous spoke, his voice low and deliberate. "I understand your predicament, Muhammed. I am willing to help you, but I trust you know what you are asking."

Muhammed nodded vigorously. "In return, you can keep one suckling tree for yourself," he offered, his words rushing out in a mix of hope and determination.

A slow smile spread across Anonymous' face. "Agreed," he said, extending his hand. Muhammed shook it firmly, sealing their pact.

They quickly drafted a non-disclosure agreement, the flicker of the candle casting a warm glow on the parchment. As they signed, the reality of their conspiracy settled over them like a shroud. Muhammed felt a surge of relief mixed with a flicker of apprehension.

Anonymous had a lot of men who worked for him, each as shadowy and discreet as their master. Summoning one of his trusted aides, a lean, sharp-eyed man, Anonymous handed him a few potions of the enchantment. The flickering candlelight danced over the vials, illuminating the iridescent liquid within.

"Find Alexandre's chamber," Anonymous commanded, his voice a soft murmur that brooked no argument. "He is the stronger of the two, and likely the one holding the suckling trees. Use the potions as leverage."

The aide nodded, slipping the vials into his tunic before melting into the shadows.

Anonymous then turned to two other messengers, each cloaked in dark, nondescript robes. Their faces were partially hidden, only their eyes visible, reflecting a keen readiness.

"You," he pointed to the first, "go with him to Alexandre. And you," he gestured to the second, "go to Lambert. Announce that you come on my behalf."

The messengers inclined their heads in unison, ready to depart.

"When you speak to them," Anonymous continued, his tone measured and deliberate, "present the bargain clearly. Tell them it is a better deal than having their secrets exposed to the king. Stress the importance of discretion and the value of the trade."

The messengers left the chamber, their movements swift and silent. Anonymous watched them go, the shadows swallowing them whole.

"Now," he said, his voice a whisper in the dim light, "we wait. They will see reason. People always do."

Muhammed and Charles exchanged a glance, the weight of the conspiracy settling heavily on their shoulders. As they prepared to leave, the flickering candlelight cast long, shifting shadows on the chamber walls, a silent testament to the gravity of their plans.

The message was delivered to Alexandre and Lambert. They were shocked; they had never seen it coming. Uncertainty gnawed at them, as they were unsure which of their secrets had been uncovered. Guilt haunted them, and they believed it was time to escape.

The third messenger arrived at Lambert's chamber late at night, a hooded figure blending into the shadows. He cleared his throat, his voice low and steady. "I bring a message from Anonymous," he began, eyes flicking over Lambert. "Three suckling trees in exchange for a portion of Aza's enchantment. The location and time are specified. This is a better deal than your secrets being exposed to the king."

He passed a note with a location and time written on it.

Lambert felt his heart race, but he kept his face impassive, nodding slowly. Inside, his mind was a whirlwind of thoughts. *Which secret? How much does Anonymous know?* His palms itched to wipe away the sweat forming, but he clasped them behind his back, maintaining a facade of calm. "What proof do I have that this enchantment is real?" he asked, his voice cool but tinged with the slightest hint of tremor.

The messenger's gaze was steady. "You have the word of Anonymous. You know he doesn't make idle claims."

A cold chill ran down Lambert's spine. The word of Anonymous was usually more than enough; the man was a shadowy legend in the Tree House. Still, he tried to appear contemplative, nodding slowly. "Alright," he said, his voice measured. "I'll do it."

The messenger inclined his head slightly. "Wise choice." With that, he melted back into the darkness, leaving Lambert alone with his turbulent thoughts.

Meanwhile, the first and second messengers approached Alexandre's chamber. They knocked, their arrival synchronised to ensure the message was delivered at the same time. Alexandre, already tense from the day's events, opened the door, his eyes narrowing at the sight of the hooded figures.

"We bring a message from Anonymous," one of the messengers began, their voices harmonising in the dimly lit room. "Three suckling trees in exchange for a portion of Aza's enchantment. The location and time are specified. This is a better deal than your secrets being exposed to the king."

They also left him a note.

Alexandre forced a casual stance, arms crossed. His mind raced. *We've been careful. How could this have happened?* He squinted slightly as if trying to pierce through the messengers' hoods to see their eyes. "Why should I trust this deal?" he asked, trying to maintain his composure. "How do I know Anonymous won't double-cross us?"

The messengers' gazes remained steady. "Anonymous values his reputation. He knows things about you that would make you vulnerable if revealed. This is a fair exchange."

Blackmail? he thought.

Alexandre's thoughts churned, but he knew they had no leverage. The weight of Anonymous' knowledge pressed down on him. "Fine," he said, voice gruff. "I agree to the terms."

The messengers nodded in unison. "A wise decision," one of them said before they slipped back into the shadows, leaving Alexandre to grapple with his decision.

The instructions were precise: drop three suckling trees at a designated location and pick up a portion of Aza's enchantment. Alexandre and Lambert felt the urgency of leaving the Tree House before their secrets could be unveiled. Despite their doubts about the authenticity of the enchantment, they had no choice but to trust Anonymous who had sent this classified information.

They both reconvened later on, at their hideouts, to share their peculiar encounters. It was a relief to both of them when they discovered that they were on the same page regarding the deal; that they had both accepted the terms. Alexandre decided that they would both meet with Anonymous, together. He could not see the point of their meeting separately.

At the appointed time, Alexandre and Lambert made their way to the exchange spot, a secluded area on the underside of the tree house. The air was thick with anticipation. Shadows danced in the flickering torchlight, and every sound seemed amplified in the stillness.

As he approached, he saw a figure waiting, face entirely hidden behind a mask, blending seamlessly with the darkness. The figure's posture was relaxed but alert, exuding an air of quiet authority.

Alexandre's heart raced, but he kept his composure, gripping the bundle containing the three suckling trees tightly. Their delicate roots were wrapped carefully in damp cloths to protect them. He stepped forward, his eyes scanning the surroundings for any signs of treachery.

His eyes seemed to show a sliver of surprise on seeing Lambert there with Alexandre. And, in all honesty, their duo did not know what to make about this reaction.

The exchange was swift and silent. Alexandre handed over the bundle (for him and his friend), the weight of the transaction heavy in the still night air. The masked figure took the trees, examining them briefly before nodding in satisfaction. In return, he presented a small vial containing the enchantment, the liquid inside glowing faintly in the dim light.

No words were exchanged, only nods of understanding. The atmosphere was tense, yet there was an unspoken agreement between them. Alexandre pocketed the vial, his fingers curling around it protectively. He nodded once more to the masked figure, a silent acknowledgement of their mutual trust.

After the transaction, they both realised that this was their cue to disappear, to leave the Tree House and forge their path far from the reach of the king and his impending wrath.

Anonymous, ever the strategist, poured himself a portion of the enchantment, knowing the value of growing the suckling tree in his possession. He understood that if Alexandre and Lambert were planning to leave the tree house, it would be wise to advise everyone in the Alliance to depart on the same night. His initial plan had been to meet with Alexandre and Lambert separately, testing their loyalty and possibly turning them against each other. However, seeing them both appear at Alexandre's appointed meeting time proved that their greed had not eclipsed their…peculiar relationship.

Anonymous arranged a brief follow-up meeting with Alexandre and Lambert. In the dim, secretive chamber, he impressed upon them the importance of following his advice and orders to ensure the success of their plan.

"Are you planning to leave the tree house soon?" he asked, his voice a low murmur.

Alexandre and Lambert exchanged a glance before nodding.

"Yes," Alexandre replied.

"Good," Anonymous said. "Wait for my order. You and the other socialites will leave on the same night. Coordination is key to avoid detection."

Alexandre and Lambert agreed, understanding the gravity of the situation. They were dismissed, their minds racing with the implications of what was to come.

Chapter Twenty-Eight
Voyage to Sanctuary

The dim light of the chamber flickered softly, casting long shadows on the walls, as Charles and Mohammad stood before Anonymous. The scent of aged wood and earth filled the air, mingling with the faint aroma of the burning candles. The room, filled with maps, ancient scrolls, and enigmatic artefacts, felt like the very heart of mystery and strategy.

Anonymous handed over two carefully wrapped suckling trees, their delicate roots swaddled in a damp cloth to keep them nourished. Beside them, a small vial containing the remainder of Aza's enchantment shimmered in the candlelight. The weight of the moment hung heavily in the air.

"Here they are," Anonymous said, his voice a quiet murmur that seemed to resonate with the gravity of their pact. He looked intently at Mohammad, his eyes sharp and knowing. "You must ensure absolute confidentiality. Any slip, any whisper, and the king's wrath will be upon us all."

Charles, holding one of the suckling trees, nodded solemnly. "You have our word. No one will know."

Anonymous turned to Mohammad, his expression softening slightly. "Mohammad, I consider you more than an acquaintance. You've sought my counsel before, and I have never steered you wrong. Trust me now as you did then. You must leave on the same night as Alexandre and Lambert. The king's wrath is not something to be underestimated."

Mohammad, feeling the weight of Anonymous' words, looked around the chamber, taking in the layers of history and knowledge that surrounded them. It was the first time that Anonymous chamber was this well-lit, he realised. He felt a chill run down his spine, not from the cold, but from the realisation of the stakes involved. He met Anonymous' gaze and saw a flicker of genuine concern.

"I understand," Mohammad replied, his voice steady but filled with an undercurrent of tension. "We will be ready. But…are you sure this is the only way?"

Anonymous' lips curved into a slight, enigmatic smile. "Trust in my judgement. The timing is crucial. The king's suspicions are like wildfire; they can spread rapidly and uncontrollably. We must act with precision."

The air seemed to thicken with the weight of their decision.

Mohammed and Charles nodded firmly.

Anonymous' eyes flickered with approval. "Good. Now, go. Prepare. Time is of the essence."

As they turned to leave, the flickering candlelight casting its elongated shadows on the ancient walls, Mohammad paused for a moment, feeling a pang of unease. He looked back at Anonymous, who stood silently behind his mask. Mohammad knew that this alliance was their best chance, their only chance, to escape the looming threat. He gave one more nod and continued on his way.

Anonymous sent a messenger to Alexandre and Lambert, informing them that the entire Alliance would depart in two nights. The message was clear: any delay could mean exposure.

The messenger moved silently through the dimly lit corridors, his footsteps barely audible against the creaking wooden floors. Reaching Alexandre's chamber, he knocked softly, a series of coded taps that only those in the know would recognise. The door creaked open, revealing Alexandre's tense face.

"The time is set," the messenger whispered, eyes darting around to ensure no one was eavesdropping. "Two nights from now. Delay, and you risk everything."

Alexandre nodded, his mind racing. "Understood. Lambert and I will be ready." He glanced towards the dim interior of his chamber, where Lambert sat, anxiously waiting.

After the messenger left, Lambert stood and approached Alexandre. "What's the plan now?" he asked, his voice a low murmur filled with apprehension.

"We need to inform the rest of the Alliance," Alexandre replied, a determined glint in his eyes. "There's no time to waste. I know just the right guy to relay the message."

Alexandre called for their trusted comrade, a person so simple and unnoticeable, added to the fact that he was adept at moving through the shadows, undetected and unheard.

"You have a crucial task," Alexandre began, his tone urgent, some fifteen minutes later when he arrived. "The Alliance must be informed. Two nights from now, we depart. Ensure everyone knows the exact time. Any delay could mean our exposure and doom."

The young-looking man nodded, understanding the gravity of the mission.

With a swift, silent departure, he took to his mission, moving with purpose and precision. The corridors of the tree house, usually bustling with activity, seemed eerily quiet as he navigated through them, slipping past groups of guards.

"Hello, beautiful evening, don't you think?" he would say, and they would always grunt something about him quitting his skedaddling.

Every member of the Alliance received the message in hushed whispers and secretive gestures. The atmosphere was charged with tension, every glance and every movement infused with the knowledge of their imminent departure.

As the final preparations were set in motion, Alexandre and Lambert felt a mixture of anxiety and resolve. They knew the risks were high, but the promise of freedom for them, and the looming threat of the king's wrath left them no choice.

The tree house, with its labyrinthine passages and hidden corners, had been their home and their prison. Now, it was a ticking clock, each passing moment bringing them closer to their escape or their doom. And as the appointed night approached, the Alliance steeled themselves for the journey ahead, bound by their shared determination and the enigmatic guidance of Anonymous.

Anonymous sat in a high-backed chair, slowly sipping a light beverage. The air was cool and still, the only sound being the faint creaking of the wooden structure around him. As he pondered his plans, the flickering candlelight cast dancing shadows on the walls, adding to the chamber's mysterious atmosphere.

Anonymous had his own ambitions. He had promised to help Charles and Mohammad elude the tree house on the same night, leveraging their long-term relationship. Taking another thoughtful sip, he considered the intricacies of his scheme. Sailing to a place called Sand Dunes was his ultimate goal, a location he had learnt about through his extensive network of spies and informants.

Setting his drink down, Anonymous unfurled an old, weathered map on the table before him. The map detailed a hidden path through the treacherous seas, leading to Sand Dunes—a land of vast wealth and opportunity. His fingers traced the route he had studied countless times. He envisioned building a home for his men there, establishing his own kingdom where his power would be absolute.

However, Anonymous knew he needed Charles and Mohammad's assistance to realise this dream. One crucial element was missing from his plan: the iron glass. This piece of the puzzle eluded him, and he knew that without it, his vision of a prosperous kingdom in Sand Dunes would remain incomplete.

His knowledge of Sand Dunes had come from this very map, acquired years ago through a series of covert operations. His obsession with wealth and power had driven him to learn everything he could about potential havens. Sand Dunes, with its promise of untapped riches and strategic advantage, had always been his ultimate goal. Now, with the chaos brewing in the tree house, the opportunity had finally presented itself.

As he took another sip, Anonymous' mind raced with plans and contingencies. The flickering candlelight illuminated his face, revealing a determined and calculating expression. The time was ripe, and every move had to be precise. His network of spies had ensured he knew more than anyone else in the tree house, and it was this knowledge that gave him the upper hand.

He was ready. The pieces were falling into place, and with Charles and Mohammad by his side, he was confident they could navigate the perilous journey to Sand Dunes. He envisioned the future, a kingdom of his own making, where his wealth and power would know no bounds. The anticipation was palpable as he planned his next steps, his mind as sharp as ever, ready to seize the opportunity that lay ahead.

In his secret chamber, surrounded by maps and ancient texts, Anonymous felt a surge of determination. He knew just too much, and it was this mysterious knowledge that gave him an edge. People whispered about his uncanny ability to predict events and his seemingly endless reservoir of information. As he prepared for the night of the escape, he felt a sense of destiny. His plans were in motion, and soon, he would achieve the wealth and power he had always desired.

In stark contrast, Alexandre and Lambert had secretly built a formidable force of thousands of thugs who lived under the guise of the Alliance. They had stockpiled a significant amount of iron glasses and were prepared to elude the tree house at a moment's notice, taking women and children with them under their command.

Warriorisborn, the king, remained oblivious to this looming threat. The oligarchic structure of the tree house meant that most of the soldiers patrolled the lower levels, leaving the upper regions less guarded. This oversight granted

Alexandre and Lambert a strategic advantage over the king's forces. When the time came, they swiftly mobilised their thugs.

The assault was brutal and efficient. Under the cover of the night, the Alliance launched their attack. The soldiers stationed at the downside of the tree house were caught off guard, unable to mount a significant defence. Alexandre and Lambert's men, driven by desperation and a desire for freedom, overpowered the soldiers with ruthless efficiency. The patrols were ambushed, overwhelmed, and systematically slaughtered.

As the bodies of the fallen soldiers lay strewn across the lower levels, Alexandre and Lambert's forces moved swiftly to consolidate their position. The air was thick with the scent of blood and the sounds of battle, but within the chaos, a grim sense of order prevailed among the thugs. Their leaders had promised them a new life away from the tree house, and this brutal display of power was the first step towards that goal.

Immediately, Anonymous, accompanied by Mohammad and Charles, moved swiftly under the cover of night. Guarded by his secret members, whose numbers had quietly grown into the thousands within the tree house, they made their way to the king's ships. The air was thick with anticipation as they boarded, their destination clear: the Sand Dunes.

As the ships set sail, the water lapping rhythmically against their hulls, Anonymous' mind raced with thoughts of the new kingdom he envisioned. The journey to Sand Dunes, a land of untold wealth and opportunity, was fraught with danger, but Anonymous felt a sense of purpose driving him forward.

Meanwhile, Alexandre and Lambert had their own plans. They knew of a secret place called the Hillside, located hundreds of miles away from Mount Ganjak. This hidden haven had come to their attention through whispered tales and hushed conversations, many of which had originated from Anonymous himself, who had an uncanny ability to gather information from the most obscure sources.

The Hillside was said to be a secluded, fertile region where one could start anew. However, reaching it was not simple. They needed to gain passage through the territory controlled by the Landers. Alexandre and Lambert, determined to find a safe place for themselves and their followers, knew they had to negotiate a treaty with the Landers. Despite the uncertainty of acceptance, especially with their intent to live on the Hillside as husband and wife, they decided to take their shot.

Their plan began to take shape. They would approach the Landers with a proposal of peaceful coexistence and mutual benefit. The Landers, known for their structured society and strategic alliances, might be swayed by the promise of trade and cooperation.

Anonymous' recommendations had always carried weight, and this time was no different. The tales he had shared about the Hillside painted it as an ideal refuge, free from the turmoil of the tree house. This emboldened Alexandre and Lambert, giving them the confidence to proceed.

As they prepared for their diplomatic mission, Alexandre and Lambert coordinated their departure with the rest of the Alliance. Stealth and caution were paramount.

Chapter Twenty-Nine
The Great Ganjak

The canopy of the forest was thick, allowing only slivers of sunlight to pierce through, creating a mosaic of light and shadow on the ground. Wealth of God moved with quiet determination along the forested paths, each step purposeful and deliberate. The air was rich with the scent of pine and moss, the earthy aroma grounding her as she navigated the winding trail. Her heart pounded not only from the urgency of her mission but also from the weight of the secret she carried.

Servant of Allah was more than just a prisoner to her, unlike the rest of the Landers.

Well, he was still her husband, and she feared that he might have to remain in his prison bonds for a while. The delay in her efforts to rescue him stemmed from the necessity of maintaining this secret, protecting him and herself from the political backlash that could arise if their union were discovered.

First things first, however. She figured she would have to comfort him before he blew into a fit and started calling to have an audience with his wife. Her family might really not take a blow like that lightly.

As she approached the heavily guarded compound, Wealth of God paused, taking a deep breath to steady her nerves.

There were a couple of guards in sight, around the perimeters. She straightened her poise to exude the confidence she was known for, striding her steps and inclining her jaw.

The guards, recognising her authority, nodded respectfully and allowed her entrance, without as much as a word. The interior of the prison was dim and musty, the scent of damp stone and rusted iron mingling in the air. The sounds of distant murmurs and clinking chains echoed off the cold, hard walls, adding to the oppressive atmosphere.

"Lead me to the foreigner," she said to one of the guards. She recognised this guard from a few years back when her father recruited him to this service. He seemed to be enjoying his job.

"Yes, my lady," he replied curtly with a nod.

Wrongdoers often found themselves here, she recalled. It has been how the Landers have been able to maintain outlaws and the like for years.

Wealth of God was led down a narrow corridor, her footsteps echoing in the silence.

Finally, she arrived at a small, dimly lit cell. There, behind the iron bars, sat Servant of Allah in a dusty corner, his once-strong form now gaunt and weary from months of confinement. His hair, which had grown long and unruly, framed a face etched with lines of worry and fatigue.

The clothes that hung loosely on his frame were tattered and stained, a stark reminder of the harsh conditions he had endured.

"You may leave us," she told the guard.

He nodded curtly and turned away, returning back to his post.

Servant of Allah's eyes, which had been dull with despair, lit up with a mix of relief and surprise as he saw her. Those eyes, once-vibrant and full of life, now held a glimmer of hope, their dark depths reflecting the flickering torchlight and the rekindling of a long-suppressed strength.

He scrambled to his feet, a spark of his former self emerging from the shadows as he beheld the woman he loved standing before him.

Wealth of God stepped closer, gripping the bars tightly, her heart aching at the sight of him, as she wrapped her hands around his.

"My love," she whispered, her voice a blend of urgency and tenderness. "I am here. I will get you out of here soon."

Servant of Allah leaned closer to the bars, his expression a mixture of hope and frustration. "Wealth of God, I've been waiting. What took so long? Have you brought help from the king?"

She hesitated, choosing her words carefully. "The king…did not send any reinforcements or envoys to negotiate your release."

A flicker of anger crossed Servant of Allah's face. "Why? Why did he not act? Am I not valuable to him?"

Wealth of God reached through the bars, taking his hand in hers. "You are valuable, but the king has his own agenda." She then glanced around to make sure they were not being watched and pulled a small bundle from within her cloak. "Here, I brought you some food," she whispered, passing him the bundle through the bars. The scent of fresh bread and cured meat wafted up, a stark contrast to the stale, meagre rations he had been surviving on.

This gesture, small yet significant, brought a soft smile to Servant of Allah's lips. He squeezed her hand, his eyes softening. "I trust you, Wealth of God. Just promise me we'll be together soon."

"I promise," she said, her voice strong and resolute.

With one last lingering look, Wealth of God turned and left the cell, the determination in her stride unshaken. As she made her way back through the prison and into the forest, she couldn't help but think about the delicate balance she had to maintain. Her secret marriage mate and the political intricacies of their world all weighed heavily on her. But she was resolute. She would rescue him, and together they would navigate the uncertain future ahead. She would definitely find a way.

***

Followmehome had learnt from the past endangerment faced by the tree house's occupants, and so he decided to initiate a few ideas of the king's to develop his own structure. In a similar model to the king's tree house, and besides the steps that led to respective chambers and the elevators that were built to enhance the flow of movement within the tree, no wide step was constructed to avoid the same predicament faced by the tree house occupant. This enhanced plan was given to Wealth of God and Mighty to design a house structure on the tree house on Mount Ganjak, hoping this would defend them against the king and, by extension, the Angels of Death in the future.

Followmehome received the letter in the most unexpected way. A talking raven, its feathers a glossy black that shimmered with hints of blue in the sunlight, swooped down gracefully from the sky. The bird landed on the stone ledge outside his cave, fixing its sharp eyes on him. Its beak clutched a small, rolled parchment bound with a piece of crimson ribbon. Followmehome approached cautiously, his heart racing with curiosity. The raven gave a low caw and tilted its head, offering the letter. He gently took the letter from the bird, which gave a sharp nod before flying back into the vast blue sky, its call echoing through the mountains.

With the letter in hand, Followmehome retreated to the cool, dim interior of the Moon Cave. The scent of damp earth and ancient stone filled the air. He sat down at his sturdy oak desk, unrolling the parchment with care. The letter was from his daughter, urging him to come and see the completion of the tree house on Mount Ganjak.

Eager to witness the fruits of their labour, Followmehome wasted no time. He packed a small satchel with essentials, grabbed his walking staff, and set out on the winding path that led to Mount Ganjak. The journey was long, taking him through dense forests where the scent of pine needles and fresh earth was invigorating. He crossed bubbling streams whose crystal-clear waters sparkled in the sunlight and climbed steep, rocky inclines that tested his endurance.

As he neared Mount Ganjak, the trees began to thin, revealing glimpses of the majestic tree house in the distance. His pace quickened, spurred on by anticipation. The closer he got, the more details he could see, and each one filled him with awe.

Finally, he arrived at the base of the grand tree house. The sight before him took his breath away. The structure stood tall and majestic, an intricate weave of wooden beams and lush foliage, blending seamlessly with the natural environment. The sunlight filtered through the leaves, casting dappled shadows on the ground. It was a vivid reality of what he had imagined, and more.

Followmehome took a deep breath, the crisp mountain air filling his lungs, and began to ascend the winding staircase that spiralled up the massive trunk of the tree. Each step brought him closer to the masterpiece his first son had crafted. As he climbed, he marvelled at the fine details—the carved railings, the sturdy platforms, and the way the branches had been carefully integrated into the structure, creating natural supports and shaded alcoves.

At the top, he was greeted by his daughter, her face beaming with pride. "Father, you made it!" she exclaimed, throwing her arms around him in a warm embrace.

He hugged her tightly, his eyes scanning the surroundings. "This is beyond anything I could have hoped for," he said, his voice filled with wonder. "You and your brother have truly outdone yourselves."

She led him through the tree house, showing him each room and walkway. The interior was just as impressive as the exterior, with rooms that felt both grand and cosy, filled with handmade furniture and decorated with natural elements.

The scent of fresh wood and wildflowers filled the air, creating a sense of peace and harmony.

"This is where we will build our future," his daughter said, her eyes shining with excitement. "A place where we can live in balance with nature, where our family and community can thrive."

Followmehome nodded, feeling a deep sense of satisfaction. "You have built not just a home, but a legacy," he said. "One that will stand the test of time and inspire generations to come."

As they stood together, looking out over the sprawling landscape from their lofty perch, Followmehome felt a profound connection to this place and to his family. The journey had been long and arduous, but it had been worth every step. He knew that this tree house on Mount Ganjak was more than just a structure—it was a symbol of their unity, their strength and their enduring spirit.

Followmehome walked through the structure, feeling the smoothness of the wooden railings and the sturdiness of the platforms beneath his feet. It was a marvel of enginecring and creativity. Each detail, from the intricate carvings to the seamless integration of nature and architecture, spoke of the love and effort poured into its creation.

"This tree house," he said, his voice echoing with emotion as he paused to take in the grandeur of the place, "shall be called the Great Ganjak."

The name resonated through the air, carrying with it a sense of reverence and triumph. The Landers around him, who had gathered to witness this moment, erupted into cheers. Their faces beamed with pride and joy, their voices rising in a harmonious chorus that filled the twilight sky. The Great Ganjak stood as a beacon of hope and strength, a symbol of their resilience and unity.

As night fell, the tree house was illuminated by lanterns hung from the branches and platforms, casting a warm, inviting glow over the scene. The soft light danced off the wooden surfaces, creating a magical atmosphere. The Landers gathered in clusters, sharing stories and laughter, their voices mingling with the sounds of nature around them. The air was filled with the scent of pine and fresh wood, mingling with the aroma of food being prepared for the evening feast.

Children ran about, their laughter ringing through the night, while elders sat together, reminiscing about days past and marvelling at the new beginnings the Great Ganjak represented. The sense of community was palpable, each person contributing to the shared celebration in their own way.

Followmehome watched from a higher platform, his heart swelling with pride as he observed his people. He saw his daughter moving through the crowd, her face lit with joy as she engaged in conversations and accepted congratulations. His son stood nearby, a quiet but proud smile on his face, acknowledging the praise for his craftsmanship.

He knew that this tree house, the Great Ganjak, would be more than just a home. It would be a fortress against future threats, a safe haven for his people. It would be a place where they could live in harmony with nature, drawing strength from their surroundings and each other.

As the festivities continued, Followmehome found a moment to reflect. He thought about the journey that had led them here, the challenges they had faced and overcome. Each obstacle had only strengthened their resolve; each victory had brought them closer together.

He turned his gaze to the horizon, where the first stars of the night began to twinkle. The future was uncertain, but at this moment, surrounded by the warmth and light of the Great Ganjak and the love of his people, he felt a profound sense of peace. He knew that whatever lay ahead, they would face it together, united and strong.

With a final look at the bustling scene below, he stepped back into the shadows, content to let the celebration continue without him. He knew that his presence, while significant, was just one part of the greater whole. The true strength of the Great Ganjak lay in the hearts and hands of the Landers who had built it and would continue to nurture it.

And so, under the canopy of stars and the watchful eyes of the forest, the Landers celebrated their new sanctuary, the Great Ganjak, a testament to their enduring spirit and a promise of hope for generations to come.

Requin stood at the precipice of destiny, the tree house looming like a spectre of impending doom. He knew its shadow promised peril, yet within that darkness, he glimpsed a chance to kill two birds with one stone. Loyalty to the Treehouse King had become a dangerous gamble, so Requin devised a daring strategy to play both sides as a double agent.

The magnificent Mount Ganjak's craft was finally complete, its divine wealth shimmering like a promise of glory.

In the heart of this splendour, Wealth of God had congregated her most trusted crew.

She stood straight and tall, her eyes scanning their faces. The urgency in her voice cut through the ambient hum of anticipation. "I call you here today because I have a big task for one of you. Aza, the blossom whisperer, is crucial to our future. Thus, we need a hero to retrieve her from the clutches of the king's tree house."

Upon the completion of the new tree house on Mount Ganjak, Wealth of God felt the need to have Aza on her side as she would soon begin ruling. She had earlier requested her father's raven and sent a message to Aza in the tree house. The raven, a sleek black bird, flew swiftly through the forest and over waters, carrying a tiny scroll tied to its leg.

A hush fell over the gathered assembly. The task was perilous, almost suicidal. The exchange of glances and under breath exchange spoke volumes. No one was willing to go.

Well, except not everybody was the devil's advocate…like Requin.

Chapter Thirty
Requin

Requin, standing at the edge of the crowd, felt a jolt of surprise at the demand. His mind raced, spinning wild fantasies of glory and power. In that split second, he imagined the accolades, the elevated status and the unique position he would secure by undertaking such a mission.

He saw himself in the grand halls of Mount Ganjak, praised and revered. The chance to play both sides as a double agent had just presented itself in the most fortuitous manner. With a deep breath, he slipped into the facade of a loyal, dedicated hero.

Requin stepped forward, his face a mask of steely determination. "I will go," he declared, his voice strong and unwavering. "I will bring Aza back safely, even if it costs me my life."

Wealth of God's eyes met his, searching for any flicker of doubt. Finding none, she nodded, her trust placed in his seemingly unwavering resolve. "Your courage is commendable, Requin. May the spirits guide you."

As he accepted the mission, Requin's heart pounded with a mix of fear and exhilaration. His outward appearance remained composed, but inside, he revelled in the myriad opportunities this mission promised. He was ready to navigate the treacherous path ahead, his true motives hidden beneath a cloak of feigned loyalty.

I should've been an actor in some distant land had I been extended that opportunity, Requin thought, hiding a smile.

As the Landers placed their trust in him, unaware of his treachery, Requin prepared to embark on his perilous journey. It was time to visit the tree house, to update the king on the Landers' movements and schemes. The whispers of the Moon Cave and Mount Ganjak had reached his ears, but their exact locations remained elusive, shrouded in mystery by the cunning of Followmehome, guardian of the Landers' secrets.

As he sailed towards the tree house, Requin's heart beat with a mix of fear and determination. He was a player in a deadly game, where loyalty and betrayal wove a tangled web. His fate hung in the balance, but Requin was resolved to navigate the shadows and seize his moment, whatever the cost.

Aza stood before Warriorisborn, her heart heavy with the knowledge of impending doom. "Your Majesty," she began, her voice trembling slightly, "I implore you to desist from making reckless decisions that could endanger the tree house and its occupants. I can sense a looming disaster."

The king, seated on his ornate throne, glanced at her with a mixture of disdain and amusement. "Aza, your concerns are noted, but the wizard's wisdom guides me. His counsel is sufficient."

Aza felt a chill run down her spine. The wizard's influence over the king was overpowering, and her own warnings seemed futile. She bowed deeply and left the king's premises, her mind racing with thoughts of escape.

Aza received the Wealth of God's message in the stillness of her chamber. The raven did a dramatic landing on her window, and being who she was, Aza could tell from a glance that this was no ordinary raven. And she was right. She found a wrapped paper under its claws. Unrolling the scroll, she read: "Join me at Mount Ganjak. Your safety is assured. Await my signal."

She replied, detailing her evident limitations. Wealth of God's reply came swiftly: "Stay prepared. You will get a signal when it's the perfect time."

Requin strode into the throne room with a dramatic flourish, his cloak billowing behind him as the heavy wooden doors creaked open. The scent of aged wood and burning torches filled the air, mingling with the tension that crackled like static. He moved with purpose, each step echoing in the cavernous space until he stood before the king. Dropping to one knee, he bowed deeply, the flickering torch light casting shadows on his determined face.

"Your Majesty," he began, his voice resonating with urgency, "I faced many challenges that hindered me from stealing the poison, but I am not backing down. I have returned to give you updates about the Landers' developments."

The king's eyes narrowed, a glint of interest sparking within them as he leaned forward, eager to hear what Requin had to say. "Speak, Requin."

"The Landers plan to rule on Mount Ganjak," Requin revealed, watching the king's face twist in fury. "They have fortified their defences, and whispers of a werewolf and a hidden Moon Cave have reached my ears. However, I have yet to discover the werewolf's identity or the Moon Cave's location."

The king's eyes blazed with determination. "Continue your mission. Find the werewolf's identity and the exact location of the Moon Cave."

"Thank you, my lord. I shall leave tomorrow night before the crew notices my absence."

The king nodded with a smirk. *His choice of a spy had proven perfect,* he thought to himself.

Late, the following night, Aza sat by her window, the moonlight casting a soft glow over her anxious face. The room was silent except for the distant hum of nocturnal creatures. Her thoughts were heavy, tangled with fear and hope. Suddenly, a soft, insistent knock broke the stillness. Her heart leapt into her throat.

Quickly, she gathered her belongings, making sure not to leave any trace of her departure. The knock came again, more urgent this time. She had received a letter earlier that day that she was to leave tonight.

Aza opened it, her eyes wide and filled with a mix of hope and fear. The sight of Requin, his face partially hidden beneath the hood, sent a shiver down her spine.

"It's time, dear Aza," he whispered, his voice low and reassuring. "I'm on Wealth of God's side. She sent me to you."

With a nod, Aza stepped into the corridor, the tension palpable between them. They moved like phantoms through the darkened halls, every creak of the floorboards amplifying their shared anxiety. The cool night air greeted them as they slipped out of the tree house, the vast canopy of stars above a silent witness to their escape.

Requin led her to his little ship. The vessel bobbed gently in the water, waiting to carry them to safety. As they boarded, Aza glanced back at the looming silhouette of the tree house, a mixture of relief and apprehension washing over her.

The king, unaware of Aza's escape, had allowed Requin to leave, trusting his loyal spy. Little did he know that Requin was now playing both sides, his true allegiance hidden behind a mask of deceit.

As the ship set sail, the gentle lapping of the waves against the hull seemed to echo their shared determination. The night swallowed them, leaving the tree house and its secrets behind, their fates now intertwined in a dangerous game of survival and loyalty.

Finally, they reached the edge of the Landers' territory, where Wealth of God's loyalists were waiting.

Requin and Aza were welcomed with open arms. Wealth of God embraced Aza, relief washing over her face. "You are safe now," she whispered.

Requin stood back, watching the reunion. He had played his part well. The Great Ganjak stood tall in the distance, a beacon of hope and resilience.

As they made their way to the heart of Mount Ganjak, Requin couldn't help but feel a sense of accomplishment. He had navigated the shadows and seized his moment, and now, the future held endless possibilities.

After the departure of the tree house chiefs, excluding Cyril, the king had plunged into a brooding silence. In his private chamber, the atmosphere was thick with tension. The room, dimly lit by flickering torches, cast long, dancing shadows on the walls. Ornate tapestries depicting scenes of past glories seemed to mock him now, reminding him of a time when his rule was unquestioned.

The king paced back and forth, his footsteps heavy and deliberate on the polished wooden floor. Each step echoed his inner turmoil. His hands clenched and unclenched at his sides, the muscles in his jaw working furiously as he bit back the torrent of emotions threatening to break free.

"How could they?" he muttered to himself, his voice a low growl, almost swallowed by the oppressive silence of the chamber. His eyes, normally sharp and commanding, now flickered with a mix of anger and hurt. He stopped abruptly in front of a grand window overlooking the dark expanse of the sea, the moonlight casting a cold, silver sheen on his regal attire.

He felt disrespected by his chiefs and betrayed by those he had trusted implicitly. The sting of their departure was a deep wound, festering with each passing moment. He had no idea where they had escaped to, no leads to follow, and this uncertainty gnawed at him, fuelling his frustration.

The king resumed his pacing, his mind a whirlwind of thoughts. *Who could he hold responsible for this disgrace? How could he restore his authority?*

Cyril's presence was a small consolation, but the king knew he needed more than loyalty; he needed answers. His heart pounded with a mix of determination and despair. He paused once more, staring into the shadows as if hoping they might whisper the secrets he sought.

"Find them," he whispered fiercely to himself, a vow more than a command. "Bring them back. Make them pay."

The words hung in the air, a stark contrast to the silence that had enveloped him for days. The king stood still, the weight of his resolve settling over him like a cloak. He would not rest until his authority was restored until those who had betrayed him were brought to justice. And as the first light of dawn began to creep into the room, he knew his course of action was set.

Gandoki was in deep agony, unsure of his next move. Terror gripped him, a chilling sense of desertion gnawing at his core. He felt unsafe and paranoid, his once-familiar surroundings now menacing and alien.

Clad in a hood-like apparel, he descended to the downside of the tree house. The shadows seemed to close in around him, amplifying his anxiety. Each step echoed his internal turmoil, the usually comforting rustle of leaves now an ominous whisper of betrayal.

Alexandre and Lambert had deserted him, not taking him along in their escape. Their betrayal stung deeply, a sharp reminder of his newfound isolation. His mind raced, seeking an escape from the looming threat that seemed to lurk in every corner of the tree house.

Reaching the base of the tree, Gandoki's eyes scanned the dark expanse. He spotted one of his father's small ships, a lifeline in his desperate state. He hurried towards it, his heart pounding with fear and determination.

The ship, modest in size but sturdy, rocked gently in the water. Gandoki climbed aboard, his hands trembling as he unfurled the sail. The hood of his cloak shadowed his face, hiding the tears that threatened to fall.

With a final, lingering look at the tree house, Gandoki set sail towards the land. The night was calm, the sea a dark, endless expanse before him. The gentle lapping of the waves was the only sound, a stark contrast to the chaos in his mind.

As the ship moved away from the tree house, Gandoki felt a mix of relief and sorrow. The betrayal of Alexandre and Lambert weighed heavily on him, but the open sea offered a glimmer of hope. He knew he had to survive, to find safety on the land and to rebuild from the fragments of his shattered trust.

The journey ahead was uncertain, but Gandoki was resolved. The betrayal had wounded him, but it had also ignited a spark of resilience. As the first light of dawn began to break, he steered the ship with a newfound determination, ready to face whatever challenges lay ahead.

Chapter Thirty-One
Asylum

Alexandre and Lambert were nearing the shore, the sight of land just within reach, when they were unexpectedly confronted by a formidable ship blocking their path. The ship, weathered countless journeys, was adorned with intricate symbols and emitted an otherworldly glow in the twilight.

At its helm stood a figure they vaguely recognised –a man whose presence exuded authority and power. They remembered him from a few years ago during the Stairs of Horror competition, but his name eluded them. Whatever the case, it meant that he was also a Lander.

The sea, a deep, mysterious blue, churned restlessly beneath them, its waves lapping against the ship's hull with a rhythmic intensity. The air was thick with the scent of salt and the cries of distant seabirds. The man at the helm, cloaked in a dark, flowing robe, watched them with piercing eyes that seemed to see into their very souls.

"Who dares approach my waters?" the man demanded, his voice stern and authoritative, carrying a gravitas that matched the power of the sea itself.

My waters?

Alexandre and Lambert exchanged a startled glance, their hearts racing. They had been told about an enigmatic figure who claimed domain over these parts of the water, but never had they anticipated that this enigmatic figure would be one of the sons of Followmehome, Lord of the Landers. They quickly scrambled to gather their composure. Steering their ship closer, they raised their hands in a gesture of peace. The wood of their vessel creaked underfoot, and the cool, damp sea air filled their lungs.

"Great Sea King," Alexandre began, his tone measured and sincere, carefully choosing his words. "We come in peace, seeking asylum under the rules of the Landers. We are aware of the protocols and are prepared to follow them."

Lambert nodded in agreement, his eyes reflecting the gravity of their situation. "We humbly request an audience with Followmehome. We seek refuge and protection from the Landers."

The Sea King regarded them with a piercing gaze, his scepticism palpable. The sea seemed to quieten around them as if waiting for his judgement. His eyes narrowed, studying their every move, their every breath.

"Why should I trust you?" he asked, his voice low but firm, laden with unspoken doubts and concerns. "What assurance do I have that your intentions are pure?"

Alexandre stepped forward, his eyes unwavering, the tension of the moment making his muscles taut. "We come with confessions and a desire for refuge. We are not here to deceive or to harm, not like we could with someone as sage as you are, either way. Our only wish is to find safety and a new beginning among the Landers."

There was a long pause, the air thick with tension. The Sea King's gaze flickered with a mix of emotions—suspicion, curiosity and a hint of understanding. Finally, he nodded, his expression stern but accepting.

Upon their arrival, Alexandre and Lambert were guarded to land, alighting from their ship with a mix of apprehension and hope. They felt the sand under their feet, a stark contrast to the swaying deck of their vessel. They were escorted to the Landers' domain, where, to their relief, they were treated with respect and dignity while awaiting the presence of their leaders.

Magnus the Messenger, having swiftly dispatched his men, ensured that his father, Followmehome, was informed about the arrival of the chiefs. The sun had dipped below the horizon, casting long shadows as Followmehome read the message by the flickering light of a torch. Upon receiving this information, he instructed Wealth of God to welcome them with open arms. He trusted her strength and believed she could uphold the rules of the tree house and make a fair demand on behalf of the Landers.

A few days later, Wealth of God met with the chiefs. The atmosphere was tense but courteous. Wealth of God, exuding confidence and authority, approached them with a warm smile, her presence commanding respect.

"Welcome," she said, her voice steady and inviting, carrying the weight of her authority. "We understand you have come seeking asylum."

Alexandre stepped forward, bowing respectfully. His voice trembled slightly as he spoke, the gravity of their situation evident. "We seek refuge and protection among the Landers. Our past is marred with mistakes, and we come with genuine intentions to start anew. We are prepared to follow the rules and contribute to your community."

Lambert nodded in agreement, his expression earnest and sincere. "We are willing to abide by your laws. We seek a chance for redemption and to live in peace."

Wealth of God listened intently, her piercing gaze assessing their sincerity. Her eyes narrowed slightly as she considered their words, weighing their honesty. She was secretly impressed by how well they avoided mentioning her grandfather in it all. Her eyes were screwed. If they weren't going to take the lead down that conversation, then she wouldn't push.

After a moment of contemplation, she nodded.

"We appreciate your honesty and willingness to adhere to our rules," she said. "Asylum will not be granted lightly, but your earnestness speaks volumes. You will have to prove your loyalty and dedication to our community."

Alexandre and Lambert exchanged hopeful glances, feeling a weight lifted off their shoulders. They bowed deeply to Wealth of God, their voices filled with gratitude.

"Thank you," Alexandre said. "We will not disappoint you."

Wealth of God smiled though her eyes remained calculating. "Welcome to our domain. Follow our rules, contribute positively, and we will protect you as we would our own people."

With that, Alexandre and Lambert were led to their new quarters, their hearts filled with cautious hope. They knew the path to redemption would be arduous, but they were ready to embrace it fully, grateful for the chance to start anew under the watchful eyes of the Landers.

Alexandre was uncertain if it was the right time to reveal their sexual orientation. He decided to keep this aspect of their lives hidden from the Landers for now. Instead, he focused on their primary goal: securing passage to the Hillside, their intended destination.

"Wealth of God," Alexandre began, choosing his words carefully, the weight of his hidden secret pressing on him. "We seek more than just asylum; we seek safe passage to the Hillside. It is there we hope to find a new beginning. In return, we vow to abide by your rules and, if ever needed, we will fight alongside the Landers as loyal allies."

Wealth of God nodded, a small smile playing at her lips, the flicker of a lantern reflecting in her eyes. "Very well. We shall grant you passage to the Hillside. In return, you will uphold your promise to stand with us if ever called upon."

A treaty was quickly drafted and signed with the Queen of the Ganjak, symbolising their agreement. Alexandre and Lambert felt a mix of relief and determination. They knew their journey was far from over, but with this agreement, they had taken a significant step towards their new life. The Great Ganjak, now illuminated by the soft glow of lanterns, stood as a testament to their resilience and the beginning of their new chapter.

Chapter Thirty-Two
Hillside

Alexandre and Lambert, along with the rest of the Alliance, over a thousand strong including women and children, were granted passage to the Hillside, after a week of resting with the people of the Great Ganjak.

Alexandre and Lambert had seen, first hand, what the tree sucklings can develop into, and they had already begun mapping out in their minds some of the intricate patterns that they had seen.

The air was thick with tension as they prepared for the journey, knowing they needed to remain vigilant for the king's inevitable retaliation. The Hillside promised a new beginning, but they needed to hide behind the protection of the Landers until they could grow their kingdom strong enough to stand on its own.

As they gathered their people and prepared for the move, it became clear that they needed a leader with the courage and cunning to guide them through these tumultuous times. Among them, one name stood out: Sylvester Seditious, the son of the renowned Seditious, who had been poisoned by the Treehouse King.

Sylvester's reputation as a fearless rogue preceded him. He had inherited his father's strength and rebellious spirit, qualities that made him the perfect candidate to lead the Alliance.

"We need someone who can stand up to the king, someone who understands the risks and isn't afraid to take them," Alexandre said, addressing the gathered members of the Alliance. "Sylvester Seditious is that leader. His father was a great man, and Sylvester has the same fire burning within him."

Lambert nodded in agreement, adding, "Sylvester knows the Treehouse King's tactics and has the strength and resolve to guide us through the challenges ahead, in the near future."

Sylvester stepped forward, his presence commanding attention. "I accept this responsibility," he declared, his voice steady and strong. "We will move to the Hillside, and we will build our kingdom. The king will not find us unprepared."

The crowd murmured in approval, their spirits lifted by Sylvester's confidence. With their new leader at the helm, the Alliance felt a renewed sense of purpose. They began their migration to the Hillside, ready to face whatever challenges lay ahead, determined to protect their people and build a future free from the Treehouse King's tyranny.

Sylvester Seditious, the first son of Seditious, was cut from the same rough cloth as his father and his uncle Dino. Known for his animalistic behaviour and ever ready for war, Sylvester harboured a deep, unyielding hatred for the Treehouse King. He had lost many close to him, and the scars of those losses had forged him into a fierce, unrelenting force.

Sylvester stood on a rocky outcrop overlooking the vast expanse of the forest. The sky above was a canvas of swirling grey clouds, promising a storm. The wind whipped through his dark, unruly hair and his eyes, cold and calculating, scanned the horizon. His face was a mask of hardened resolve, each line and scar telling a story of battles fought and loved ones lost.

The memories of his father and uncle, Dino, were a constant presence in his mind, their voices echoing in his thoughts as he clenched his fists, feeling the roughness of his calloused palms. He could almost hear his father's gruff encouragement and Dino's wild laughter, pushing him to be stronger, fiercer. These memories fuelled his rage, and his hatred for the Treehouse King burned with an intensity that seemed to match the storm brewing overhead.

Sylvester's thoughts drifted to the Treehouse King, his sworn enemy. The image of the king, with his regal bearing and calm authority, was a stark contrast to Sylvester's own rough, battle-hardened appearance. The king represented everything Sylvester despised His jaw tightened, and a low growl escaped his lips as he imagined the Treehouse King's face.

As he stood there, Sylvester's mind raced with plans for his next move. He envisioned the king's downfall, picturing the look of defeat in his enemy's eyes. He could feel the weight of his weapons at his side, the familiar comfort of the sword's hilt and the sharp edge of his dagger. These tools of war were extensions of himself, symbols of his unyielding determination and readiness for battle.

The sound of the approaching storm, the distant rumble of thunder, mirrored the turmoil within Sylvester. He remembered the fallen comrades, the battles lost and the promises of vengeance he had made over the years. Each memory was a wound that never fully healed, driving him forward with a relentless need for retribution.

In the dim light of the approaching dusk, Sylvester's figure was a silhouette of defiance against the darkening sky. He was a man forged in the fires of loss and anger, a warrior whose life was defined by his hatred for the Treehouse King. His eyes narrowed as he made a silent vow to himself: the king would pay for the pain he had caused, and Sylvester would be the one to deliver that justice.

Turning away from the edge, Sylvester began to descend the rocky path back to his camp. Each step was heavy with purpose, his mind focused on the battle that lay ahead. He would gather his forces, sharpen his weapons and prepare for the inevitable clash. The storm was coming, and Sylvester Seditious would be its harbinger, a force of nature driven by a deep, unyielding rage.

When Alexandre and Lambert presented him with the opportunity to lead the Alliance, Sylvester saw it as his chance to prove himself. He was determined to show them that he was the right person to rebel against the Treehouse King and defend the Hillsiders against any threat.

The Hillside, hundreds of miles away from Mount Ganjak, was a domain surrounded by countless hills. It was an ideal hiding spot, a natural fortress where they could build their new kingdom. Alexandre and Lambert knew that it would take about two years for the trees to grow if mixed with Aza's enchantment. In the meantime, they needed a temporary shelter.

"Sylvester," Alexandre said, "gather your thugs. We need to set up a tent city to serve as our shelter until the Hillside kingdom is complete."

Sylvester nodded, his eyes gleaming with a fierce determination. "Consider it done," he replied. "We will make the Hillside our stronghold, and we will be ready for anything the Treehouse King throws at us."

With that, Sylvester rallied his men, a group as rough and ready as he was. They began the arduous task of setting up tents and fortifying their temporary home. The Hillside buzzed with activity as everyone worked together, driven by the promise of a new beginning and the determination to protect their people.

As the tents went up and plans for the future took shape, the Alliance felt a renewed sense of purpose. They knew the road ahead would be difficult, but with Sylvester Seditious leading the charge, they were confident in their ability to face whatever challenges came their way. The Hillside would be their refuge, a place where they could build a kingdom strong enough to withstand the Treehouse King's wrath.

However, Anonymous, along with Charles and Muhammad, had reached the Sand Dunes, only to find themselves stranded. They lacked the iron glasses necessary to carve into the tree, even if it were planted. After several months, their hopes were nearly shattered. Just as Muhammad and Charles were on the verge of giving up, Anonymous decided to explore the desert beyond the Sand Dunes, driven by a faint memory of a conversation he'd overheard about a precious resource hidden in the sands.

The desert was a harsh and unforgiving place, but Anonymous pressed on. After days of arduous trekking, he made a remarkable discovery: a portion of the desert covered in a shimmering, almost otherworldly metal known as Starstone. This rare material was renowned for its incredible strength, luminescent properties and the ability to harness and amplify magical energies. Coveted by blacksmiths, alchemists and enchanters, Starstone was believed to be the key to creating indestructible weapons and powerful artefacts. Overwhelmed with joy, Anonymous started to head back to the Sand Dunes to share the news.

On his way back, he stumbled upon a half-buried chest. Intrigued, he dug it out, revealing a trove of gold. His eyes widened at the sight of such wealth, but he quickly decided to keep this newfound treasure a secret. He knew the value of the Starstone would be enough to spark excitement among his companions.

Returning to the Sand Dunes, Anonymous shared the discovery of the Starstone with Charles and Muhammad, omitting any mention of the gold chest. The trio was elated at the prospect of the valuable resource. Anonymous, however, knew that the true value of the Starstone was only known to a select few foreigners. To capitalise on this discovery, he needed to travel to a distant land, one he'd heard about from a trusted ally.

He prepared for his journey, concealing his true intentions and the secret of the gold. As he set off, the weight of his dual discoveries sat heavy in his mind. The Starstone would bring them wealth and power, but the gold chest—his hidden ace—might just ensure his supremacy in whatever future awaited them.

Anonymous called Mohammad and Charles to a secluded spot beneath the shade of a weathered dune. The sun hung low, casting long shadows that danced on the sand. As they gathered, Anonymous' eyes glinted with a determined resolve.

"I've decided to travel north," he began, his voice steady yet filled with a sense of urgency. "I will seek out the foreigners interested in the Starstone trade. After that, I promise to secure the iron glasses from the tree house king."

Charles and Mohammad exchanged wary glances, their scepticism evident. Charles, frowning, crossed his arms and leaned in slightly. "How can we be sure you'll return? We've faced so much together, but this…"

Anonymous placed a reassuring hand on Charles' shoulder, his grip firm. "I understand your doubts, Charles. But trust in what we've achieved together. We have no choice but to move forward with faith."

Mohammad, his brow furrowed, nodded slowly. "We've come this far. We must believe in each other."

The next morning, the air was crisp with a hint of desert chill as Anonymous prepared for his journey. He donned a hooded cloak, the gold chest securely strapped to his back. He turned to his companions, a resolute look on his face.

"I will return," he vowed, his eyes locking with theirs. "And when I do, we'll have everything we need." His words were a promise, but there was a flicker in his eyes that hinted at plans known only to him.

Charles and Mohammad watched as Anonymous set off towards the northern horizon, his figure growing smaller against the vast expanse of sand. The determination in his stride was clear, each step taken with purpose, yet shrouded in mystery. They had no inkling of the true extent of his intentions.

Left behind, Charles and Mohammad set to work, their hands moving in practised synchrony as they began to build the suckling trees with their enchantment. The air buzzed with the hum of magic, mingling with the scent of the desert as they toiled under the sun's watchful gaze.

Despite their doubts, they knew they had to place their trust in Anonymous. As they worked, they shared silent glances of hope, each gesture a testament to their unspoken belief in his return. But lingering in their minds was the unsettling thought: what exactly was he planning?

Chapter Thirty-Three
The Slavers' Bay

The sunset in a blazing display of reds and oranges, casting long shadows across the Sand Dunes. The wind whispered secrets as it danced through the desert, rustling the sparse vegetation. Anonymous stood on a high dune, his eyes fixed on the horizon where the sun dipped below the sand. He was lost in thought, contemplating the complex web of alliances, betrayals and power-plays that had brought him here.

The sky above was a canvas of fiery hues, the dying light of day painting the sands in shades of gold and crimson. Each grain of sand seemed to catch the light, creating an ethereal glow that made the desert appear almost otherworldly. The air was thick with the scent of warm earth and the faint, lingering traces of the day's heat.

The wind, a constant companion in this desolate landscape, murmured softly in his ears, carrying with it the ancient tales of the desert. It swept across the dunes, lifting fine particles of sand into the air, creating a shimmering haze that blurred the line between earth and sky. The sparse vegetation, hardy and resilient, swayed gently, their shadows stretching long and thin across the undulating terrain.

Anonymous felt the coolness of the evening air against his skin, a stark contrast to the searing heat of the day. He stood tall, his silhouette a dark figure against the vibrant backdrop of the setting sun. His cloak billowed around him, caught in the playful gusts of wind and, his eyes, sharp and contemplative, remained fixed on the horizon.

In the distance, the sun's final rays dipped below the sand, casting the world into a twilight glow. The sky transitioned from fiery reds to deep purples and blues, stars beginning to twinkle faintly in the encroaching darkness. Anonymous' thoughts were as turbulent as the shifting sands beneath his feet.

He knew that the king of the Tree House, with his insatiable ambition, was enslaving the Angels of Death to tighten his grip on power. Anonymous had learnt of the king's sinister plans to use these supernatural beings to control the world. The mere thought of the Angels of Death, their ethereal forms bound in servitude, sent a shiver down his spine. The king's desire for power knew no bounds, and the Angels were his most formidable weapon.

But he also understood that such a plan required secrecy and a constant supply of resources to sustain the beasts that the king intended to unleash. The population of the Tree House people was dwindling, a fact that could not be hidden forever. The whispers of their decline were beginning to reach even the farthest corners of the land.

Anonymous knew that, eventually, the king would need to procure human beings to feed the beasts and maintain his hold on power. This grim reality loomed over him like a dark cloud, threatening to engulf everything he held dear. Anticipating this, Anonymous had devised a plan to ensure his own influence and survival in this new world order.

Several months after his departure, during one of his expeditions, Anonymous had stumbled upon an island far from the Sand Dunes, beyond the reach of the known kingdoms. It was a grim place, an island where men of colour were held captive by foreigners. They were chained in cages, subjected to horrific torture and used as mere commodities. The island was a place of unimaginable suffering, a testament to the cruelty of those who sought power through oppression. At the time he discovered it, it had a million captives. It was a place that he called 'Slavers' Bay'.

The memories of that discovery haunted him, seeping into his thoughts with an unsettling persistence. He recalled the oppressive heat of the island, the air thick with humidity and the stench of decay. The sight of the captives was etched deeply into his mind—emaciated bodies covered in sores, their eyes hollow and devoid of hope. Each prisoner bore the scars of relentless abuse, their spirits crushed under the weight of their torment.

The cries of the captives echoed in his memory, a cacophony of anguish that seemed to permeate the very soil of the island. He had witnessed the foreigners' cruelty firsthand—their whips lashing out with a sickening crack, the dull thud of fists meeting flesh and the guttural cries of pain that followed. The slaves' suffering was palpable, their every movement a testament to their endurance amidst unimaginable hardship.

Yet Anonymous maintained a taciturn attitude toward their circumstances. His face remained a mask of stoic determination, betraying no hint of the turmoil within. He walked among the cages with a measured stride, his eyes scanning the scene with cold detachment. His heart may have ached for the captives, but his mind was focused on the larger picture—the strategic advantage this island represented.

He remembered the moment he approached one of the cages, the prisoner within a gaunt figure with sunken eyes. The man's gaze met his, a flicker of curiosity breaking through the veil of despair. Anonymous had offered no words of comfort, no promises of liberation. Instead, he had studied the man's condition, assessing his strength and resilience with a clinical eye.

The island was a grim tableau of human suffering. The captives were forced to labour under the scorching sun, their backs bent and muscles straining as they toiled endlessly. The foreigners watched over them with sadistic glee, their laughter mingling with the groans of the oppressed. Anonymous observed it all in silence, his mind calculating the potential uses of such a place.

He recalled the night he spent on the island, the air heavy with the scent of sweat and blood. The cries of the captives had persisted into the darkness, a haunting chorus that seemed to rise and fall with the rhythm of the waves. The stars above offered a stark contrast to the hellish reality below, their distant light indifferent to the suffering on the ground.

Despite the grimness of the scene, Anonymous had seen an opportunity. The island, with its captive population, represented a resource he could exploit. He knew the king of the Tree House would eventually require human beings to sustain his beasts, and this island offered a solution. The captives could be traded, their suffering turned into a commodity that would secure their own position of power.

His decision to buy the island was made with the same cold pragmatism that had guided his actions thus far. He negotiated with the foreigners, his expression unreadable as he struck the deal. The transaction was conducted with a chilling efficiency, and the captives' fate was sealed with the exchange of gold. Anonymous had secured his leverage, the island now under his control.

As he stood on the high dune, lost in thought, the memories of the island played out in his mind like a dark, twisted tale. The wind whispered around him, carrying the faint echoes of the captives' cries. He knew that his actions were driven by necessity, a ruthless pragmatism that left no room for sentiment. The path he had chosen was one of power and survival, and he would navigate it with unwavering resolve.

The island, with its grim tableau of suffering, was a cornerstone of his plan. It represented the harsh realities of the world he inhabited, a world where power was won through cunning and cruelty. Anonymous's taciturn attitude was both a shield and a weapon, allowing him to manoeuvre through the treacherous landscape of alliances and betrayals with calculated precision. In the end, the suffering of the captives was a means to an end, a necessary sacrifice in his relentless pursuit of power.

He navigated the treacherous waters surrounding the island, negotiating with the ruthless traders who controlled the human cargo. The negotiations were brutal, but Anonymous was relentless. He used the gold from the chest he had found in the desert to secure the purchase, a transaction that made his stomach churn but one he knew was necessary for his plan.

The island was a desolate place, surrounded by cliffs and treacherous waters that made escape nearly impossible. The captives, shackled and broken, watched him with hollow eyes as he surveyed the terrain. He knew that he needed to keep these people alive, to ensure they could be traded to the king when the time came. Anonymous established a harsh regime, one that balanced survival with control, ensuring that the captives were kept in a state of fear and obedience.

He established a secret channel by which he communicated with the king through secret, courtesy of the resources he had acquired. The king, always eager for power, was intrigued by the prospect of an endless supply of human beings to sustain his beasts. Anonymous played his cards carefully, never revealing too much, but enough to keep the king's interest piqued.

As he solidified his hold on Slavers' Bay, Anonymous also kept an eye on the other emerging kingdoms. He had spies in Mount Ganjak, where Wealth of God was establishing her rule. He watched as Charles and Mohammad worked tirelessly to build their kingdom in the Sand Dunes, using their enchantments to create a new home. He monitored the progress of Alexandre and Lambert at the Hillside, knowing that they too were preparing for the inevitable conflict with the Tree House king.

Each kingdom was a piece in a larger game, one that Anonymous intended to control. He knew that alliances would shift, and loyalties would be tested. But with Slavers' Bay under his command, he had a powerful bargaining chip that could tip the scales in his favour.

One evening, as the sun set over Slavers' Bay, casting long shadows across the cages, Anonymous stood on a cliff overlooking the island. He could hear the distant cries of the captives, a haunting reminder of the price of power. He knew that his actions were driven by necessity, but the weight of his decisions bore heavily on his soul.

"Am I not a wonder?" he asked himself aloud. "Here I am keeping the balance of the world in check through uncanny means. Still, if I don't dirty my hands through these slaves and the thirst of the Angels of Death can no longer be contained, can the rest of the world deal with that consequence? Tsk…the monsters we make…"

As he gazed at the horizon, he reflected on the kingdoms that were rising from the ashes of the old world. The Sand Dunes, with its mystical enchantments and hidden treasures; Mount Ganjak, a fortress of strength and wisdom; The Hillside, a sanctuary for those seeking refuge from tyranny; and now Slavers' Bay, a dark testament to the lengths he would go to secure his future.

Anonymous knew that the coming days would be filled with challenges. The king of the Tree House was a formidable adversary, and the other kingdoms would soon realise the stakes of the game they were playing. But he was prepared. He had positioned himself strategically, with allies in unexpected places and a resource that could turn the tide of any conflict.

As night fell, Anonymous made his way back to his quarters, his mind racing with plans and contingencies. He knew that the path ahead was fraught with danger, but he was ready to face it. He had embraced the darkness, knowing that sometimes, the ends justified the means.

In the quiet of his room, he unfurled a map, tracing the routes between the kingdoms. Each line represented a potential alliance, a possible betrayal, or a path to power. He knew that the future was uncertain, but he was determined to carve out his place in this new world.

As he plotted his next move, Anonymous allowed himself a moment of reflection. He thought of the captives in Slavers' Bay, the people who had become pawns in his game. He vowed that one day when the time was right, he would find a way to free them…

Scratch that. It wouldn't make him less of a bad person, either way.

For now, he had to focus on the immediate goal: securing his power and outmanoeuvring the king.

The kingdoms were rising, and with them, the stakes of the game. Anonymous knew that the coming days would test his resolve, his cunning and his capacity for ruthlessness. But he was ready. The future belonged to those who could see beyond the immediate, to those who could navigate the shadows and emerge victorious.

The dawn of a new era was upon them, and Anonymous was poised to be at its forefront. As the first light of day broke over the horizon, he felt a surge of determination. He would ensure that Slavers' Bay, and the other emerging kingdoms, would be the foundation of a new world order. And in this new world, he intended to be the one who held the reins of power.

—Book One Ends Here—

Book One ends on a note of rising tension and anticipation, with the emergence of new kingdoms and the intricate web of power-plays setting the stage for Book Two. The readers are left with a sense of impending conflict and the promise of further intrigue as the characters navigate their alliances and rivalries in the quest for dominance.